Claire's FOREVER LOVE

RUBY JAMES

For Everyone looking for a place to belong.

Contents

Animals of Hawkins Ridge

As a sanctuary ran by a family who loves animals, many will play side characters in the series. For Claire's Forever Love, you will meet the following dogs. You can use this as a reference.

Oriole—Jace's Lab Mix

Cammie—Jace's Blind Pomeranian

Luna—Claire's Boxer

Balty—Rue's Mix breed

Duke—Rescue Pitbull

Lenny—Rescue senior Terrier Mix

Shorty—Naomi's long-haired Dachshund

Rosebud, Tulip and Bluebell—Logan and Naomi's Pug sisters

Mika and Tam—Logan and Naomi's Terrier mix sisters

Brutus—Ophelia Norris Newfoundland

Chapter One

The rich aroma of dew-covered grass hit Claire Everson when she opened her kitchen window. The late winter rainstorm the night before reminded her spring was just around the corner. A thought that put a shimmy into her curvy hips.

It was the first day of her needed time off as the vet tech for Hawkins Ridge Animal Sanctuary and Farms. Her cousin, Garrett, moved to the mountain town after meeting his wife four years ago and recommended Claire when he heard of the opening. The position came with a tiny house on the property. She worked five days a week and on-call the remaining time. Her boss, Logan Beckett, rarely called her unless it was an emergency. Even when he did, Claire didn't mind. Caring for animals was her calling. A career she didn't think she'd ever have given her upbringing.

Living in Oak Mountain Maryland was the polar opposite of growing up at the Sunny View Trailer Park in rural Virginia. Rue, Claire's aunt, raised her after losing her mother, Dorothy, in a fire caused by a faulty heater in her bedroom when she was seven.

Claire's heart pounded as she traced a finger over the pink compression glove encasing the puckered skin of her left hand. The burns there were worse than the scars on her face and shoulder, and the glove eased the nerve damage she'd endured. A constant reminder of what she'd been through and how far she'd come.

Money was an issue growing up. Public assistance didn't see the need for Claire to have cosmetic surgery. Depression at a young age was constant. Her aunt fought for years to have the surgery. They did, however, approved for her to see a counselor. During that waiting period, she endured taunts and bullying from classmates. If it wasn't for her counselor and aunt, Claire didn't think she would have made it out of middle school. Almost ten years later, they approved for surgery on her face. Just in time for graduation.

Her hometown had few options for advancement: working at the fulfillment center, meatpacking plant, joining the military, or earning money illegally. Less than three percent of the residents left the area. Rue made sure she and Garrett were part of that three percent. She pushed them to apply for positions in the larger town fifty miles away after high school. Claire would be forever grateful for her aunt and couldn't wait to see her the next day when she came for a month-long visit.

The buzzer on the timer dinged, pulling Claire from her spiraling thoughts. She tightened the pink band holding her dark hair from her face. She slipped on the oven mitt. Steam momentarily fogged her glasses when she pulled the silicone molds from the oven. The stack of cooling racks on her small kitchen table held four previous batches. She made room and set the latest pumpkin banana treat.

Making the dog treats was her way of giving back to the Beckett family. They didn't care about the nerve damage in her hand and trusted her to do her job. Lifting animals was hard if she was having a bad pain day. Logan didn't hold it against her if she asked for help. Claire wanted to make sure there was enough to last the pack of rescues.

An alert on her phone had her pulling off the mitt and tugging her phone from her pocket. A text from her friend, and Logan's brother, Jace.

Jace: Are you home? I found something for you.

Claire stifled a girly sigh. Now was not the time to think of Jace in that way. Her handsome, caring friend with deep dimples and dark blond hair. She had a schedule to keep if she wanted to finish ten dozen doggie treats and eight dozen cookies before packing.

Claire: Yep. I'm home and may have sugary goodness for you.

She placed her phone on the counter and quickly popped in two bone shaped molds filled with sweet potato and banana batter. Claire stopped in front of the second-hand, full-length mirror on the front of her bathroom door to check for wayward flour splotches, despite the apron. The mirror was one purchase she made when she moved into her first apartment. She'd painted the wood frame purple at least five times over the years. Though she could afford a newer one now, the item reminded Claire of how far she'd come.

And to do everything she could *not* to go back.

Flushed cheeks from the warm oven and bright green eyes from her caffeine addiction stared back at her. Claire kept her make-up to a minimal. Mascara and color lip gloss were sufficient when dealing with animals all day.

A rhythmic rapping on her front door brought a smile to Claire's face. Jace. She wiped her damp palms on the polka dot ruffle apron and hurried to the door, flinging it open with a flare. Standing before her, dressed in a navy flannel with an adhesive name tag on the spot above his heart, stood her friend. Claire tilted her head and mentally ran over excuses why he would need a name tag.

"Nice to meet you, Jace. My name is Claire," she quipped, holding out her hand. "Why?"

Jace rolled his eyes despite the hint of a smile. "I'm going with Mom to a luncheon at the community center to discuss the upcoming seed exchange."

"Everyone in town knows you," she said, stepping to the side to let him in.

"Not the new mayor and people from the next town. The committee wants to expand the offerings of flower and plant seeds. So name tags it is. Of course, Dad, Logan, and Caden were all too busy to go with her."

It was rare for anyone in the family to say no to his mother, Josie. Jace was the youngest of the Beckett family and usually bent over backwards to accommodate his mother.

"I think it's sweet you're going to be your mom's date," Claire teased as she closed the door.

"Having fun, are you?" Jace's admonishment held no heat. "I have resigned myself to endless stories of how much I've grown or how their daughter or niece is single now and looking for husband number two or three. Mom will tell them to mind their own business while appearing to be the pillar of the community. Then she'll sit at the table with her friends and gossip. Basically, the usual. The food is worth the torture, though."

Claire giggled. "That's the payoff, uh."

"I'm not stupid. Maeve is making her macaroni and cheese and promised to set aside a dish for me to take home. She told me since Logan is too busy to come with his mother, I can eat it all."

Maeve was Logan's mother-in-law and one of Josie's best friends. She now lived with her fiancé a couple of miles down the road.

"Of course you're going to eat it right in front of him."

"You know me too well, Buttercup."

Jace gifted her with the nickname shortly after seeing her wear several scrub tops with various versions of the petite flower. It was her favorite flower because it grew wild in the trailer park. Claire would always pick a bunch and place them in old jars.

Jace pulled a screwdriver out of his back pocket. "You said the light fixture in the bedroom was wobbly?"

It didn't surprise Claire he remembered her mentioning the problem in passing yesterday. That's just the kind of man he was.

"You didn't have to make a special trip," Claire said, leading him to the bedroom. "It could have waited."

"It's not a problem. I'm meeting Mom in thirty minutes, and you're five hundred feet away." He tilted his nose in the air. "What smells good?"

The buzzer sounded before Claire could answer. "Sweet potato banana treats. Or it could be the white chocolate fudge which you can have a few pieces."

She hurried from the room and pulled the current molds from the oven and set them on a kitchen towel. She slipped the tray that held the oatmeal and carob mixture in and set the timer. Jace was strolling into the living room when she turned around.

"All done. If you want a newer fixture, it's no big deal to change it."

Claire shook her head and tugged a freezer bag from the holder. "It's fine. I mostly use the lamps, but I had to dig my craft things from the closet and it provides better light."

She used a plastic knife to cut into the cooled fudge. A nerve spasm ran from her wrist to her elbow, causing her to stop. Jace missed nothing and hurried over when the knife hit the floor.

"Are you okay?"

It was past the time for her dose of medication and cursed herself for getting caught up in baking. Claire nodded and reached for her pill bottle on the counter. Jace already had the refrigerator door open, pulling her filter pitcher from the bottom shelf.

The Becketts understood she had nerve damage. Surgery couldn't guarantee it would correct the problem. When she took her medication as prescribed, she rarely had problems. Logan could read when she was overdoing it and gently suggested she work on emails to give her hand time to relax.

Jace was different.

They were friends, but there were feelings. On both sides. The last thing she wanted was his pity.

Their fingers brushed when Claire took the offered cup of water. She ignored the tingle in her heart and swallowed her large caplets. She would need to rest for forty minutes while they kicked in. "You're going to be late meeting Josie," Claire commented, taking a seat in the kitchen chair. "I'll have the fudge cut and packaged by the time you get back."

Jace shook his head, picking the knife up from the floor. "I have five minutes. She knew I was stopping here first. What do you need to finish?"

"You don't need to do anything. I can take what's in the oven out with one hand and put the cooled treats in containers. The batter for the cookies can rest in the fridge for a bit. Seriously, I'm fine."

"I know, but I can at least put this to the side for you." He moved the mixing bowl into the refrigerator. "Tell me what else you need before I go."

"Nothing. Thank you for getting me the water. Go before Josie comes over here looking for you."

That was the last thing Claire wanted. The matriarch of the family was a natural nurturer and would make herself late for her luncheon if she knew Claire had an episode. She appreciated the woman's concern, but there was nothing she could do now that she'd taken her medicine. Claire dealt with the nerve damage long enough. Being babied wouldn't help.

Jace studied Claire for a moment before offering a quick nod. "Fine. I have time to store the treats for you."

She didn't want to argue. Instead, she motioned towards the two tin canisters labeled with the flavor of treats. Claire watched as he quickly plopped the crunchy nibbles from their mold.

When Claire took the job at Hawkins Ridge, she didn't expect to find a place that felt like home. She had a dream job making more money than her mother had working for the fulfillment center back home. She now had friends who saw past her burn scars and her humble beginnings to the woman she was. It was a life she wished she could share with her mother. But she couldn't wait to show her aunt that she was happy.

Despite her feelings for Jace.

"Okay, Buttercup," Jace said, pulling Claire out of her thoughts. "I'll check on you when we return."

"Thank you for fixing the light and everything else." Claire stood, the pain in her arm subsiding. "I'll have the fudge ready. Tell Josie and Maeve I said hi."

Jace wrapped his arms around her for a quick hug. The soft material held his patent, woodsy cologne.

"Don't overdo it when you feel better." Jace stepped back and sighed. "Wish me luck with Mom's friends."

Claire giggled as he made his way out the door. A glance out the window showed Jace jogging to his truck across the road, where his mother stood saying goodbye to Logan. She sighed and turned away from the scene. Her gaze fell onto her high school graduation photo sitting on her mantel. Claire stood between Rue and Garrett. All three flashed huge smiles.

Her job, home, and friends were the life her mother and aunt wanted for Claire. She moved past the heartache of her ex-fiancé, Andy, and landed on her feet again. Jace's declaration at Logan's wedding months earlier still played in the back of her mind. He wanted something more and gave Claire time to think about a possibility. She massaged her hand as the memory washed over her.

Jace and their friend, Noah, returned with small plates of appetizers.

"Nibble on these while we walk outside." Jace plucked a stuffed mushroom cap and held it in front of her lips. Confused, Claire opened her mouth for him to feed her. "If you were hungry, why didn't you say something? Do you have food in the house? We can go shopping this evening."

The earthy flavor of the appetizer lodged in her throat momentarily before she could swallow. "Why do you think I don't have food? Why would you even care?"

"Your stomach growled."

Claire rolled her eyes. "I didn't eat breakfast because I was nervous. I have food. Even if I didn't, I can buy my own."

"I didn't like hearing that sound. To answer your other question, of course I care, why wouldn't I?" He held the door for her to step out into the autumn sun first. Claire squinted for a moment while her glasses darkened.

"I don't know. You confuse me sometimes."

Claire snagged a brownie bite and popped it in her mouth. Jace held her elbow, bringing her to a stop. The photographer had the wedding party stand to the side while she positioned Logan and Naomi for their couple photo. Claire sucked in a breath when Jace bent and held her gaze.

"I'm going to make this clear so there's no more confusion. I like you. For some unknown reason, you think that my compliments, the expression of how I feel, is a joke. I'm not kidding, Buttercup. I like everything about you. The way you talk to the dogs before you give them their medicine. How you nibble your lower lip when you measure out the cat's food. The way you twirl your hair around your finger when you're reading an email. How you wear your red *rimmed glasses every Monday because you want to start the week off in a positive mood." Jace took a step closer. "The way your cheeks turn pink when I wink at you. So why I care is because I want more than what we have."*

Despite being aware that her mouth was open, Claire couldn't remember how to close it. Jace was serious. Did he stop flirting to give her a chance to truly know him? It was only when he did that; she opened herself up to seeing him as a friend. Now came the question: did she want more? She felt at ease and content with him in the friend zone. Too much was at stake if things didn't work out, including her job, a place to live, and her friends.

"I don't know what—"

"Don't say anything," Jace interrupted. "I'll give you until the new year to wrap your head around what I said. Just know that I have an answer for every argument you can think of as to why we wouldn't be good together. Now let's go get our picture taken so we can eat a decent meal."

Claire blinked back to the present. She enjoyed Jace in the friend zone. It was safe. Losing all she worked for, a life in the Oak Mountain community and her friends to start over if it didn't work out, held her from taking the step. Jace's reputation of a man that couldn't commit also played a big factor.

Claire shook her head, running her fingers over the paper mâché covered frame. Jace held the role as the face of Hawkins Ridge and has a standing in the Oak Mountain community. Claire may be confident in her abilities as a vet tech and finally slayed the taunts from childhood about her scars. The scrutiny from Jace's former dating pool was something Claire didn't want.

Keeping Jace as a friend would probably be the best for her mental and emotional well-being.

Right?

Chapter Two

Puffs of white air escaped Jace's mouth as he rounded the bend past the stables on Hawkins Ridge. The small lamp band around his head lit his way as his feet pounded the hard dirt. Oriole, his rescued orange and black retriever mix, happily kept pace during their morning jog. Dressed in matching white hoodies to ward off the early March cold, Jace never thought he'd be one of those pet owners to wear matching outfits.

If his old colleagues from the firehouse could see him now.

Technically, Jace still helped the fire department when major emergencies hit the small town of Oak Mountain. He took a step back nine months earlier to focus on his position with the family business started by his great grandfather.

Initially, a horse farm started by his great grandfather. Over the decades, Hawkins Ridge grew into what it is today. A sanctuary who rescues strays and takes in dogs and cats from regional shelters. Most were prepared for adoption or trained to be support animals. The rest lived their remaining lives on the property, receiving unconditional love. Instead of breeding, they now offer horse boarding and training. Chickens, eggs, creating goat milk products and growing fruits and veggies for the local co-ops and farmer markets, rounded out the rest of the property's function.

It's a sustainable business that supports the needs of the community and protects the animals in the region. At least, that's how Jace presents it to potential clients and partners now that he and his brothers handle the day-to-day operations.

They wanted to expand the reach of Hawkins Ridge past the county to regional. His ability to bring in business could make their dreams a reality. Deep down, doubts churned in his gut, wondering if he could live up to the expectation of being the face of the business and negotiating deals.

No pressure.

Jace adjusted the hood covering his dark blond hair back over his ears as he passed his parents' house. A light glowed behind the drawn curtains. Knowing his parents, he wagered they were attending to the cat sanctuary. His parents and his brother Logan switched houses after the first of the year, when the stairs in the main house were too much for them. Besides, Logan, his daughter, Fiona, and new wife, Naomi, needed more space. Six dogs, no matter how small, needed room.

The first morning rays dotted through the barren oak trees on the property. This was his favorite time of the day. The quiet calm before the organized chaos of workers, animals, family, and responsibility ate up the day. At thirty-five, this was the life he knew and now finally accepted. His playboy days were behind him thanks to the empty house across from his parents.

A handmade stick wreath decorated Claire's front door. She'd left three days ago to spend time with her cousin and aunt on the other side of town. Jace missed seeing her around the property, but understood she needed this time. They've texted to say good morning, but Jace didn't want to come across as needy.

Claire was his one. He knew within a week of her arriving on the property. Unfortunately, his reputation as someone who couldn't commit was almost legendary—and half true.

Jace refused to settle. He'd seen his two brothers and best friend go through painful divorces of women who were only interested in having the Beckett or Garrison name. He, too, had his own heartbreak when his college girlfriend moved overseas. Jace wouldn't go through that again.

Leah was the first girl he developed actual feelings for. They met in a public relations class during their junior year. After being placed on a class project together, they became close. Leah was a small-town girl from Ohio, and Jace figured she would want to return to that lifestyle after they finished at the University of Pittsburgh.

He was wrong.

Leah applied for jobs in their senior year in Pittsburgh. Jace, still unsure about what he wanted to do with the family business, figured a couple of years in a large city would help him when he returned home later in life. Sometimes, youth and stupidity go hand in hand. Offers poured in and he assumed they would start a future together. It devastated him when Leah announced her true plans of starting a life as a single expat. Jace retreated to his mind and almost failed the final semester of school.

So, he came home. Lost, unsure, and bitter.

Jace assumed they would be the four bachelors running Hawkins Ridge and passing everything to his niece when it was time. Then Logan found the love of his life last year. It's what made Jace accept his feelings for Claire as true.

First, he had to show her there was more to him than his reputation. Hence, why he went the friend route. He wanted Claire to see the real Jace Beckett. If he was honest, he wanted to prove to himself that he was worthy of Claire.

Jace took a bold step at Logan's wedding. While waiting for the wedding party pictures, he laid his cards on the table and said he wanted more from their relationship. He valued their friendship and the last thing he wanted was to pressure her. So, he wanted to give her time to think and see the possibility.

Jace also had to settle into his role in the family business full time. Something he fought but now embraced because he spent his time on the property instead of the firehouse. Time spent with his family and Claire.

Clearing his mind, Jace slowed to an easy trot on the last leg of his run, unclipping his water bottle from his waist. Coming up to the goat barn, the two large livestock guard dogs trotted over to say hello to their friend. Oriole hurried over, tail whipping in the wind. His brother, not by blood but by heart, stepped out of the goat barn to the pasture and tossed up a wave.

Noah Garrison propped a shovel against a tree stump and adjusted his fleece band covering his ears. A tinge of redness from the cold dotted his medium-brown complexion. The two were born two weeks apart and thick as thieves. Their parents were best friends and claimed they didn't plan their births. Noah and his father had a stake in the business.

"You have coffee yet?" Noah asked, closing the distance.

Jace walked in circles, stretching intermittently. "No. You coming over to get some? I had the timer set."

Noah glanced at his watch. "Give me thirty minutes to feed the goats. Dad brought over cinnamon rolls last night. I'll grab you a few."

His mouth watered. Noah's father, Owen, and Jace's mother kept the family fed and happy. That would change soon when their folks embraced retirement and started traveling.

"That works. I need to take Cammie out first."

Jace said his goodbye and strolled into the cluster of trees. Oriole trotted past and met him at the front door of his house. The entrance to his driveway was a turnoff from the greenhouse. Jace purposely had his home built away from the bustle of the property. When he worked as a firefighter, his hours varied and if he needed sleep, he didn't need the normal, everyday noise keeping him awake.

"Let's get you warmed up. Your sister may need company while she does her business."

He opened the door and Oriole let out a small bark. From her spot on the heated blanket near the ottoman, Cammie darted to the sound of her brother and owner. The blind Pomeranian was a year old. She had the same energy as any of the pets and kept up with Oriole when they played. Nothing stopped his little dynamo from getting around the house. If Cammie headed towards danger, Oriole always nudged her back on track.

Having an open floor plan helped Cammie adjust when he bought her home after rescuing her. When he had the home built, it was with the purpose of starting a family and having gatherings. He was happy Cammie could benefit from it, at least.

Jace scooped the dog up when she stopped in front of him and nuzzled his nose against her tan fur. She rewarded him with kisses on his neck. He slipped on her sweater before placing her on the cool tile to follow Oriole out the door. Cammie dropped her nose to the ground to sniff her way around the front yard. Jace knew Oriole wouldn't let anything happen to his sister, freeing up a minute for him to start a fire in the fireplace. He positioned both dog beds near the hearth before stepping into the kitchen to start the oven for the bacon.

Before the switch in residences, Jace and Noah would have breakfast at the main house. Now, until things settled, everyone was on their own. Most mornings, though, the two friends still shared coffee and a quick bite before starting the day.

Jace made his way to the front door and let out a loud whistle. Both dogs scurried in and gave matching body shakes. After disrobing both dogs, they followed him back to the kitchen, where Jace scooped a serving of the fresh, wet food Logan made. He sat the bowl on the mat and tapped the side of Cammie's so she would know where it was located. While they ate, Jace hopped in the shower and thought of his day.

He had plans with his brothers to move the rest of Naomi's boxes out of storage and help unpack. He also needed to talk to them about getting an assistant. Jace needed help keeping everything straight.

Posting on social media, rescuing dogs from their shelter partners, contacting new businesses for their products and lining up homes to foster the animals was a lot. The last thing he wanted was to disappoint his brothers. Not that they would be mad if he couldn't get another diner or co-op to use their eggs or cheese.

No, Jace wanted to make his brothers proud. He wanted to do his part in bringing the business to the next level. He wanted to prove to Claire he was worthy of her affection.

Jace finished his shower and padded back into his bedroom. He designed it with his and her closets. Something he thought he would have with Leah. After she ended their two-year relationship, Jace swore off getting serious with anyone. He understood finding someone to spend his life with was ideal, but the women he dated were only interested in the Beckett name. They weren't willing to put in the work necessary to build their future. He'd all but given up and began looking at adoption.

Then Claire showed up.

Long silky dark hair Jace itched to brush. Twinkling green eyes, behind a pair of fashionable glasses. Voluptuous soft curves any man with eyes would want to cuddle with in front of a roaring fire. He chuckled, thinking about her sharp wit while he slipped on a navy blue henley and a pair of worn jeans. The woman was the entire package. But she saw his flirting as a game and tossed him in the friend zone before he knew what happened. Now he wanted to show her his interest was legit.

First, she had to come home from visiting her family.

He stepped into the living room just as Noah walked through the front door. Both dogs greeted him as he passed off the plastic container filled with sweet sugary goodness. Noah gave each dog equal lovings before following Jace into the kitchen.

"Remind me to grab eggs after we're done with Logan," Jace commented and pulled the bowl of fresh eggs from the fridge.

Noah nodded and picked up the dogs' empty bowls and set them in the sink. "I ran into Tinsley when I dropped off the cheese this morning. Wanted me to tell you hi."

Jace rolled his eyes. "We had a date last year, and she's still trying to get another one out of me. I told her it wasn't working for me before dinner was even over."

"Was it the gum popping or the fact she thought roosters lay eggs?"

A grin graced Jace's lips. "You're taught in elementary school the difference between the two. I know cause all three of us sat in the same row when Mr. Brooks told us."

"To be fair, Tinsley's interests during that time were boy bands and becoming the next reality TV star." Noah sat the last of the bowl on the drying rack and took the eggs to crack. "Did you talk to Logan and Caden about getting you help?"

Jace carefully placed the bacon on the cookie sheet rack and shook his head. "I wanted to find time today to bring up the subject. I don't see where it should be a problem. Trying to round up more foster homes for the animals is a challenge. The time to interview them and do home visit before we can add them to the list."

One of the brothers' goals was to partner with shelters across the state over the next two years. For that to happen, they needed foster homes to help prepare dogs and cats for their forever homes. As a firefighter, Jace witnessed firsthand the conditions in which some animals were kept. He would always return on his day off or call his brothers to go to the homes and talk the owners into surrendering them. It was how he got Cammie. The Pomeranian's previous owners didn't know what to do with the blind puppy and kept her outdoors so she wouldn't knock over items in their house. Jace parked the firetruck when he saw her aimlessly walking in circles. It took all of two minutes to convince the young couple to give her up.

Jace slid the tray into the oven before glancing at his baby curled up next to her brother in front of the fire. Best decision he ever made. He turned his attention back to Noah.

"Are you still planning on doing soaps next weekend?"

Noah nodded while crumbling herb infused goat cheese over the cooking eggs and moved it around the skillet. "Will Claire be back by then? She loves helping."

Jace pulled plates and silverware out before pouring them both coffee. "I think so. We've been texting a little. I didn't want to bother her with her aunt's visit."

"Are you still planning on pursuing her?"

Jace handed him his mug just as the oven buzzed. He nudged his friend out of the way so he could pull the bacon out.

"I am. Agreeing to go the friend route was for her to see the real me. Not the town's playboy that her cousin made me out to be when she moved here. I also needed the time to get a handle on working the family business full time." Jace slid the bacon onto paper towels, then went about scooping cheesy eggs onto their plates. "I still feel like I'm floundering sometimes." He had to be honest.

"You're not. You, me, Logan, and Caden know what we're doing. If we didn't, the folks wouldn't have trusted us to fully take over at the start of the new year. We've already increased orders for the goat products and produce because of you." Noah clapped him on the shoulder. "Don't sell yourself short and don't give up on Claire."

Jace gave a tight nod and picked up his plate, including the extra slices of bacon for the dogs, and headed to the breakfast bar. He appreciated Noah's words, but he still felt the pressure of sealing enough contracts so they could still stay small and yet be profitable. After all, it would always be a family-owned business. They knew how far they wanted to grow to make that happen, which was why they had different ventures. Getting a grip on his feelings for Claire added to his unsettled mind.

Jace crumbled pieces of bacon onto two saucers and carried it over to the dogs. Both popped up from a dead sleep and gobbled their treats. He and Noah tucked into their breakfast in silence as he went back to his mental checklist for the day. He added, confirming with Logan when Claire was returning, followed by putting together an email campaign for the upcoming spring sale.

Priorities, after all.

Chapter Three

The light from the diner lit the interior of Claire's car. Her left hand shook as she tried to get the child safety cap off the bottle of acetaminophen. Her head pounded from days without caffeine. It was the only reason she would sit in the diner's parking lot, in thirty-four-degree weather, at five thirty in the morning, dressed in her flannel jammies to get a cup of coffee. She had the brilliance to braid her long dark hair before going to bed the night before. No one in Oak Mountain wanted to see the horror of her bed hair.

Once the cap was off, she dry-swallowed two pills, then focused on blowing on the hot liquid. The steam fogged her glasses, but she didn't care as she took a sizable gulp. Claire's eyes rolled back in her head as the first taste warmed her body.

Garrett didn't mention he and his wife were only drinking decaf because she was pregnant. If he had, she would have bought her single serve coffee maker. She could have stayed at Hawkins Ridge and drove to her cousin's daily, but she had the time off and wanted to get away. Sort of mini staycation.

Claire took another fortifying sip before backing out of the parking spot. She hoped to get back to her cousin's home before anyone woke up. Driving through the quiet of Oak Mountain helped calm her frayed nerves.

Her cousin managed the town's feed store. When he told her about the position, it was during a time Claire needed to leave Virginia.

Her ex-fiancé, Andy, cheated on her with one of his co-workers. He was her first long-term relationship. Working towards her goal of becoming a vet tech and financial stability didn't allow time for romance. Andy wormed his way in her heart and Claire let her guard down. They were together six months before he proposed. It was a happy day.

A week after the big question, Claire stopped by his apartment to share the good news of receiving a raise. The woman who answered the door dressed in a towel prevented her from telling Andy. Claire politely handed her the ring, told Andy it was over when he appeared behind the mysterious person, and fled to her place.

For a month, Andy became mentally abusive. Texts and notes on her car about her weight and burns brought back memories of childhood bullying. When she found herself spiraling into depression and losing her self-esteem, Claire did what most people would. She went home. Quitting her job was hard, but Claire had to protect her sanity. She moved back to her hometown and into the trailer with Aunt Rue and healed, finding her self-worth again. She also knew staying in that hateful town would only send her spiraling again.

Claire didn't think twice when Logan offered her the position.

Since being in Oak Mountain, she'd formed a close friendship with Naomi, Logan's wife. Both were new to the small town when they met and bonded over their goal of starting over in a new place. It was something Claire had no desire to jeopardize.

No matter how tempting Jace Beckett was.

At Naomi and Logan's wedding, Jace proclaimed he wanted something more than their friendship. He said he would give her time to think about the possibility. It was another reason she spent her aunt's visit off the property. She wanted to get Rue's opinion on the subject but hadn't had a moment alone.

The thought excited and scared Claire. Yes, it flattered her that the most handsome, sweetest man in Oak Mountain was interested in a short, bespectacled, extra curvy bookworm. But the fear of losing everything she'd built the past year and having to start over was real.

Oak Mountain had three veterinarians. Logan Beckett, Thomas Beckett, and Naomi Hendrix-Beckett. There were no other practices in town she could go to. Claire wanted a place to settle down. The town had everything she was looking for: a friendly atmosphere, a diverse population, an incredible view of the leaves in the fall, and one of the two people left in her family. The possibility of throwing that away if things didn't work out with Jace made the coffee in her stomach roll.

Light of the morning sun set the sky a pinkish hue. Claire turned onto her cousin's street. A looming figure sat on the top step of the front porch, watching a dog sniff every diameter of the mature pine tree in the front yard. Claire pulled to a stop behind her aunt's simple pickup truck. Her cousin's quaint three-bedroom single story brick home was on the east side of town. The family-oriented neighborhood was another reminder of how far they came.

Her mother would be proud of what the two had accomplished.

Balty, Rue's mix breed dog, met her at the driver's side door, his tail wagging high in the wind.

"Good morning to you, kind sir," Claire cooed, scratching behind his ear. It was Balty's cue to go into a case of zoomies around the yard.

"The last time I've seen you leave the house in your pajamas was when you picked me up from Eric Seavers' house 'cause I missed curfew," Garrett teased from his spot. His light brown hair still had the signs of sleep. Dressed in a thick sweatshirt and flannel sleep pants, he looked like an expectant father waiting for their daughter to come home from a date.

"You missed curfew because you pissed off your girlfriend and she left your butt at the party." Claire took a seat beside him and clutched her coffee tighter. "Did you get my note?"

He nodded. "I'm surprised it took you three days to give in to your caffeine withdrawals."

"The only reason I didn't go to the diner yesterday is because Rue was already up making breakfast. Why didn't you tell me you'd gone to the dark side and started drinking decaf?"

"I haven't. I guzzle about three cups of the good stuff at work." Garrett called for Balty, who wasted no time coming to heel. "I'm showing solidarity with Sara since she had to give it up for the baby. She allows me to drink it at work just as long as I don't brag about doing it."

Garrett's wife was four months pregnant with their first child. Claire loved her cousin-in-law. The blonde, waif beauty had a heart of gold. Garrett met her while she was in grad school in Virginia, and he worked as the supervisor for the grounds crew. When Sara returned to Oak Mountain to be a pre-school teacher, Garrett came with her.

Claire patted his knee and rose to her feet. "You're a good husband."

"Aren't I?" He pointed to Claire's left hand. "Where's your glove?"

"The need for coffee muddled my brain to put it on. I also can't really drive in it."

"Good thing we're going in."

Garrett held the door for her and Balty. She sighed in relief as the heat warmed her bones. The numbness in her hand supported her cousin's argument. The nerve damage to her hand was worse in colder temperatures.

"You okay?" Garrett said from behind her, bringing her back to the present.

"Just taking a minute to enjoy the quiet. Workers are already getting the morning feed ready back at the sanctuary. I didn't realize how used to the dull noise I'd become." She gave him a soft smile and snagged her compression glove from the coffee table. She slipped it on before picking up her coffee. "What time do you have to be at work?"

Garrett studied her for a moment. Claire poked his side to show she was okay. Though younger by a year, he took on a big brother role when his height shot past her in middle school. He returned the affectionate poke with one of his own.

"Seven. Between the garden sale and a truckload of gravel, it's going to be a busy day."

"Josie is going to help Naomi and I put together window boxes."

Garrett chuckled. "Her garden club has an order in for potting soil." He led her into the kitchen and started a pot of decaf. "I'm glad you like it here. I'm going to try to talk Mom into moving. Now that her disability has come through, she doesn't need to be in that town alone."

Claire settled at the kitchen table. "It would be great for her to be close, especially with the baby coming."

"That's what I was thinking. I was hoping you could help me talk her in to it."

Claire snorted before guzzling her last sip of coffee. "Rue's not the type to be talked into anything. Since she's here for over a month, I think we have time to *show* her the best part of Oak Mountain. Once I catch up on everything, I'll bring her out to Hawkins Ridge, introduce her to Josie."

It seemed the matriarch of the Beckett clan was part of the welcoming committee for new residents over the age of fifty-five. Unofficially, of course. If Garrett was serious about Rue moving, Josie would be their co-conspirator.

"Thanks. I'm going to hop in the shower. I think Sara is going with her mother and sister shopping if you and Mom want to go."

Claire liked Sara's family well enough. Walking around the mall in the next town over was not her idea of fun. She didn't think Rue would be on board with the invitation, either. It would also give her a chance to talk to her aunt about what she was going through.

"I'll probably pass. If Rue wants to do something special, I'll take her."

"Thank you." Garrett patted Balty on the head as he headed out of the kitchen. "I'm glad you stayed these days instead of going back and forth every day."

Claire was too, but he was gone before she could respond. Hope swelled in her at the thought of Rue moving to Oak Mountain. She had Josie and Naomi's mother, but it wasn't the same as having her aunt. As she pulled an English muffin from the bag, she thought of spending the day with her aunt. Perhaps she would get the nerve to talk to Rue about her feelings for Jace. Maybe even get a handle on her fear of losing everything she worked so hard for.

The intoxicating aroma of warm apple and cinnamon teased Jace as he stepped into his family home. He stopped in the kitchen and took a deep inhale. Apple cider and homemade lemon sugar cookies had his stomach growling. A hard shove brought him out of his food induced fantasy.

"Why are you just standing there?" Noah growled around the two boxes he held. "The faster we get this done, the faster we can eat."

"Logan should have fed us first," Jace responded as he continued to the living room and dropped the two boxes he held onto the couch.

"If I had done that, none of y'all would have helped," his oldest brother said as he jogged down the steps.

Noah placed his load in the corner next to the artificial olive trees. "Why didn't you just have the movers do this when you made the switch?"

"Because Naomi didn't want to pay the movers for a second day to get her things out of storage," Caden, his middle brother, commented as he rounded the corner from the den.

Jace fell back into the recliner and ran his fingers through his shoulder length hair.

"Except for a few totes, I think we're done." Jace's lower back throbbed. "I'm going to need my massage chair when I get home."

"You're thirty-five," Logan fussed, taking a spot on the couch. "Wait until you get to be my age."

"Yep, thirty-nine is ancient." Noah squeezed in between Logan and a stack of books. "Our folks are in their sixties and in better shape than we are."

"That's because they had us to pass off chores to when they were our age," Caden quipped, taking the last chair in the crowded living room. Everyone nodded in agreement.

Jace loved his brothers. They each held specific positions in their family business. Logan was a veterinarian and took care of the well-being of the animals, including the horses they boarded. He also had patients on the surrounding farms. Caden ran the stables and training of the animals who would be available for adoption. Noah oversaw the small farm, the goats, and their goat milk-based products they sold.

"Where do we stand with food?" Noah asked, rising to his feet.

"I could eat." Logan pressed his fists into his lower back. "We need to talk about the next few days, anyway."

They all agreed and headed to the kitchen. A plastic wrap tray of thick ham sandwiches sat in the fridge. Jace couldn't stop the smile that graced his lips as he sat their lunch on the large island. Noah stepped out of the walk-in pantry with paper plates and a party-size bag of chips. They made small talk of college basketball and plans to watch that weekend's game together while making their plates and ladling warm cider into cups. Once settled at the family table, set between the kitchen and living room area, Logan started speaking.

"They're calling for temps in the upper fifties this coming week. We talked about doing a major cleaning and airing out the enclosures. Do we have enough people scheduled?"

Caden nodded. "We should. No one scheduled time to take their horses out. We're also expanding the chicken run."

"I want to use the trees we cut during the blizzard to make obstacles for the goats to play on," Noah added. "The gardeners plan to take the coverings off the in-ground crops to see what we have to work with."

Jace reached for a chip. "Have you scheduled second interviews for the new manager of staff?"

Logan swallowed his bite. "Yep. I'll email everyone later today."

With Noah's father retiring as manager of staff, it would be the first time in fifty years someone without the last name Beckett or Garrison would hold the position. The family had hoped Jace would take over for Owen, but the family agreed his skills were the strongest brokering partnerships with other sanctuaries, retail for the organic products and build support for the service dog training.

Caden cleared his throat as he wiped his mouth. "I'm going to ask the question no one is brave enough to bring up. What about family meals? Do you or Naomi plan on taking over cooking duties?"

Everyone laughed, including Logan. Jace wondered the same thing. The back screen door slammed shut, followed by light footsteps. Josie strolled in carrying a plastic container.

"What's so funny?" She pulled the lid off and sat the round tub in the middle of the table. All four hands dove for the warm chocolate chip goodness.

Logan slid over a chair to let her sit while Jace spoke around a mouthful. "We're concerned that since Logan and Naomi took over the big house, we're going to starve."

"All of you know how to cook." Josie grinned, taking a cookie. "But Naomi has offered the kitchen to Owen and me for dinners, and we'll still have family breakfasts on the weekend."

"That's a relief," Caden mocked, wiping his brow.

Josie ignored her middle son and turned towards Logan. "Will Claire be back tomorrow?"

The name alone warmed Jace from head to toe.

"I still don't understand why she couldn't come home every day." Jace shoved another cookie in his mouth, keeping his gaze on his plate.

"Ignore him." Noah patted him on the shoulder. "He'd gotten used to seeing her every day and now he's going through withdrawals."

His family knew he had feelings for the woman. The twinkle in his mother's voice softly admonished him.

"She wanted time with her aunt. I know we see her as one of the family, but she needed the break."

"It's only been three days," Logan added. "Are you going to follow through with asking if she wants more?"

Jace nodded. "I want her to know I'm serious."

"I think she knows." Josie crossed her legs and held her son's gaze. "You need to remember, she's barely been in Oak Mountain a year. She's a shy person most people in town know nothing about, except that she's Garrett's cousin. Somehow, she has garnered the attention of one of the town's most eligible bachelors. That's a lot for someone like her."

Jace raked his fingers through his hair. "I know. No one outside the family knows I have feelings for her."

"And when the women who have had their hearts broken will see Claire as the one able to do what they couldn't, the cattiness towards her will be on a new level." Caden pointed a finger. "Make sure this is what you want because you're going to have people trying to put a wedge between you two."

Logan agreed. "Naomi still gets looks from the single mothers when she's out with Fiona. They don't have the guts to say something to her. Those superficial vipers you surrounded yourself with will have no problem approaching Claire."

His family spoke the truth. Since he realized Claire was the one for him, he hadn't been on any dates and had ended all contact with his special friends. Jace wanted to show Claire he was more than his reputation. He also needed to show his family he was ready to step up and do what they needed him to.

"I hear what you're saying. My previous actions may bounce back onto Claire. Am I supposed to ignore how I feel because of what other women may or may not do?" Jace blew out a breath. "I haven't felt this way about a woman since Leah, and we haven't been on one date. All I can say is that if people have a problem, I will help her deal with it."

"We all will," Noah said, clapping Jace on the shoulder. His family mumbled the same sentiment.

"We care for Claire." The love in his mother's eyes was obvious. "You let me know if any of those women say something. I'm sure I have their mothers' numbers on speed dial." Everyone laughed as they rose to clear the table.

Jace knew his family had his back with Claire and his responsibility at the sanctuary. Now he just had to convince Claire to give him a chance.

Chapter Four

Claire pushed up her glasses after closing the dishwasher door. Her cousin-in-law understood when Claire and Rue declined her offer for shopping. It was her last day of vacation and really wanted to spend time with her aunt. Balty nudged her hip, looking for lovings or a biscuit.

"You've had more than enough this morning," she cooed, giving him a scratch behind the ear. "I'll try to sneak you a piece of chicken later."

"When you do it in front of everyone, it's no longer sneaking," Aunt Rue teased as she strolled into the kitchen braiding her damp, long gray hair.

"How could I say no? Look at those eyes."

"You've always had a hard time saying no to animals." Rue tugged open the cabinet door by the refrigerator. "Do you want some tea?"

Now that Claire felt more like herself after her coffee fix, she nodded and filled the stovetop kettle. Neither Garrett nor his wife were tea drinkers, but his mother was. He stocked up on all of her favorites whenever she visited.

"Tell me about your job." Rue placed a citrus tea bag in their mugs. "Garrett said the town has nothing but respect for the family."

"That's true. The Becketts are a warm and giving family and I love working for the sanctuary. I'm glad this is an extended visit because I want to introduce you to them. Balty would love my friend's dogs. There's enough room for you to stay a day or two." Claire's home was a one-bedroom, but she'd give up her bed to Rue and sleep on the couch.

"Then we'll have to go out there soon. I miss seeing you."

Claire wrapped her arm around her aunt's shoulder and gave her a side hug. "I miss you too."

Rue didn't hesitate to take Claire in after the death of her mother. Both were single mothers and worked at the same fulfillment plant. Rue and Dorothy adjusted their schedule so the other could babysit the kids. Even when Claire moved out after high school, she always visited her aunt once a month.

The whistle of the kettle ended their moment. Claire turned off the stove and poured the water into the cups. Rue carried the cups to the kitchen table while Claire snagged the tin of cookies. This was the first time she'd been alone with her aunt since she arrived.

Rue brought the warm mug to her mouth and gave a gentle blow. The same green eyes as Claire's held her gaze. "So tell me what is on your mind. You've been chewing on something for a couple of days."

"How do you know I'm thinking about something?"

"You've been nibbling on your nails."

Claire glanced down at the ragged edges. Heat rose to her cheeks. Deep down, she was glad her aunt brought up the need to talk. She snagged a bird shape cookie to stare at while she spoke.

"There's a man."

"It's about time."

Claire playfully rolled her eyes, calming her nerves. "Anyway, the man is the brother, well one of them, of the doctor I work for. Before you say anything, let me finish."

Rue held up her hand and motioned for her to continue.

"His name is Jace. He's made his feelings known shortly after I started that he's interested. The problem is, he has a reputation as a ladies' man. Izzy, that's a woman I work with, has said Jace hasn't had a relationship since college."

"So you think he is only interested in one thing?" Rue took a sip.

"At first, yes. According to Naomi, Logan's wife—"

"You're going to write these names down, so I remember. My mind isn't what it used to be."

Rue was fifty-eight and had one of the sharpest minds Claire knew. Though she was on disability for the past two years because of a back injury, it didn't affect her memory.

"Okay quickly. Logan Beckett is the doctor I work for. His new wife, Naomi, is also a veterinarian. Her practice is at the sanctuary. Izzy is her vet tech."

"Got it. Go on." The smirk on her aunt's face had Claire laughing.

"Anyway, Jace backed off about a month later and said he wanted to be friends. Naomi said he wanted me to see that he was more than his reputation."

"And now?"

Claire exhaled, leaning back in her seat. "Now, I know he wants to see if there could be something between the two of us. I enjoy having him as a friend. It's safe for me if we stay that way."

"Safe in what way?"

The question gave Claire pause. Putting into words why it was safe to keep Jace in the friend zone may seem cowardly to some. A good number of women in Oak Mountain would jump at the chance to say they were in a relationship with Jace. But Claire had a lot to lose.

"He's my boss' brother. If things don't work out, why would they keep me on? The only other practicing vet in town is Naomi. So it's not like I have employment options. Besides, I still don't think he wants a relationship. Nothing about me is his type."

"Have you ever considered that could be why he's attracted to you?" Rue ran her hand down Balty's back.

"No, I haven't and not sure I could think that." Claire ran her hand along her left arm. "These burns don't attract people." She then motioned along her body. "Some men can appreciate my short, fat curves. I can't see Jace being one of those people. You know, he went out with Sara's sister in high school."

Claire's cousin-in-law and her sister were willowy with blonde hair. She and Sara shared a love of books and would text suggestions to one another. Though the young high school relationship lasted a month in eleventh grade, she always spoke kindly of him. Maybe Jace had a thing for nerds. Claire would have to think more about that later.

"Please don't tell Garrett," Claire whispered to Rue. "He warned me about Jace when he set up the interview with Logan."

Rue waved away her concern. "I won't say a thing. Remember, you're the one responsible for your happiness. No one has a say in who you can and can't date. Not Garrett or anyone else."

"I know." Deep down, Claire believed it.

Love coated Rue's tone. "Why are you hesitant about this?"

Claire twirled loose strands of her dark hair around her finger, thinking of the right words. "I'm finally in a place where I feel accepted, doing what I want to do. I have friends who truly care for me. Heck, the Becketts have welcomed me with open arms and invite me to join some family meals. If I decide to give Jace a chance and we break up, I could lose that." She met her aunt's eyes. "I don't know if I have it in me to start over again."

Rue vehemently shook her head, taking hold of Claire's hands. "Don't you dare think that. You know if you find yourself in a position to start over, you have the strength to do it. Period. You've overcome so much. Women always have to start over at various stages in their lives. We have so many roles to fulfill, we don't look at it as starting over." Her aunt leaned forward.

"Regarding this young man, I understand you're scared. After your last relationship, it's only natural. But do not let that stop you from seeing what may come of this. You said yourself, Jace has been pining over you for almost a year. If that's true, I think you owe it to yourself to see what the man is offering."

Naomi and Izzy told her the same thing. Jace had opportunities to push her to the side and pursue women that would give up a pinky toe to date him. Still, the fear of losing everything had her heartbeat rising. Despite the encouraging words from her aunt, the question remained: was Jace worth it?

She mentally shook the "woe is me" attitude away. In a possible futile effort to change the subject so she could think about her aunt's question, she gave Rue a genuine smile.

"I've been thinking about getting into gardening. Naomi and I want to make window boxes. Mrs. Beckett is the head of a gardening club. They mostly focus on crops and flowers for resale, but they also have annuals and perennials."

Rue studied her for a moment. "This family seems to like you. Do you really think they would turn their back on you if things between you and this young man didn't work out?"

Claire mentally kicked herself. She'd never been good at casually changing subjects. Rue caught her every time. Claire sighed and grasped her cup. Since she left home fourteen years ago, she made it a mission to save money. She'd learn to budget, and Hawkins Ridge allowed her to build a tiny nest egg. Losing her dream job meant going through her savings to move to another town, place deposits on another apartment and having to find new friends. Claire had confidence she would find something else, but she'd lose her emotional support.

Claire shrugged. "My gut is saying no."

"You said you've been friends with him." Rue stood to turn the heat on again under the kettle. "During that time, has Jace ever given you a reason he would be mean or disrespectful to you?"

Claire broke off a piece of her cookie and thought about their friendship. A shy smile creased her lips as a memory came to mind.

"Two months ago, I tripped over a goat kid. The fluffy thing came from out of nowhere. I ended up twisting my ankle. Jace went to the store for me to get things I needed. He brought me meals. Jace's mother and even Naomi offered to do it, but he said he had it." Claire met her aunt's caring gaze. "He's sweeter than I think he shows the town."

"It sounds like you're *also* interested in something more."

"I'm not going to lie and say I'm not, but I've been through one relationship where I wasn't enough." And she didn't want to go through it again.

Rue patted Claire's cheek. "That right there is the source of your fear. Yes, the possibility of maybe leaving a place you've grown attached to is legitimate. However, it's Jace's reputation and your past that is making you second guess this."

Her aunt went about making another cup of herbal tea. It gave Claire a chance to think while slipping Balty a dog biscuit from the bag on the table. As always, her aunt was right. It was Jace's reputation that put him in the friend zone. She'd seen his determination to prove to himself and his family, his commitment to helping grow the business.

Could that be the reason he put aside his chasing of women, because he's too busy? What if things slowed down, and he had more time on his hands? Even with his reputation, no one ever said he was a cheater. Could it be the women he spent time with in the past weren't looking for a relationship, either?

Claire exhaled and stood to give her aunt a hug. "Thank you for listening."

"Always. Think about talking to him before you start anything. Explain to him why you're hesitant. When he says you have nothing to worry about, he'll need to prove it."

"You're right. I'll talk to him after we get through the spring chores this week." She thought of Garrett's mission and gently broached the subject. "You know, if you move here, you could be my sounding board all the time."

Rue's light laugh bounced off the wall. She picked up her mug and headed to the doorway. "Subtle is not one of your strong points. Sara already mentioned the idea. We'll see how this month goes. Now, let's go watch that movie Garrett groaned about last night."

Claire poured herself a glass of water before following. Having her aunt put everything into perspective calmed her mind. Talking to Jace was a good idea. Maybe everything would work out and she'd have her happily ever after with the guy and the job.

Stranger things have happened.

Chapter Five

Thick soupy fog rolling across the foothills had Claire easing her foot off the gas and flicking on her lights. It didn't dim the soft smile gracing Claire's lips as she turned onto Hawkins Ridge. No matter how much she enjoyed spending time with her family, she realized this was her home.

As she passed the barren trees and covered soil for root vegetables, she waved to Noah emerging from the small greenhouse. Off in the distance, the goats played silly games on fallen logs. She pressed the remote to open the gate that took her to the sanctuary, the main house, and her home. However, seeing Izzy's car led her to pull in next to her friend. The mere thought of a steaming cup of coffee put going home to change on hold.

Claire tugged on her gloves and waved to a goat handler chugging past in an UTV when she exited the car. Moments later, the rich aroma of caffeine gold drifted up her nose as she stepped into the clinic building. The double wide modular building housed Naomi's veterinarian practice and the office for the sanctuary. Her tattooed friend with long red hair greeted her with an enthusiastic grin.

"I thought you were coming in later," Izzy said, coming around the desk and enveloping a laughing Claire in a bear hug.

"I knew you would have coffee." Claire stepped back and spotted the half full carafe. "My aunt drinks tea in the morning and Sara has Garrett on decaf because of the pregnancy. Yesterday I couldn't take it anymore and snuck out at five-thirty to get coffee from the diner."

"You have suffered, my friend. I'll make you a cup while you get comfortable."

Claire handed Izzy her pink travel mug from beside her computer before hanging her jacket on the rack in the waiting room. By the time she made it around the desk, Izzy had the cinnamon creamer out and handed her a spoon.

"How is your aunt liking Oak Mountain?" Izzy took a seat in her desk chair and picked up her own mug.

Claire held up a finger and took her first sip of caffeine for the day and groaned with pleasure. "Man, that's good. We really need to get the name of the company Owen orders his beans from." She took another sip and headed to her chair. "She likes it a lot. Garrett is trying to talk her into moving. She has a few friends back home, but I don't think it would be enough to keep her knowing her only grandchild is here."

"Between Josie and her crew of women, your aunt will have friends in no time."

"I hope so. I didn't know how much I missed her until this visit." Claire swallowed a sudden lump in her throat when the thought of her mother surfaced. "Where is everyone?"

"Sam is feeding the pack. Naomi should be here soon. She took Fiona to school today. Josie tossed up a wave as she walked by."

Naomi's practice was closed that week and Logan wouldn't go out to any of the farms unless it was an emergency. The couple wanted to focus on grooming the animals, perform exams, administer vaccines, and do inventory. Claire would need to change clothes before they started.

"Are you and Mike doing anything for your anniversary?" Claire asked before taking another healthy sip.

Izzy's husband was a deputy for Oak Mountain Police. She shook her head. "He's on duty. He has an upcoming three-day weekend, so we are talking about getting away and leaving the kids with the grandparents."

"I hope it works out. You two need a break."

"Tell me something I don't know." Izzy leaned back in her chair and clutched her cup. "Jace left early to meet with a co-op the next county over. Just in case you were curious."

Claire wasn't curious because Jace texted the night before to let her know. It was a larger co-op than the one in Oak Mountain and would mean a boost in their reach. Before Claire could comment, the front door opened to a hurried Naomi.

"Morning!" The brown-skinned woman unzipped her oversized Hawkins Ridge jacket. "I thought you were coming in at ten?"

All three women were best friends, but Claire had a special bond with Naomi. "I needed coffee and stopped in real quick. It saves me from making a pot at home."

"And I shared Jace's whereabouts before she could ask. You know, since I'm a good friend and all." Izzy batted her lashes for emphasis.

Naomi smiled while playfully rolling her eyes. She stepped behind the desk and took a seat. "Ignore her. How was your time off? By the way, the cookies and fudge you left are gone. Jace mentioned the fudge, and that was all she wrote."

Claire couldn't swallow the light chuckle fast enough. It warmed her heart that the Becketts enjoyed it. She loved making homemade items. During her time at the sanctuary, she learned the family was food motivated.

Claire gave her friends a summary of her time off and the activities they did around the county. When she mentioned Garrett's plans, both women were nodding.

"We can set her up in the mother-in-law suite at the main house for her visit," Naomi volunteered. "We have six dogs to keep Balty busy. Josie would have her at every luncheon, meetups at the diner and anything else our mothers are doing."

"She'll also try to set her up with ever widower and divorcé in a fifty-mile radius," Izzy added. They all laughed because she did the same thing with Naomi's mother, who was now engaged.

"I have only seen Rue date once, and it was after Garrett and I were on our own. I don't know if she would be interested."

"My mother wasn't looking either, and Harold swept her off her feet," Naomi said while booting up her computer. "The point is, if it's important to you and benefits Rue, we'll help sell Oak Mountain to her."

"Thank you." Claire didn't expect the possibility of being part of a matchmaking scheme to appeal to Rue. Showing her the appeals of the town, a list of activities to keep her busy, and being close to her first grandchild is what would motivate her to give it considerable thoughts.

"Oh!" Naomi slapped her hand on the desk. "Jace dropped off leftover chicken he cooked in the air fryer. He said you didn't like that Sara put cilantro on her baked chicken."

Izzy nodded. "Her family loves that stuff. Her mother brought a three-bean casserole to a potluck last year with that stuff sprinkled on top. You know, like you would green onion or parsley. Anyway, the flavor seeped into the dish." Izzy shuddered. "You don't mix that with the fried onions. Ruined the whole dish."

"Sara said she had a craving," Claire added.

"Vanilla wafers and cherry ice cream are cravings. The pregnant women in my family never craved an herb."

Naomi shook her head before turning her focus back to Claire. "Anyway, it's in the house in a blue container if I'm not around at lunch."

If the women were in the same area around noon, they would either gather at Naomi's or Claire's for lunch, depending on whether anyone else was joining them.

"I didn't know Jace makes meals for you." Mischief lit Izzy's hazel eyes.

"I don't think leaving leftovers equals him making it for me. He's probably saying thanks for the cookies and fudge I gave him before I left." Claire shrugged. "It's what friends do. I left some for you two."

Naomi and Izzy snorted in unison. It was Naomi who spoke. "You're right, we always share food. Deep down, you know his offer was more than friendly."

Claire didn't know that for sure. She hoped there was more to it, but she didn't want to go down that mental path. She needed to keep her expectations realistic.

The sanctuary was a dream job. It allowed her to work with great people and save money with a goal of buying her own place in town. Spending time with Balty strengthened the desire for her own pet. She'd fostered animals in the past, but working and going to school didn't allow her the time needed for a full-time pet. Now she could.

Claire wanted a simple life and to stay with Hawkins Ridge for the long haul. Could she have everything she wanted with Jace?

She met the gazes of her friends and attempted to sound confident. "We're just friends. He did the same thing either of you would have done."

Izzy rolled her eyes while Naomi leaned forward and spoke. "This is the same man who, at my wedding, confessed he wanted to pursue something more down the road. Have you thought more about that?"

Claire clutched her cup to her chest. "I have. Honestly, it's all I thought about while I was at Garrett's. I still don't know. He hasn't mentioned anything since that day. That was months ago. Maybe he realized I'm not worth the effort, or he was kidding and happy staying friends." Claire didn't want to examine the wave of disappointment at the thought of Jace thinking she wasn't worth the effort. Was he expecting her to make the first move?

Naomi and Izzy looked at each other before doubling over in laughter. Heat rose to Claire's cheeks as she scowled at her friends. Naomi rested her hand on Claire's scarred arm and gave it a squeeze.

"We're not laughing at you. I swear. It's just adorable that you haven't noticed how he looks at you. Jace wants more."

"I've known him my entire life." Izzy crossed her legs and pointed a manicured finger. "Jace Beckett does not give up once he wants something. He's wanted you since you stepped on the property. He's giving you time to come to terms with it."

"Let's approach this from your point of view." Naomi shifted Claire's chair towards her. "If you didn't know Jace and only saw him walking down the street, would you find him attractive?"

Claire tilted her mug to her lips to hide the blush. "You know I do."

"Okay. Is it his reputation stopping you from taking him seriously?" Naomi's dark brown eyes clouded with warmth as she asked, "I ask because he hasn't seen anyone in a long time."

Izzy nodded in agreement. "My brother told me when Jace and Noah meet them for beer, he only shoots pool and turned away hoochies trying to get his attention."

"Hoochies?" Claire snickered.

Izzy waved her hand dismissively. "I'm sticking with it. Floozy seems judgmental. My point is, Jace is trying to prove to you—and I think to himself—that he is more than his looks and reputation."

"Agreed," Naomi said, pulling Claire's attention back to her. "Logan's told me how impressed he is that Jace has stepped up and taking his role in the business seriously. What else is bothering you?"

"What if it doesn't work out?" Claire dropped her head back and stared at the ceiling. "I would lose everything and be forced to move out of Oak Mountain. I worked too hard to go back to waiting tables because there were no other veterinary clinics in town. Even if there were and I stayed, do you know how hard it would be to see Jace traipsing around town with some other woman? Again, that would be too hard and I'd have to move. I wouldn't see you two anymore and would have to give up Owen's special coffee bean blend." Claire shook her head and sat straight in the chair. "Nope, we'll stay friends. Nothing more." She hadn't told her friends that her ex-fiancé cheated on her. She still harbored embarrassment and didn't want pity eyes.

Naomi rapidly blinked. "Wow. That's a lot of what ifs."

"No, that was a reality TV meltdown is what that was." Izzy grinned to lighten the mood. Naomi rolled Izzy's chair out of the way and moved in front of Claire.

"Sweetie, everyone has that same fear of uncertainty in a new relationship. When I moved the practice to Hawkins Ridge instead of finding a new office space to rent, I worried about something similar. I'm still adjusting to my name being on the paperwork for Logan's business." Naomi took her hand. "Regret is the only thing that's guaranteed. Don't regret not giving Jace a chance. You enjoy being friends with him, helping when he's trying to find foster homes for the animals. Why do you think that would change or he would treat you differently?"

"And why do you think you'd get rid of Naomi and me? We're going to be the old biddies running this town in thirty years." Izzy finished with a nod.

"I dare you to tell Josie or our mothers they're old biddies," Naomi challenged.

Izzy snorted. "I'm not stupid."

The women giggled like high school girls. Claire felt better sharing most of her fears with her friends. If Jace brought up dating again, she would say yes. Rue's words filtered back in her mind. Talking to Jace and explaining her concerns made sense. They were adults, not kids. He knew his reputation and her gut told her he'd understand her hesitation.

Besides, if things didn't work out, she could always stay in Oak Mountain and maybe find a job at a vet office in the next town over and commute. She'd done it before, after her engagement ended two years ago. She could do it again.

CHAPTER SIX

Jace tapped his fingers on the steering wheel to the beat of one of his favorite songs. His meeting with the co-op went better than expected, and he couldn't wait to tell his brothers. He even secured two foster homes with the manager and owner.

He pressed the button for the gate leading to the sanctuary. The sight of Claire's car parked beside her home had his lips spread into an enormous grin. It was three o'clock. This was the time she checked emails. That would mean she'd probably be in the office, and he could get a dose of her smile before finding Logan.

He parked his truck in the lot for Naomi's clinic and jogged the few feet to the office door. Hope crashed when the only person behind the desk was Thomas Beckett, tugging a shirt over his head. Though all the brothers had their mother's eyes, their chiseled jaw line and handsome features came from Thomas. Jace was also the only brother to inherit his mother's dark blonde locks.

"Why are you getting undressed?" Jace took in the overall appearance of his father and cocked his head. "Why are you wet?"

Despite his disheveled look, joy lit up Thomas' face. "I was helping your brother bathe the dogs. By the time we got to the livestock dogs, we were both soaking wet."

"You live mere yards from here. Why didn't you change your clothes there?"

"Your mother is finishing up the cat quarantine room. If I had gone home to change, she would have roped me into helping."

Jace laughed. No one said no to Josie Beckett. He strolled over to the water cooler in the corner, yanking a paper cup from the dispenser. "Where's everyone?" He wanted to ask about Claire specifically, but figured he'd show concern for the rest of the family.

Thomas sat in one of the multicolor waiting room chairs and stretched out his long legs. "Logan's passing out treats to the pack. He should be here any minute. Naomi and Izzy are at the stables, taking samples from the horses. Sam and Claire took the livestock guard dogs back to the goats and then will take samples of the kids. Noah is checking in with the head gardener. Caden is picking up Fiona from school. More importantly, Owen is in the main house, putting together a batch of chili for tonight."

Something else they took after their father—the love for food. Jace took a seat facing his father and linked his fingers behind his head. Before he could ask if Owen planned cornbread or biscuits, Logan strolled in through the sliding back door that led to the fenced in play area for the dogs. He, too, had changed given the tight sweatshirt he currently wore.

"I didn't know you were back," Logan said, hoisting himself onto the check-in desk. "How'd it go?"

"Good. They agreed to letting us sell the goat cheese for a six-month trial basis starting the middle of next month. We can also have a sample table one weekend a month. We just need to let them know in advance in case there are other companies. I already secured the first weekend we start. When I mentioned about putting up a sheet for fostering the animals, the manager and owner volunteered. They used to foster for the shelter that closed down."

Logan and Thomas nodded. It was his father who spoke. "Good job, son. We can put together a schedule later."

"That works. I wanted to wait until I had everyone present, but will toss it past you two. I need an assistant."

"You're not getting Claire," Logan teased. Or Jace hoped he was teasing. Working side-by-side with Claire would be a test of his willpower.

"Har. Har. Seriously. Keeping on top of the social media, research, setting up schedules." Jace raked his fingers through his shoulder length hair. "More for administrative things."

"I planned on looking for a part-time person myself for the same duties, since Claire is taking over for Sam in a few weeks." Logan glanced at his father. "We could combine the two positions."

"We've been trying to figure out enough duties to justify an office employee." Thomas pointed to the water cooler. Jace stood to get him a cup. "Put together a list of what you want done."

Jace already had everything written up because he thought he'd have to sell his brothers on the idea. Logan leaned forward, resting his arms on his thighs.

"I'll bring what I've put together to dinner."

Logan nodded, tugging on his too tight shirt. "Sounds good. I think Naomi asked Claire to dinner. We can get everyone's input."

A slow smile crept on his face. Spending time with Claire would make the chili taste even better.

"We have a pickup in the morning. Do you want someone to ride with you?" Thomas crushed his cup in his hand and held his youngest son's gaze. "Not your mother."

The three men laughed because Josie had the largest soft spot for the animals, especially cats. She founded the sanctuary while engaged to Thomas. Four years ago, it reached the point where the family banned her from any more pickups, as she always came home with double or triple the animals she went to collect.

Before Jace could respond, the back door slid open. A moment later, Claire and Sam strolled in, laughing. The dark-haired beauty's face was flush with happiness. They pulled up short when they saw the men.

"Sorry," Claire said, pulling the scrunchie from her ponytail. "The kids were rather rambunctious today."

Sam, Owen's husband and Noah's stepfather, nodded in agreement. "They kept going after our shoelaces. Twice they knocked the kid getting the sample taken out of the way and then played a spirted game of chase." He held out his medium brown hand to Jace. "Did Thomas tell you about the chili?"

Jace shook his hand with gusto. "Yep. I hope he's making enough for me to take a bowl home." He turned to Claire, who twirled keys around her finger. A quizzical look on her face made him pause. "How's your day going, Buttercup?"

She rolled her eyes, but he didn't miss the twinkle in them. "Not bad. You've been running your fingers through your hair. It's sticking out on the side."

Jace's hands flew to this hair and glared at Logan. "Why didn't you say something?"

His oldest brother smirked while counting the vials. "I thought it was a new look you were going for."

Claire giggled. "It's not bad. Sorta." She turned her gaze to Logan. "Unless you need me for something else, I'm going to head home to clean up before dinner."

Jace met his brother's eyes, pleading to let her go. When Logan gave her permission, he did a mental fist pump. "Mind if I walk you home?"

She flashed a shy smile and nodded. He would move his truck on his way back. If she lived further than the two-minute walk, he would offer to drive. This way, it gave them more time together. After settling on a time for dinner, they said their goodbyes. Jace held the door for her to step through first.

"Thank you for the chicken. You didn't have to leave me your leftovers," Claire commented as they walked across the lot.

Jace waved away the statement before shoving his hands in his pockets. He'd give her his leftovers every day. Better yet, he'd make sure she'd have three meals a day.

"No need to thank me. Sara's family puts cilantro on things it shouldn't be on."

"Izzy told me about the casserole."

Jace shuddered. "I'm not a fan of the dish anyway, but that was just wrong. Did she at least squeeze lime on it?"

Claire's melodious laugh brought a smile to his face. "Red pepper flakes. The green salad was good. Rue volunteered to take over dinner under the guise Garrett and Sara would be too tired after work and it was the least she could do."

"You've suffered, so leaving juicy, perfectly seasoned meat was more of a lifeline," Jace teased. They both offered waves to workers who were leaving for the day. "Did you enjoy spending time with your aunt?" Claire's face lit up.

"I did. Rue is the best. She wants to come meet everyone once we get through this week of spring tasks. Garrett is going to talk her into moving here."

"Do you think she'll do it?" If Jace needed to charm her aunt so Claire would have more family here, he would.

They waved to Naomi and Izzy as they zipped by on the UTV. He didn't miss the double thumbs up from Izzy. Pink colored Claire's cheeks, and Jace didn't think it was from the breeze. She shook her head and answered his question.

"I think Rue will think hard on it. Nothing is keeping her back home. Her first grandbaby will be here this summer." She shrugged. "It would be nice to have her here. I think she'll move."

"There's plenty of room if you ever want her to stay a few days out here. It will give Garrett and Sara a few days together."

They turned onto her walkway. The wreath she made with Fiona hung proudly on her door.

"Naomi and Logan already offered the mother-in-law suite if she wanted to stay on the property for a proper visit. Balty would love their dogs to play with."

Jace didn't want their conversation to end, but they only had ninety minutes before dinner. He too needed to freshen up, take the dogs out, and check work emails. Maybe she'd let him walk her home that evening.

"I better get going." He shoved his hands into his pocket. "I was hoping we could talk about us soon."

Claire nibbled on her bottom lip for a moment before dragging her gaze to his. "I'd like that."

A huge, goofy grin decorated Jace's face. "Great. Great. Um. I'll see you at dinner?"

"See you then."

Jace waited until she was safely inside before jogging down her stairs. Claire agreed to talk about their relationship. He brokered a new partnership. He had chili to look forward to for dinner. In his eyes, today was a good day.

Chapter Seven

Claire pressed her nose against the living room window to take in the setting sun. Dots of thick clouds decorated the sky. There was a forecast of rain overnight. Claire looked forward to falling asleep to the pitter patter of drops on her roof.

Her smile reflected off the window as she thought of Jace walking her home. When he asked if they could talk soon, she'd planned to explain her concern.

Seeing his hair mussed opened up her eyes that she noticed little things about Jace than she realized. Like how he always wore a blue shirt when he had meetings. It brought out his eyes. Whether it was for that reason, she didn't know. Also, the way his chiseled features soften when he's helped Cammie learn the terrains of a new location. Importantly, how Jace was always there for his family if they needed help.

Claire was tired of debating the pros and cons. Jace was a kind, caring man and hoped explaining her past would give them the foundation of a future.

Sparing the sky one last look, she padded through her living area towards the bedroom. Her tiny home was one of three that had a separate bedroom. It made the front room smaller, with just enough room for her navy-blue striped loveseat and chair. Her multi-color tile bistro table and two chairs were a find at a consignment store in the next town. The Becketts let her paint the walls a buttery yellow which she accented with colorful artwork. The corner fireplace heated the space, and she loved reading a good book in front of it.

Claire sat on the edge of her full-size bed and slid her feet into a pair of black cowboy boots. The collapsable crate she used for fostering caught her attention. Being around Balty the past few days stirred up her desire for a furry friend. She missed the company of the foster cats she had during the summer. The sanctuary's latest rescues have been too large for her limited space. Claire made a mental note to ask Logan if the pickup tomorrow would be one she could foster, maybe even adopt.

A quick glance at the clock had her scurrying to the front door, grabbing her keys and phone on the way. After slipping on her wool jacket, she stepped outside into the dropping temperature.

The two-story main house stood proudly steps away from the clinic. A traditional farmhouse with white-washed bricks, red trim, and a wrap-around porch. According to Logan, it has been the home for every generation of Beckett for the past one hundred years. Now it was his and Naomi's time to make it a home in their image.

She climbed the two steps and pushed open the back door. Josie told her to stop knocking after the first dinner with the Becketts. Now that it was Logan and Naomi's home, she probably should ask. The jovial voices warmed her heart. Shorty, Naomi's long-haired dachshund, hurried over to greet her. Fiona, Logan's twelve-year-old daughter, was on his paws.

"I'm so glad you're back." She wrapped her slender arms around her. "Thank you so much for the present."

Fiona's birthday was the first day of Rue's visit. With Logan and Naomi's approval, she gifted the first two months of a book subscription.

"I'm glad you like it. Did you already download the limit?" Clair looked over the girl's shoulder at her boss, who was rolling his eyes.

"Yep. She spent the weekend putting together a list of books for me to approve." Logan placed the stack of bowls in his hand on the kitchen island. "That subscription service may or may not be the best gift ever."

"Oh, it definitely is the best gift next to the new leather jacket you got me." Fiona gave a wink before skipping back into the fray of the family.

Claire laughed and slipped off her coat, hanging it on the peg near the back door. She gave Shorty another scratch before stepping further into the kitchen. Two-thirds of the lower level was one large open area. The kitchen bled into the living area, with an enormous wood table acting as a divider. To the right was a hallway that led to a full bath, the old cat sanctuary and the suite Owen and Sam called home before building their house near the stables. It would be where Rue would stay if she wanted an extended visit.

All six of Logan and Naomi's dogs played with Cammie while Oriole tugged on a rope toy with Thomas. Naomi was busy instructing Noah and Caden on where to put a piece of furniture. Fiona had joined her grandmother near the stove, making drinks for everyone. It was chaotic and something Claire hoped to have one day.

"What are you thinking about so hard, Buttercup?" Jace said from her left before sliding a glass in front of her. Sweet tea, her favorite.

"Just taking it all in." She took a small sip and turned to face him. "What do they have you doing?"

He flashed a lopsided grin. The dimple on his right cheek made an appearance. "I had to move boxes into the old cat room. Logan and Naomi still don't know what they're going to do with the space, so now it's a catchall room."

"Every house should have one of those spaces, even if it's a garage."

"I agree. My spare bedroom is mine," Jace offered.

Claire had only seen the living room and kitchen of Jace's home. She didn't want to think about the number of women who had seen more of his home. Her gut told her Jace's activities didn't take place on Hawkins Ridge property. Why? She didn't know, but the thought tamped down the rabbit hole of what ifs. It wasn't her business. So what if other women knew the color of his comforter? If she wanted to be with Jace, being jealous of his past would only lead to a failed relationship.

"Do you need help?" Her gaze scanned the room and landed on Naomi, laughing with her in-laws.

Jace strolled to a corner near the table. "I just have these two. Company would be great."

Claire's mouth went dry as she watched him squat to gather the boxes with little effort. The fitted, long-sleeve shirt stretched across his massive back and bunched up around his biceps. She took a long sip of her tea and hoped she didn't choke. Logan flashed her a smirk and a cheeky thumbs up when they walked past. She rolled her eyes at her boss, but felt the heat rising to her cheeks.

"Before my mother converted and added on to this space, this used to be our hang out room," Jace commented as they crossed the threshold.

The room was designed with two walls, mostly made of tinted glass, to catch both the morning and afternoon sun. Mounted ramps and walkways ran throughout the space, giving the cats places to race around and take sun-induced naps. Despite the dozens of boxes and small pieces of furniture, it remained one of Claire's favorite rooms in the house.

"Did you and your brother have forts in here?"

Jace sat the boxes on an old dining room chair, nodding. "We'd drag every chair we could in here and drape sheets and blankets over them. We made it so we could still see the TV when we played video games or watched cartoons. Caden had the best imagination and would take us on adventures." A warm smile graced his lips. "Our grandpa always played the villain, and our grandma would give us cookies as rewards for when we slayed him."

If Claire didn't have feelings for the man before her, she did at that moment. She'd seen pictures of the younger Beckett brothers, with Noah in the mix. Smiles were never missing in any of them.

Claire ran her fingers over a cherry wood end table she wanted in her house. She'd have to ask Naomi later.

"The nights my mom watched Garrett and I, she would do something similar in the living room. She'd drape sheets over the couch and kitchen chairs and would read us bedtime stories. Flashlights and everything." Claire hadn't thought about that moment in years. The memory wrapped around her heart like a comfy blanket.

Before Jace could respond, Oriole trotted in with all dogs on his heels. Shorty stayed close to Cammie, bringing up the rear. Immediately, all dogs dropped their noses to the floor and started sniffing.

"Residual smells of the cats," Jace explained. "Since dachshund, labradors, and terriers are hunting dogs, it's in their nature. I think the Pomeranian and pugs are just being dogs."

Claire's light giggle bounced off the wall. Each one had taken to inspecting every open space and a few boxes. It reminded Claire of her question.

"Are you picking up a dog or cat tomorrow?"

Jace had bent over and picked up Cammie to pet. "A dog. A Pitbull. Why?"

"I'm interested in another foster. Maybe permanently." She shrugged. "I like the company."

"I told you I'm willing to be your company."

Claire shook her head, but kept a smile on her face. "You said we were talking soon. I don't think minutes before eating would give us enough time."

Jace held her gaze for a moment before nodding. "We are. I have all my talking points on index cards why we'd be great together."

Her mouth dropped as she processed what he said. "You can't be serious."

"As a heart attack." Jace sat Cammie on the floor before taking a seat in one of the spare chairs. "Claire, your brain works on what ifs. I like that about you. Okay, maybe it's index cards on my tablet, but same thing."

Claire couldn't stop the laugh that bubbled up. "You're crazy."

"People may agree with that statement." Jace chuckled along with her. "You're right, though. We don't have time, especially in a house full of people we love. Back to your furry forever friend. I would suggest a cat, but you may have to fight Mom. If you trust me, I'll see if there is a dog that you'll like, and I'll text you pictures."

She studied him for a beat. Did she trust him? Without a doubt, yes. "Thank you. I trust you."

"That means more to me than you can imagine, Buttercup."

Claire smiled. Before they could confess more, a loud bellow interrupted the moment.

"Let's eat!" Thomas yelled. Every dog darted out of the room. Jace scooped up a squiggly Cammie as they headed to join the rest.

Naomi gave her a knowing look, which Claire ignored. Excited chatter about plans for the next day filled the air. Everyone lined up to the stove to dish their own serving of chili and grab a square or two of thick buttery cornbread. At that moment, a wave of acceptance washed over her.

Garrett and Rue were her family, but this caring, welcoming clan was her family as well. She spared a glance at Jace, who was laughing with Noah. Maybe, just maybe, this could be a permanent thing.

Jace lifted the fluorescent harness and nylon lead from the hook near the back door. During the daytime hours, he would let Oriole guide Cammie home because he could see them. Given that it was dark, and the drop in temperature, Jace opted to take Logan's UTV home and return it in the morning when he picked up the sanctuary truck.

Dinner was the usual boisterous affair. Laughter and various conversations melted into confirmation that family dinners had to continue. Some townspeople didn't understand even though they worked together, dinner was where they could be themselves.

It was also where they could discuss ideas for the business and get everyone's input at once. Like Jace's assistant. He emailed his list of what he needed help with earlier. Everyone came with suggestions, including spreading pickup duties with senior workers. Jace's parents, Owen and Sam, planned to spend most of the summer visiting his uncle in Florida. That meant losing four people who knew the ins and outs of all duties on the property. Jace would have to pick up the slack, solidifying his need for an assistant.

First, he and the dogs had to walk Claire home.

He headed over to the living room where all dogs surrounded Fiona on the floor. His niece's love for animals rivaled Josie and Logan. She was the beginning of the next generation of Beckett that would take over the family business. Jace wanted to make sure he did his part in making it successful when she took the reins.

"Can you put this on Cammie for me?" he asked, handing her the harness.

"Are you walking Ms. Claire home?" Fiona giggled as the fluffy Pomeranian shimmied into the apparatus. His dog understood it meant a walk.

"I am. Is that okay?"

Fiona nodded and sat the dog back on her paws. "I like her. I hope she gives you a chance. You'd make a cute couple. Do you want me to talk to her for you? You know, put in a good word?"

Man, he loved this girl. His gaze swept the area and found the woman in question laughing with his mother and Naomi. Josie pushed a canvas tote into her hands. Jace would bet all the money in his checking account that leftover chili and sweets filled the bag.

"Thank you, sweetie, but I think I got it. I'll let you know if I need an assist."

Fiona nodded and turned her attention back to the dogs. He headed to Logan and motioned to follow him off to the side. Claire's request would mean that if he found a dog for her, she would need a flexible schedule to get the dog adjusted. Maybe bringing it to work with her. He wanted to clear it with his brother before he reminded Claire on the way home.

"If you're calling me over here to ask if you should try to kiss Claire, my answer is no."

"What? Why would I ask you that?"

Logan shrugged and shoved a hand into a pocket. "What's up?"

"Just wanted to let you know Claire wants a pet. I volunteered to look around the shelter tomorrow. If I find one, we may need to make space in the office. Of course, that depends on how it adjusts to being out of the shelter. I know we have a lot planned, but it means a lot to her."

His oldest brother blew out a breath. "I can't believe I'm saying this, but why doesn't she go with you?"

"You won't need her tomorrow?" Jace fought the urge to do a happy dance.

"If she wants to go, I can spare her for the morning and ask Mom or one of the other workers to help. There's space in the office. Naomi is sending our dogs with Caden tomorrow, so it will be quiet."

"Thanks." Jace went to step away, but Logan grabbed a hold of his elbow. He stepped close and spoke in a low voice.

"Between us, Naomi mentioned that Claire's worried about if things don't work out with you two, she's going to lose our love and friendship. You said she's your one a month after meeting her. I suggest you work the Beckett charm and calm her fears. We all love both of you and want this to work."

Jace appreciated his brother looking out for both of them. His worry wasn't about them not working, but Claire not giving them a chance. If she didn't, Jace would respect her decision. The last thing he wanted was to pressure her. If she said yes, he'd do everything in his power to show how much he treasured her. He spoke the truth when he said he had an argument for every reason she could think why they shouldn't pursue something more.

He clapped Logan on the shoulder and flashed a confident smile. "Thanks. I'll do what I have to for her to see I'm a catch. By the way, I'm taking your UTV. I'll bring it back when I get the truck."

Logan gave his blessing as they headed towards Naomi and Claire, who were giving goodbye hugs. Jace picked her jacket from the peg and held it open for her. She flashed a soft smile of thanks. His heart blossomed at the gesture. Yep, he had no problem showing her how much he cared if it got him smiles like that.

After slipping on his fleece-lined jacket, Naomi passed the fabric tote to him while Logan handed off Cammie to Claire. They yelled a last goodbye to everyone and stepped out the back door. Claire put Cammie on the ground, wrapped her lead around her wrist before adjusting her compression glove.

"Does the cold aggravate the nerve damage in your hand?" If so, he'd make a mental know to either always warm them in his hands or make sure she had her gloves.

She nodded. "It goes numb quicker. I just need to wear my fingerless gloves over my compression glove. Thank you for walking me home, even though you didn't need to."

"It's called trying to woo and court you at the same time." He tucked his hands into his jacket pocket and fell into step with her. "I mentioned to Logan about the possibility of a dog for you. He suggested if you want, you could go with me."

Claire's head snapped to his. "Really? I'd love to go. Are you okay with that?"

"Buttercup, I'd love to have you ride with me."

The smile on her face lit up the night sky.

He would do anything to see her smile at him like that, even if it meant being a softy like his father and letting Claire bring home an entire shelter, just like his mother. The urge to hold her hand was strong, but he tapped it down. He didn't want to assume she was gung-ho for a relationship. It would hurt beyond measure if she decided to keep him in a lifetime friend zone, but he would have to respect her decision.

"Do they have a website? Maybe I could get an idea before-hand." Claire nibbled her bottom lip while she let Cammie and Oriole check out a spot near the dog run for the pack.

"You know, unless it's a Great Dane or a dog that size, you could consider a medium size dog. Caden would be more than happy to pick it up when he takes the rest of the dogs to the stable. Or, until it gets a feeling of being safe, Logan and Naomi wouldn't mind you bringing it to work."

Jace hated to speak for his brother, but Naomi brought Shorty, Mika, and Tam with her when they didn't go with Caden. It may also help the dog and Claire to bond. He didn't need to verbalize his thoughts when he noticed her nodding. They started walking again once the dogs had thoroughly inspected their surroundings.

"Since I've been on my own, I've always wanted a dog. I knew I couldn't. Between working two jobs and taking classes, then living in apartments, it wouldn't have been fair. That's why I stuck with fostering cats and that was only after I was working one job." Claire shrugged before turning up the path to her house. "Maybe I could get a dog and cat. Just don't let your mother come to visit."

Jace barked out a laugh. His mother loved dogs but wor-shiped cats. She'd somehow got all of her friends to adopt a cat. If word got around to Josie that there was a new cat on the premises, she'd pester Claire until she got to see it. Jace bit back a sigh as they reached her front door.

Claire pulled keys from her pocket and handed him Cammie's lead before shoving the right one into the lock. "Thank you for walking me home and letting me go with you tomor-row."

"Technically, thank Logan, but I'll take credit. Although, he wouldn't have known if I didn't ask about your new pet staying with us. So, yeah, I guess you're right. You're welcome, Buttercup."

Her angelic laugh warmed his blood. "What am I going to do with you?"

"I'd take a kiss." He puckered up his lips, amusement twinkled in his eyes.

"Good night, Jace." Claire pushed her door open. "Good night, Oriole and Cammie."

Both dogs wagged their rears, and she closed the door. Jace waited a few beats before scooping Cammie up and putting her in his jacket. He didn't want to take the chance of her jumping out of the UTV on the one-minute drive home. He jogged to the parked vehicle and climbed in. Oriole knew the routine and curled up on the passenger side floor. Jace cranked the engine and pulled out. His mind went back to his time that evening with Claire.

He surprised himself by sharing a childhood memory with her. Not that he wouldn't. He wanted her to know everything about him. But that memory always popped into his mind whenever he was around all of his brothers. His heart warmed when she let her guard down and spoke of her mother. It was only the second time she spoke of her with him. The first was explaining about her burns.

Jace cleared the cluster of trees in front of his house and slowed to a halt. He fell more in love with her when she lit up, knowing she could choose her own special pet. If something so simple could bring her such joy, he looked forward to spending the rest of his life giving Claire everything her heart desired.

CHAPTER EIGHT

Claire hummed along to the intro music for the morning news as she poured coffee into her favorite travel mug. The rich aroma tickled her nose and brushed the remaining cobwebs from her brain. A contented smile graced her lips. She was getting her own pet today.

She shimmied her full hips, taking her first fortifying sip. For fourteen years, Claire put the idea of being a pet owner on hold. She had goals and understood it required all of her focus. Her love of animals, knowing she didn't have the time or space, made the decision tolerable. Now, she was in a better position. The Becketts paid her well. Not having to spend hardly any money on rent, she paid off her small student loan last month and could finally build her savings. This was the next step in making Oak Mountain her forever home.

Even if things didn't work out with Jace.

Last night, as she sipped her chamomile tea and waited for the small batch of banana sweet potato dog biscuits to cool, she decided to give Jace a chance. This town was her home. If their relationship didn't last, she would take a job in the next town over and commute. Claire had done it before. She would do it again. When her engagement ended, she ran. Mental abuse would drive you to give up everything to seek healing from loved ones. But Jace wasn't her ex.

Claire's focus should have been on the meteorologist, instead she tossed the memories of the previous evening in her mind. Jace's story from childhood showed a side of the man she was certain, only those close to him saw.

Last month, she and Izzy went with him to visit another practice a couple of towns over to see if their clients would be interested in fostering. Jace showed his natural charm. During the meeting, however, his smile wasn't as wide as when he was with family. Naturally, the women in the office swooned when the dimples showed or he gave a practiced wink.

Only after they returned to the truck did he show the relaxed, approachable man.

Claire couldn't wrap her head around his offer to pick a pet for her. She *did* trust him to pick one for her. It was the offer that warmed her heart. Though the trip was initially a business transaction, it meant a lot that Logan let her tag along so she could experience the joy of finding her furry soul mate.

Claire kicked into gear when her gaze locked on her mother's old mantle grandfather clock. Six fifty. She had ten minutes to meet Jace at Logan's. After topping off her mug, giving the carafe a quick rinse, she picked up the small container of dog biscuits for the future residents of Hawkins Ridge, and scurried to the front door.

The shelter was a ninety-minute drive each way, and they needed to be back before lunch. It would give her new furry friend time to decompress. Claire slipped on a dark pink sanctuary hoodie as she stepped outside. The crisp, damp aroma from the overnight showers calmed her racing heart.

Claire rounded the large oak tree at the edge of her yard and spotted Jace talking to Logan in the distance, their dogs casually following each other with their noses to the ground. She put a little more pep in her step and joined them moments later. She tried not to laugh at her boss' appearance of mussed hair, worn sweatpants, and a fleece pullover.

"Morning. Sorry I'm late." She sat her mug and container on the ground and began greeting the furry companions. "Thank you again, Logan, for giving me the morning off."

He dismissively waved away her gratitude. "You're welcome. Technically, since you're going with Jace to pick up a rescue, it's work related. If you stumble across a dog or cat that tickles your fancy, good for you and the animal. You'll register with your name, but we'll cover any adoption fees." Logan stepped between Rosebud and Tulip, two of his pugs, when they went after Oriole's leash. "Why don't you work from home this afternoon checking emails and calling fosters to see how things are going? If you find a dog, you'll need that time to help them settle."

Kindness like that is why Claire loved this family.

"You don't have to do that, but thank you."

She turned her attention to Jace, who redirected Cammie away from a wood barrel planter. Dressed in a pair of comfy jeans, a blue henley, and an open flannel jacket, the man oozed casual sexiness.

"Ready to go, Buttercup?" His cocky grin stirred the butterflies in her stomach. "Do you need to top off your coffee? I know how addicted you are?"

She rolled her eyes and clutched the travel mug tighter. "Har har. I topped it off before I left."

Logan scooped up Cammie and called Shorty away from Thomas and Josie's front door. "Text Naomi, Mom, and myself when you know the dog you want so we can bring over a bed, toys, and dishes." He turned to his brother. "Let the director know we'll be back in a couple of weeks to pick up any long-time residents, dogs, and cats. If you see one that needs to be freed today, bring them with you."

Jace pulled off his baseball cap and raked his fingers through his hair before sliding it back in place. Claire noticed it was a move he did when he had built up energy. He nodded to his brother while gently nudging Claire to walk.

"If you need us to stop and get last-minute supplies, call. Otherwise, we'll be back by lunch."

Claire tossed a wave over her shoulders. Surprise showed when they stopped at the sanctuary's black Suburban.

"No van?" she asked, while Jace held the door for her.

"Logan and Dad are doing a sweep this morning."

The first time Claire heard the Becketts use the term was before the storm that brought Naomi into their lives. They would drive around the surrounding towns looking for strays. The thought of an animal stuck in the middle of bad weather bothered everyone. The town knew that if they saw an animal out or mistreated to call the sanctuary. With the rain, Claire hoped if there was an animal in need, Logan and Thomas found them.

Jace nodded to the bag on the centered console. "That's for you."

Before she could reply, he closed the door and jogged to the driver's side. Recognizing the diner's pink takeout bag, she fought the urge to squeal. Once they buckled up and Jace turned on the satellite classic rock station, he pulled out of the spot.

"You didn't make a special trip for me, did you?" Claire pulled out the foil-wrapped package and smiled. A poppy-seed bagel with cream cheese and a thick slice of tomato. Her favorite.

"Technically yes. I went with Noah to deliver the eggs and cheese order. I know you don't like to eat before eight, so I got you something."

She had no words. She stared at him and fought the urge to give him a hug. Jace understood until she got one or two cups of coffee in her, food wasn't an option. No man she's dated, though they weren't dating yet, had done something nice for her. Definitely not Andy. He expected Claire to bring him breakfast every morning, since his job was next door to hers. Her gut told her Jace wouldn't be that way, even though he loved his morning meal.

"You didn't get anything?" she asked as she re-wrapped the bagel and picked up her coffee.

"You know I did." His smile was quick. "Bacon, egg, and cheddar cheese on whole wheat. I think I shoved the last bite in my mouth when we were turning back onto the property."

"I'm surprised it lasted that long."

Jace chuckled and turned onto the highway. "Noah and I were talking."

A popular rock song from the eighties filled the cab, and the two bobbed their head to the beat. The need to not constantly talk is one thing Claire liked about Jace. They didn't have a problem holding conversations, but just being in each other's presence was enough.

"Are you serious about adopting a cat and dog?"

Claire shifted slightly in her seat to face him. "I was, but the more I think about it, trying to get a cat and dog to adjust simultaneously isn't fair to either."

Jace nodded. "True. There's another shelter close to the one we're going. We can always stop by if you don't see a dog that speaks to you."

She studied him for a moment before speaking. "You really want me to have a pet, don't you?" It wasn't really a question.

"I do. Someone that loves animals as much as you do should."

"I missed having one after I moved out." Claire took a moment to glance at the passing landscape. "Knowing I couldn't give them the time or space they needed made the decision easier. Now I'm at a place in my life where I can give them the attention they need."

Jace mumbled in agreement. "Deciding to give up the firehouse opened up the time I could give a pet."

"But you grew up with animals."

"True, but in the house, it was the cats. We didn't start building the pack until Logan married Fiona's mother. The dogs we had growing up either were guardian dogs for the chickens or helped with the horses. Any other dogs were fosters, and we prepared them for a forever home." Jace took a sip of his coffee before continuing. "We each had a chicken we had to take care of growing up."

The snort that escaped surprised Claire. "Please tell me there are pictures of you holding a chicken?" Jace joined in on the laughter.

"I'm sure there are. You'll get to see me in braces."

"I wore braces, too," Claire added. "When I got them taken off, Garrett made two bags of microwave popcorn, and we did a Star Wars marathon."

"That's better than my first day without them. Noah and my brothers bet me I couldn't chew twelve pieces of gum. Not the skinny pieces, the bubble gum balls." Jace shook his head. "I think I got nine pieces in before I started choking. The entire wad landed on Caden's brand new canvas sneakers. We all got in trouble cause we couldn't get the stuff off the laces or the material."

"It didn't land in a ball?" Claire tried to imagine the big, responsible men she knew now acting like silly teenage boys. She unwrapped her bagel and offered him half.

"There may have been some of my lunch mixed in and no one wanted to touch it. Caden yanked off his shoe and banged it against the dirt, hoping it would fall off. It didn't. That led to shoving and wrestling. It was always Noah and I against Logan and Caden. Nothing serious," he quickly added.

Claire chuckled around a bite of her breakfast. "Teenage boys are a different breed of humans. Rue would get calls from neighbors about Garrett and his friends being troublemakers around the trailer park."

"You didn't get in trouble when you were younger?"

She shook her head and turned her focus on the morning sun breaking through the remaining clouds. A sliver of hurt pierced her heart, thinking about the difference in their childhood.

"My classmates didn't want to hang with me because my burns were scary to them. I didn't make a true friend until high school. Garrett was a grade behind me, but he always stood up for me when people would tease me."

Jace shoved the last of his bagel in his mouth and reached across the center console to squeeze her compression gloved covered wrist. The move meant more than she could ever express. There wasn't pity behind it. She hated when people gave her a "poor thing" look. Until she turned thirty, she always wore her hair down to cover her neck. The plastic surgery she had at seventeen lessened the scars on her face. Rue helped her to accept everything about her. She didn't want to think about her mental health if she didn't have her aunt.

Claire placed her hand on top of his and gave it a small pat. "I'm okay. Getting lost in books and having my aunt got me through school. Once I got older, I had work or vet school friends, but nothing solid. I was okay with that because I had a goal. Now I have great friends and working my dream job. I couldn't ask for anything more."

"I can think of one thing," Jace commented with a wink. "But we can talk about that later. We'll be pulling up to the shelter in five minutes."

Claire chewed her last bite of her breakfast and washed it down with the rest of her coffee. Yes, talking would happen. She wanted to see where things went with Jace. Talking about her engagement, his reputation, and making sure there were no women with hard feelings in town. She'd seen the looks a few women gave Naomi during their weekly trip to the diner. Her friend always kept her head high and purposely made sure they saw the diamond wedding set. Could Claire approach the situation the same way? Maybe she could take lessons from Naomi and Izzy. If things got bad, she'd let Josie loose on them.

They pulled into the lot of a freestanding brick building. Claire took a deep breath and stopped Jace before he got out of the truck.

"Thank you for being with me. I'm looking forward to our chat. Maybe with a mug of hot chocolate." Claire gave a saucy wink and reached for her purse on the floor.

"If that's what it takes for us to be more, Buttercup, I'll give you all the hot chocolate you want."

The look on his face didn't hide the seriousness of his statement. It was something she'd have to think about later. Now she had to focus on finding the perfect pet.

Chapter Nine

The need to wrap Claire in a blanket and make every one of her dreams come true rode Jace's heart like the Kentucky Derby. His Buttercup had overcome a lot to be the beautiful, intelligent, caring woman he knew and loved.

Some kids weren't sensitive to other's feelings. He could only imagine what she had heard or experienced. Deep down, he would like to believe he'd be standing shoulder to shoulder with Garrett and stand up for her when others sought to tear her down.

But he was a stupid kid that sometimes made fun of others.

Thankfully, he wasn't that same immature kid. He recognized Claire's heart a week after she started, when he overheard her attempting to calm a scared cat. The stray was pregnant, covered in fleas and hissing at everyone who approached her. That didn't stop his Claire. She sat across from the crate wearing an old oven mitt and fed it small pieces of chicken. Logan said he knew hiring Claire was the best decision when he witnessed the moment. It was when Jace knew he had met the woman of his dreams.

Those close to Jace understood the type of woman he needed before he did. It was why his brothers wanted to make sure he was serious about Claire before pursuing her. He didn't understand how their suggestion that being friends first would work in his favor. Now he understood. She needed to see the real Jace, not the man the town saw who was afraid of commitment.

Jace wanted to be the man she could rely on to support whatever she wanted or needed to do. He also made a mental note to talk to Garrett down the road. It wasn't a secret he told Claire about his reputation. If that was the reason for her initial hesitation, he'd find out soon enough. He needed to reassure Garrett he cared for his cousin and wanted to make her happy.

The slamming of the passenger door brought Jace out of his thoughts. He kicked himself for missing the chance to open the door for her. He'd have another shot when they went home. Jace grabbed his phone from the holder and climbed out of the truck, meeting her at the front bumper.

"Are you okay?" she asked, uncertainty clouding her beautiful green eyes, the cold turning her nose red.

Jace pushed her glasses up before tugging the string on her hoodie. "I'm perfect, Buttercup. Every minute I spend with you, solidifies how perfect we would be together. But as we agreed, finding you a pet is important."

Claire studied him for a moment before giving him a warm smile and a nod. He hovered his palm over her lower back and guided her towards the front door. Martha, the director of the shelter, met them as they approached the glass door, swinging it open. The older woman still looked the same as Jace remembered. She had a tall, sturdy build and wore her gray hair in a simple pixie cut. Fashionable glasses highlighted mischievous eyes.

"Jace Beckett, still as handsome as ever." She pulled him in for a quick hug before taking a step back. "No Caden this time?"

Jace let a real smile form. "He has a new boarder coming and wanted to get the stall ready."

"Is Owen finally going to stick with retirement?" Martha asked.

"Noah thinks so, but he has no say in what his father does."

Owen retired at forty-five and sold his consulting business. When Josie's cousin passed away suddenly and the property manager position opened up. His parents talked Owen out of retirement until they found someone. He stayed in the position for almost twenty years and became part owner.

The older woman gave Claire a side glance. Jace gently tugged Claire from the pictures of dogs and cats who found their forever home. "This is Claire Everson. Logan's vet tech. She's also looking for a new furry friend. This is Martha, the shelter's director and a family friend."

Surprise registered on Claire's face, followed by a wide grin. "It's so nice to meet you."

Martha shot a knowing wink to Jace while giving Claire a quick hug. "Same. You're working for a great family."

Claire nodded, taking a step back. "They've made me feel welcomed."

"Well, I'm not surprised. Josie and Thomas are warm and caring people. Now," Martha slipped her arm with Claire's and guided her towards a set of double doors, "let's find you a friend."

Jace chuckled, shaking his head, and followed the women towards the back. Martha had opened the shelter early so they could spend time with the rescue before bringing it home. Once the door closed behind them, Martha explained to Claire how the shelter worked. Jace stayed a few steps behind them and waved to two workers in the process of getting breakfast ready for the animals.

The shelter worked closely with rescues and sanctuaries from around the country. Martha and her husband moved from Oak Mountain to take over operations ten years ago, when it looked like they would lose funding. His family helped their fundraising effort. Besides the small staff, volunteers from a local recovery center helped keep the place running.

Martha led them to the canine area and told Claire to take her time. She stopped Jace at the first enclosure.

"This is the pickup, Duke. Two families seemed interested, but they never followed through." Martha opened the door for the older Pittie. The black dog's cautious eyes gave Jace a once over but eagerly wagged his rear at seeing Martha. "He has a great temperament and is good with the other dogs. I think he'll do well with the pack."

Jace squatted before the beautiful beast and let him get a good sniff of his hand. He inched closer and nudged Jace's hand before retreating to the corner. Duke's hesitation made sense. Getting his doggy hopes up, only to be disappointed, made him naturally weary. Logan planned to have one of the pack employees stay with the rescue in the free-range doghouse the pack stayed in.

Jace looked over his shoulder. "What's his backstory?" He knew what his father had told him over dinner, but he wanted to make sure he didn't miss anything.

Martha joined him on the floor. Duke trotted to the older woman, keeping a cautious eye on Jace. "He came in as a stray over a year ago. Skin and bones and covered in fleas. He had a respiratory infection. A worker took him home while he recovered, but he lives in an apartment and also has a part-time job so we knew it wasn't long term. Given his temperament, we assume he was a pet and then abandoned."

"Obviously no chip."

"Nope." Martha ran her hand down Duke's back while he sniffed Jace. "There's a group in New Mexico that specializes in bully breeds. They would have space for him in six months once they adopt out a litter. He's showing signs of depression after the couple last week didn't show to pick him up. That's when I called Thomas."

Duke let Jace scratch behind his ears and agreed he would fit in with the pack, meaning he'd spend the rest of his life at the sanctuary. The last thing Jace or his brothers would want is to have another adoption fail during one of their events.

"I'll spend some time with him in the yard shortly." Jace rose to his feet before helping Martha stand. "I'm going to check on Claire first. If she's found a dog, we can be out there together since the two dogs would have a ninety-minute drive together."

"So you and Claire?" The twinkle in Martha's eyes had his cheeks warm.

"Always the matchmaker." Jace winked at his friend. "There's interest there, and I hope something happens soon. For now, we're just friends."

"She's different from women I've seen you have dinner with."

"She is, and that's why I like her. I didn't think I'd meet someone more in tune with animals than my mother and Caden. I was wrong." Jace let a soft smile appear on his lips as he ran his hand over Duke's head. "Claire's the type that would go against someone twice her size if she saw they were mistreating animals. Everyone adores her. She's best friends with Naomi and Izzy."

Martha laughed as she slipped a hemp lead over Duke's head. "Izzy is more comfortable with men as friends than women. For her to take to Naomi and now Claire, that says a lot about your young woman's character. Go, we'll meet you out back."

Jace gave Duke another scratch, then exited the enclosure. Canines of every shape, size and age filled the plexiglass spaces. Some barking to get his attention and some resigned, knowing he wasn't there to take them home. He rubbed the ache in the middle of his chest. If he could take most home, he would. They truly didn't have the space until the expansion on the doghouse was complete in a couple of weeks.

Jace quickly scanned each window until a huddle mass caught his eye. Its head rested on Claire's lap, who had her face tucked into the dog's neck.

His Buttercup found her forever pet.

He slid the door open and met her gaze. Tears flowed down her cheek. Not wanting to startle the dog, he eased in and sat beside her. It was his first look at the animal. Large spots of white dotted the common brown fur found on the Boxer breed. Its stubbed tail barely moved in a wag.

"Her owner surrendered her when the vitiligo appeared." Claire's voice was barely above a whisper. "She couldn't breed because the skin disease could pass on to her litter. They felt she wasn't enough."

Jace had seen the condition on humans, but was rare among dogs and cats. It didn't harm the dog's health and could still breed. Before he could respond, Claire continued.

"She's been here for eleven months with no one showing any interest in her. People walk past her like she's nothing. She's only two." The fire in her eyes made him smile. "I don't like people. She's a healthy dog. Just because of a skin condition, she is *not* acceptable. Maybe we should find out where her previous owners live and take all their dogs. They clearly don't deserve them."

Jace chuckled and reached to let the dog sniff his hand. "As much as I agree with you, going to jail wouldn't help this beauty find a home. What's her name?"

"Sally. What kind of name is that for a dog? I'm going to name her Luna."

"That's perfect." Jace tapped down on the desire to press his lips to her forehead. Instead, he climbed to his feet and brushed the back of his jeans. "Martha is taking Duke out back so we can do a little bonding. Why don't we get a worker to take Luna? You two can bond and she can meet Duke. They have a long car ride ahead."

"I'll wait here until they come with a lead."

"Sounds good." Claire rested her hand on his leg to stop his departure.

"Did you see the dog about two stalls down?"

"I focused on finding you. Why?"

"Senior dog. Ten if I'm not mistaken. A terrier like Mika and Tam. He was going to be my pick until I met this good girl."

Sally, soon to be Luna, wagged her tail but kept her head on Claire's lap. Naomi's terriers were supposed to be foster dogs. Within twenty-four hours stranded at the sanctuary with the pups, Naomi knew they would be Shorty's siblings. Mika and Tam were also gentle around Cammie and Fiona's senior pugs.

Jace nodded. "Okay. Let me get someone to help you take her outside and you can meet Duke. I'll see about the senior and call Caden to make room at his place."

He stepped into the hallway and stopped at the stall Claire indicated. Huddled in the corner was a black and gray mass of fur who shifted his eyes to Jace but didn't bother lifting his head. He glanced at the information sheet. The owner surrendered the dog before going into hospice eighteen months prior. Jace decided on the spot that if Caden didn't have room, he would take him.

"I'll be back for you in a bit."

He pulled out his phone as he walked down the hall and shot his brother a text. Jace had to spend time with his brothers soon to figure how they could help more animals…and apologize to their mother. Now he understood how she came home with more animals.

Most shelters had their pickups ready or in the greeting yard when they arrived. The walk past hopeful pups and cats tore his heart in two. Jace wasn't naïve to think they could save every animal. Life didn't work that way. But he and his brothers wanted to make a difference. Jace had to do his part. That meant finding unique ways to do what they could.

The makings of an idea formed in his mind as he waved down a worker for Claire. He shot off a quick text to Noah to come to his place for dinner and watch the game. The two worked out all their brainstorming ideas before taking them to his brothers and the folks.

Jace would need Noah for what he had in mind.

Chapter Ten

Claire sipped her iced tea as she scrolled through the selection of dog sweaters on her laptop. She didn't want to think about the cost of the items in her virtual cart.

She glanced over the top of her laptop at Luna's sleeping form in the oversized dog bed. Someone—she's thinking Josie—left the fleece lined bed, several stuffed toys and dishes near the small corner fireplace.

Each dog reacted differently when they returned to Hawkins Ridge. Duke eagerly greeted Logan and the worker responsible for his care while he adjusted. Claire didn't think Duke would have a problem with the pack after his examination. Lenny, the senior terrier, perked up in the truck. He'd been a pet longer than the other two and understood being in the truck meant he was leaving the shelter. However, he wasn't too keen when they stopped in front of Caden's cabin near the stables. The middle Beckett brother met them with a smile on his face. It was when Scout, Caden's therapy dog, trotted up that Lenny's tail frantically wagged and he let Caden lead him from the back of the truck.

Then there was Luna.

Her girl was hesitant when Jace lifted her out of the truck and sat her on the packed gravel. Hawkins Ridge is noisy, and Luna attempted to take it all in. It was when Thomas approached, holding a wiggly Cammie, that Luna's stubby tail resembled a propeller. Claire kept a tight grasp on her lead while she sniffed the fluffy Pomeranian and the patriarch of the family. After several minutes, Claire led her home. Luna cataloged every scent in the house while she set up her dishes and folded an old blanket in the bed. Claire wanted to give the dog breathing room while she took in her new home and decompressed.

She sat her laptop on the cushion beside her and grabbed her phone. She hadn't spoken with Rue that day and wanted to share the good news. Her aunt picked up on the second ring.

"Did you find a dog?" Rue said as a way of greeting. Claire chuckled, causing Luna to lift her head.

"I did. A two-year-old boxer with a skin condition. She's a sweetie. It will take a couple of days for her personality to show. Hold on while I send you a picture."

Claire took several photos while they were outside at the shelter. She hit send and put the phone to her ear.

"I changed her name to Luna. I know it's going to take some time for her to know I'm talking to her."

"What was her name before?" Rue asked. "Oh, she's gorgeous!"

"Isn't she!? Her name was Sally."

"That's not a dog's name."

"Tell me about it. I don't have a problem with the name itself, just it's a human name." Claire shook her head. "I'm taking her with me to the office tomorrow. I hope it doesn't give her anxiety, thinking she's back at another shelter."

She hadn't thought about the possibility until she said it. The sanctuary had crates for the animals recovering from surgery, but they weren't out in the open. It had an enormous room with toys and access to a fenced in grassy area. If Luna showed any sign of stress, Claire would have to talk to Logan or Naomi about options. Rue's voice brought her back to the conversation.

"I think as long as she can roam and see you, she'll be okay. What about patients?"

"Unless it's a property animal, Logan always goes to the various farms. Naomi isn't seeing any patients this week. If there is an emergency, she'll make a house call unless they have to do a procedure." Claire didn't want to monopolize the conversation. "How was your day? What did you do?"

"I met Garrett for lunch at the diner. Then went grocery shopping. I found the library and want to spend time there tomorrow."

"Are you and Garrett still going to Martinsburg this weekend?" Her cousin wanted to take Rue to the large town to see a play and dinner. Garrett arranged for them to stay at a nice hotel. Sara planned to watch Balty.

"Yes, even though I told him I would be just as happy putting some burgers on the grill or going to the movies here."

"He wants to do something nice and spend time with you. Let him."

"Whatever," Rue mumbled. "What about you and your young man?"

Claire exhaled, reaching for her iced tea. She didn't fight the smile when she thought of the bagel or when she let her emotions run wild with Luna. Seeing Jace toss a ball with Duke and his patience with Lenny only confirmed she wanted to give him a chance. Claire took a sip of her drink before answering.

"He mentioned us having a talk yesterday when he walked me home after work. I told him it sounded like a good idea. Before you ask, I don't know when, but I'm sure it will be soon. He mentioned introducing Luna and his dog Oriole this weekend. They're roughly the same size and age." Claire shrugged, even though her aunt couldn't see her. "I think it may be, then."

"I'm proud of you for taking the chance. Remember to be honest."

"I will." A knock at the door brought Luna to her feet and scurrying to Claire. "Someone's at the door. I'll talk to you tomorrow."

She ended the call and gave a gentle pat to Luna's head. A quick peek out the front window had her opening the door to a smiling Naomi.

"Hey. I hope I'm not disturbing you?"

Claire took a step back to let her friend in. Her hand tightened around Luna's new collar. "Not at all. I was finishing up a call with Rue."

"I take it this is Luna."

The pup in question gave Naomi a solid sniff, probably smelling her and Logan's dogs. Naomi stood in place and even offered her hand for inspection. Once Luna gave her friend the okay, she wagged her tail.

"She is a beauty," Naomi commented, going to her knees. "Did Logan look her over?"

Claire shook her head and let go of the collar. Naomi was an excellent vet and had experience with unfamiliar animals.

Luna showed no signs of aggression, so Claire felt comfortable letting the two feel each other out.

"I figure you would check her out tomorrow. I planned on bringing her to work. Logan mentioned something about Duke being there."

Naomi ran her hands over Luna while she spoke. "He examined him this afternoon. He's still under weight, needs a couple of teeth pulled and neutered, but overall, he's healthy. I'll look at Luna first thing. Logan's taking Fiona to school because he has to get some things from the feed store, so we have time. How long was she at the shelter?"

Claire answered from the kitchen area as she poured Naomi a glass of tea. "Eleven months. She went into heat about three months ago. I have a cart full of shirts for her."

"Something tells me Ms. Luna is going to be spoiled." Naomi thanked her for the tea, then joined Claire on the couch. Luna went back to her bed but remained alert. "I'm positive we have the dog-friendly sunscreen in the medication room. We'll get you a tube until her shirts come in."

"Thank you. Where's Fiona?" Logan's daughter loved Naomi like a mother, and the two spent a lot of time together.

Naomi snorted. "Her grandparents offered her a better dinner of steak and fries. I was tempted to join her, but then Logan would have pouted. So we had a quiet meal of soup and sandwiches. I'm sure Josie also promised she could help feed the cats."

"I'm surprised she hasn't talked you guys into adding a cat."

"Six dogs is enough. Her grandparents are a thirty-second walk away. She can get her fill of cats there." Naomi set her tea on a coaster and studied Luna. "Jace said you were thinking about Lenny at first, then decided on Luna. Was it the vitiligo that made your decision?"

Claire exhaled, tucking her feet under her. She spared a glance at Luna, who rested her head on a stuffed worm.

"I really wanted Lenny. He gave off an air of giving up, and my heart went out to him. There were workers at the end of the hall, and I set out to ask them to open the door. It was the spotted white discoloration that grabbed my attention. She, too, just looked resigned. It was her story that did it." Claire reached for her tea, taking a sip to get her emotions under control. She hadn't shared with Jace why Luna's history touched her. She could talk to Naomi.

"I missed a year of school after my accident going through skin graphs, therapy, counseling sessions. Every friend I had dumped me because I looked different. I felt alone. I had Garrett, but he had his own friends. It's why I drown myself in books." She sighed. "All children and animals want is to be loved and feel safe. "

"Adults too," Naomi added as she reached for Claire's hand and gave it a squeeze.

"It's why I mentioned Lenny to Jace. The dog spent his entire life with a person who physically couldn't care for him anymore. He needed a second chance at feeling love. I don't know if Luna ever felt that. To her previous owners, she was a commodity that couldn't produce."

"Now she'll have that acceptance she deserves." Naomi glanced at her phone when it pinged, rolling her eyes. "I have to go. Mika and Tam are ignoring Logan and have cornered a raccoon near the dog run."

Claire laughed. "Do you need help?"

"No. Normally, they listen when he calls. However, when they get a raccoon or a squirrel in their sights, his voice is just background noise."

Naomi typed a response before draining the rest of her tea. Claire needed to take Luna for a final out and grabbed her lead. She ordered a reflective version, since a harness would rub against her sensitive spots. For now, she would stay within the area around the house.

"Thank you again for looking at her tomorrow."

Naomi waved off the gratitude and pulled Claire in for a hug. "I'm glad you landed at a place where you feel accepted."

"Me too."

And Claire wanted to keep it that way.

"Would you really have adopted the senior dog?" Noah asked before stuffing chips in his mouth.

Jace stepped back into the living room and passed a cold beer to his friend. He plopped into the recliner and sighed.

"Without giving it a second thought. He was depressed and didn't show any sign of life until we helped him into the SUV." Jace took the bottle opener from Noah, flipping the cap off. "I know we have senior dogs in the pack, but my gut told me he wouldn't have thrived."

"Besides, Caden has Rocky, so it was a better fit."

Caden adopted a senior dog when they picked up Logan's pugs last year. The twelve-year-old mix breed was satisfied sunning on the porch and doing rounds with the stable cats.

Caden only wanted Scout and Rocky, but Jace knew his brother wouldn't say no to Lenny.

"It's also quieter on that side of the property," Jace continued.

"Which is why Dad and Sam built their module over there," Noah added.

The two returned their focus to the college basketball tournament game. Jace kept Claire's reaction to Luna to himself. Not that Noah would tease her, but it was a vulnerable moment she shared with him. He'd built trust with Claire and wanted to keep it that way.

On the way home, he mentioned introducing Luna and Oriole. Boxers are playful and figured Oriole would help Luna exercise some of her energy. When Luna met Cammie, she gently sniffed the Pomeranian. He didn't know if the dog could detect Cammie's blindness, but their one-on-one interaction would require Jace and Claire's full concentration.

Jace also hoped they could talk about taking the next step together. He didn't want the subject hanging over them like an anvil. If they started dating, Luna would spend more time with his dogs. They would have to get Cammie used to Claire's house.

He mentally shook his head and cheered when his team scored. Jace couldn't jump to the future until he knew for sure Claire would be interested. For now, he had to run something by Noah.

"I think we should figure out a way to take in more animals."

Noah shifted his gaze. "What do you mean? That's why we're putting the addition on the doghouse so we can house fifty dogs."

"I know." Jace raked his hair and figured out the best way to explain his thoughts. "Caden wants to expand the support dog training. What if there was a way to house those dogs away from the pack? He's working with the PTSD counselor in Stark Valley so the support dogs would rotate. Giving them their own space would free up the quantity allowed for the sanctuary."

"Huh." Noah tapped his chin. "We're sending out grant proposals for the program in the fall. Showing it as a truly separate non-profit from the sanctuary would work in our favor. We'd have to get your parents' approval to clear a couple of acres."

Josie, Thomas, and Owen transferred ownership of the business, buildings, and land to Jace, his brothers, and Noah at the beginning of the year. The private residences and the land belonged to the owner of the houses. However, the unoccupied land belonged to Jace's parents. He didn't see them saying no.

"There's something else I'm thinking about."

"You're just a fountain of ideas this evening," Noah teased. Jace ignored the ribbing and continued.

"I think we have to expand the foster homes list beyond the three counties. I'm thinking possible homes within a four-hour drive time radius."

Noah shook his head and muted the TV. "Where is all this coming from? It's a good idea, but a lot of work."

"I know." Jace rested his forearms on his thighs and gave Oriole a scratch behind the ear. Cammie slept on her back at the end of the couch. "Doing the pickup today got to me. The other shelters will lead us to a separate area and bring the dogs or cats to us. Martha's place isn't that big, so she moves the pickups to the front enclosures. Walking to find Claire just made me understand why Mom always came home with more."

"Which is why I only pick up the goats. I know I'm a softy," Noah said. He, like Josie, had cats as pets.

"I'm proud to admit I'm a marshmallow wrapped in muscles."

"Which is why the women love you."

Jace rolled his eyes but laughed along with his brother by choice. "Whatever, man. You act like they aren't all over you, too."

"But I always say no." Noah pointed a finger. "There's a difference."

Jace tried not to think about his old lifestyle. After Leah ended the relationship, he thought casual was safe. Seeing his brothers' and Noah's marriages end, he felt he made the right decision. Jace didn't want to make the same mistake and marry a woman who didn't understand what they were doing at Hawkins Ridge. He also didn't think he could recover if another woman crushed him like his ex. When his family asked if he was sure about Claire, a part was because they wanted them to work. The other part is they were fearful Jace wouldn't bounce back.

But they had nothing to worry about. Claire loved Hawkins Ridge, and he could watch her talk to animals for days. They had chemistry. When she smiled at him, he felt warmth coursing through his veins. The urge to date other women dried like a sponge on the surface of the sun. No one tempted him. That's how he knew Claire was the one.

Of course, his family would tease him senseless if they heard his thoughts.

"The more I think about your idea, it might work," Noah's statement cut into Jace's thoughts. "I'm going to crunch numbers this week. Figure out the details, and we can mention it to Logan and Caden at the poker game on Saturday."

Jace planned to work on the property for the rest of the week, so putting together the information wouldn't be a problem.

"I'll show you what I come up with beforehand."

The two turned their focus back to the game. A few minutes later, Jace's phone beeped. He smiled, seeing the picture Claire sent him of a sleeping Luna.

Claire: I have to get her a bed for my room. Is a pink collar too much?

He quietly chuckled and typed his reply.

Jace: If the other dogs don't tease Cammie about her camo sweater, I think Luna's safe with the color of her collar. Just leave off the spikes.

Claire: Good point. Thank you again for everything today. Night.

Jace: You're welcome. Night.

Chapter Eleven

Claire nibbled on her bottom lip as she studied her reflection in the mirror. She didn't want to overthink her outfit, but she hoped to strike a balance between relaxed and cute. Luna nibbled on a bully stick while keeping an eye on Claire's actions.

The two bonded the three days since she rescued the boxer. Claire brought her to work each day. Izzy gushed over her baby and snuck her treats when she thought no one was looking.

Naomi's exam revealed Luna had an ear infection and was slightly underweight. They started antibiotic drops and vitamins immediately, and Claire noticed a difference in the dog's energy after twenty-four hours.

"What about a tank top under an open shirt?" Luna responded to Claire's question with a wag.

Claire glanced at her watch. They were going to Jace's so Luna could meet Oriole and the two could talk. She had thirty minutes to change and make the walk. Claire wanted the privacy and vetoed meeting at her home. Hawkins Ridge slowed down on the weekend, but it still had a lot of activity.

Nerves rode her as she threw her hair into a low ponytail. She didn't know how the conversation would start. Would he expect her to bring up the subject? Would he understand when she explained her hesitation? What if Luna and Oriole hated each other? Would they put the talk on hold?

It was too late to over think everything. Slipping her cell phone into her pocket, she spared another glance in the mirror and let out a deep breath.

"Okay, let's get you ready for your play date."

Claire already rubbed the sunscreen on Luna and helped her into a new tie dye shirt. She wondered if her previous owners dressed the pup because Luna easily stepped into the openings without complaint.

After snapping on the lead and picking up the baggie that held Oriole's present from Luna, the two were on their way. Luna hadn't traveled past the clinic and took in the unfamiliar smells. When they stopped at the chicken enclosure, a UTV pulled up beside them. Josie greeted them with a wide smile.

"Beautiful day for a walk," she said, resting her arm on the steering wheel. "I thought you were coming to family dinner last night."

Claire fought the urge to check her watch. She hated being late for things. "I didn't know how Luna would be with that many people and the dogs. It's why we're heading to Jace's. We want to see her interaction with Oriole."

Josie nodded in agreement. "That's smart. You don't want to overwhelm her. If she hasn't freaked out with the noise and activity the past few days, then seeing how she interacts with other dogs is the next step. Hop in, I'll give you a ride over. I was heading to the greenhouse, anyway."

"Thank you." Claire guided Luna to the passenger side and climbed in. Luna's large black eyes studied the area Claire pointed to on the floor between her legs. Josie patiently waited. Once Luna gathered enough nerve, she slowly hoisted herself into position and rested her head on Claire's thigh. She praised her with comforting strokes along her head.

"She is a cutie," Josie said and eased the accelerator.

Cutting through the trees past the goat area was normally faster to get to Jace. Since this was Luna's first time in the UTV, Josie stayed on the packed gravel. It gave Luna a chance to see the property. Though she sought comfort from Claire, her gaze bounced to any new sounds.

A few minutes later, they came to a stop in front of Jace's single story home. He and Oriole stood on the porch playing tug with a rope. The retriever mix dropped his end, causing Jace to stumble back. He recovered quick enough to get a firm grasp on the dog's collar.

"I wasn't expecting to see you, Mom." He guided Oriole to the driveway but kept a safe distance. Luna's head popped up and eyed Oriole. Claire had her lead wrapped around her good wrist in case Luna wanted to jump out during the drive.

"I saw them on my way to the greenhouse and offered a ride." Josie put the vehicle in park and climbed out. "Where's Cammie?"

"Logan picked her up about an hour ago. Fiona wanted to groom her." Jace locked eyes with Claire. "You okay, Buttercup?"

"Yep. Trying to figure out the best way to get out without losing control of Luna."

"Let me help, dear." Josie hurried over to the passenger side. "Give me the lead. Once she's out, then you can take over."

Oriole whimpered and tugged, trying to meet the visitors. Once he saw Luna's full body, a gleeful yip and excited tail wagging had Jace dig his feet in place. Claire quickly exited and took control of the dog. The last thing she wanted was for Luna to drag Josie.

The humans were quiet as Jace and Claire slowly closed the distance between them. Jace gave the command for Oriole to sit. It surprised everyone when Luna did the same.

"Good to know she knows that command," Claire said, easing the tension. "It's okay. Let's go say hi."

She led Luna to the excited dog and let the two get a feel for one another. When Luna wagged her rear and went to a downward facing dog pose, everyone relaxed. Jace released his grip on the collar, but remained close while the two sniffed each other in a circle.

"Well, my work here is done," Josie announced before giving Jace a hug. "I made a batch of cream cheese dip this morning. Logan will have some at the poker game." She faced Claire. "Naomi is bringing some with her for your movie night."

Claire's mouth watered. Josie's addictive cream cheese dip had bacon and cheddar cheese.

"Thanks, Mom. I'll give Claire and Luna a ride back," Jace offered.

Claire didn't know if he mentioned to anyone about their talk. She'd only told Rue. Jace's statement conveyed they didn't need any pop-ins. The knowing smile on the matriarch's face set Claire's cheeks on fire.

"I'll take that as my cue to leave. Have fun. I hope you can make it to dinner tomorrow evening, Claire." Josie gave them each a hug before heading on to her original destination.

"You know you weren't subtle," Claire teased as she moved closer to Luna, who followed Oriole along the treeline.

"I wasn't trying to be. Mom would've found a reason to stay longer if I hadn't."

"You know she's going to go back and tell Thomas we're up to something."

"We are." Jace winked. "Is Luna adjusting?"

"I think so. She's only been to the clinic. We've stuck to the area around the house during our walks, but she's seen the workers come in and out of the surrounding buildings. I'll see how she does with Logan and Naomi's dogs tomorrow."

"I think she was around other dogs, especially if she came from a breeder." Jace tilted his head towards Luna and Oriole as they chased a squirrel. "She's letting him take the lead. I will be curious to see her around Cammie with the other dogs. If she will notice their protectiveness of her and be gentle."

"I guess we'll find out tomorrow."

Claire could sense the awkwardness between them. She didn't have a problem talking about Luna, but it's been months since they just made idle chit-chat. Yes, the seriousness of this conversation would change things, but she didn't know how to start the conversation. Secretly wished he would. However, if she wanted to be on equal footing in the relationship, she needed to bite the bullet.

"You said you wanted more from us. Is that still the case?" Heat rose to her cheeks as she studied her shoes.

Jace blew out a breath, shoving his hands in his pockets. "It's always been the case since day one. Let's take a seat on the porch. I'll grab us something to drink."

Luna noticed Claire was moving and trotted over. Oriole continued to sniff the tree for the squirrel, but soon gave up. Jace returned from inside with two bottled waters and two chew sticks before darting back in and returning with water for the dogs.

Claire made herself comfortable on the outdoor chair. She wiped her hands down her thigh and took calming breaths. She'd mentally worked through points she wanted to bring up while eating breakfast. There was a difference between confessing her fears to Rue and even Naomi than to Jace. But she wanted this. That couldn't happen unless she shared everything.

After another trip inside, Jace returned with a plate of herb infused goat cheese, pita chips, and grapes. Once Luna and Oriole settled down with their treat, Jace turned his chair to face her.

"Sorry. I wanted us to be comfortable and have the dogs distracted for a bit." Jace leaned forward and snagged a chip. "To finish answering your question. You know I want more. I'm also glad we became friends first."

"I am too."

"When I asked you out a month after you started, I didn't take into account you were new, not just to Hawkins Ridge but also Oak Mountain. I also didn't know my folks were serious about us taking over at the beginning of the year." Jace raked his fingers through his hair. "There were changes I had to deal with over those ten months. Proving to my family, and myself, that I was ready would have taken away from a serious relationship. It also gave me a chance to show I am more than my reputation."

Claire sighed. She saw Jace struggle early on when he left the firehouse and went full time at Hawkins Ridge. Even if Jace didn't have the reputation in town, would she have been enough at the time? She also focused on doing a good job and laying roots. Neither would have been in the proper head space to give their all to a relationship.

"I get that. Oak Mountain was a new start for me." Claire took a sip of her water. "When Garrett told me about the position, I had moved back to the trailer with my aunt because I ended my engagement."

"You were engaged?" Jace furrowed his brows. "I didn't know that."

"No one here does. It's embarrassing. I just wanted to move past my ex-fiancé and didn't want the pity stares."

"Wow. Do you mind me asking what happened?"

She sucked in a breath and let the words out. "He cheated on me and then mentally abused me because of my weight and scars." She absently ran her fingers across the puckered skin on her neck. "I moved back home to heal. I didn't know what my next step would be, but I knew I couldn't stay in my hometown."

Claire met his gaze and found warmth, not pity, in his eyes. She popped a pita chip in her mouth to let Jace process what she said. He spoke after a few moments.

"He's an idiot for not realizing what an amazing woman he had. Only mentally small men would abuse a woman. So my reputation only fueled your doubts."

"Yep. Hearing from Sara that you couldn't commit, I assumed you were interested in another notch on your tally of women." She shrugged. "I didn't want that."

"I get that, even though you wouldn't have been. That explains why you never took me seriously."

"Also, you went from flirty to friend zone overnight. I felt I dodge a bullet."

Jace chuckled. "Logan told me you needed to see the real me and not how the town sees me. He and Caden also threatened me that if I wasn't serious about pursuing you to let it go. That was when he was trying to get a handle on his feelings for Naomi. The more I thought about it, I realized he was right."

"I think not having the pressure of something more helped our friendship."

"Agree." Jace nodded and passed a piece of cheese to each dog. "Did anyone ever tell you why I played the field?"

"Izzy said it had something to do with college, but it was your story to tell."

"My college girlfriend broke my heart. Leah and I were together for two years. I planned on proposing at graduation. During spring break of our senior year, she said she applied and accepted a job overseas. She also said she wanted to start her new life unattached."

Claire swallowed a gasp. "She never told you she was looking at overseas jobs?"

"No. I thought we would build something in another city, but she had no intention of us being together after college. If I didn't have Noah at school with me, I don't think I would have passed my finals."

"So you gave up on women?"

Jace shook his head. "I gave up on finding a happy ever after, not women. For five years following college, I saw Noah and my brothers' marriages fail. We grew up seeing our parents happy. Yes, Owen and Noah's mother divorced, but that was because Owen came out. He found his one in Sam a few years later."

Claire adored Owen's husband. She never experienced a two-parent household. Seeing the marriages Jace and his brothers had as examples, it made sense they would want the same. At least Logan had that now.

"You didn't think the women you were casual with could be someone special?" Claire didn't want him to realize that he and Tinsley belonged together a month into their relationship.

Jace coughed, causing Luna and Oriole to glare in his direction. "No. Most of the women I grew up with or I know their exes. A few didn't grow up on farms or assumed we just brushed horses or tossed seeds out for the chickens. Noah and Caden's ex-wives thought they supervised and let the workers do everything."

"Why would they think that? Didn't they see how things worked when they were dating?"

"They thought it was a show. Noah's ex followed him from college and wasn't used to a small town. She thought she'd get him to sell his share and move to New York City with her." Jace chuckled and tossed a piece of cheese into his mouth. "That marriage barely lasted nine months."

Claire couldn't wrap her head around that. Small towns weren't for everyone. Sure, people knew your business, but she loved the sense of community in them. She learned a lot during her time in the city, but recovering back home made her realize she wanted to spend her life in an accepting small town.

She found that in Oak Mountain.

"What do you want, Buttercup?" Jace asked, holding her gaze. "Do you want something more?"

She said she would be honest. Now was the time.

Jace wanted to get straight to the point. Talking about their past seemed necessary. He hadn't known Claire was once engaged, and a wave of anger surged through him. The idea that anyone could think someone was better than her confused him. To make matters worse, the thought that stripping her of her self-worth could make someone feel like a man was beyond him. He was sure he could talk his brothers into finding out where this man lived. Maybe Garrett knew.

It did, however, explain why she didn't think he was serious when he first asked her out. Jace hoped his explanation cleared up why he had the reputation he did.

His parents met at college. Over forty years later, his mother still swooned when his father sang love songs for her. She didn't mind that Thomas couldn't hold a key. Just last week, he stumbled on them making out behind the chicken coop. That was what he wanted in a marriage. Someone who still sparked when the other walked into a room.

He also wanted someone he could share Hawkins Ridge with. It was one of the many things he liked about Claire. Before they even approached friendship level, she wanted to be part of helping to save animals. It was her dream before Oak Mountain to take care of animals. She worked hard to be a vet tech. He wanted to support her in what she wanted out of life. If she wanted to go back to school to be a vet, he'd be right there with her cheering her on. Claire also made organic, nutritious treats for the dogs. Maybe she wanted to market to places outside of the sanctuary and Naomi's practice. Whatever she wanted.

Claire rose to her feet and rested her hands on the railing. Luna lifted her head to follow, but remained relaxed. Jace would give her as much time as she needed. She spoke after a few moments.

"Oak Mountain is everything I've wanted in a home. I have a great job with people I care deeply for. Heck, I finally have a dog." She smiled warmly at Luna before turning her gaze to him. "I'm happy."

"But?" Jace remembered Logan's words from the dinner at the beginning and stayed quiet.

"I'm afraid I will lose everything that I've worked hard for. This opportunity, if things didn't work out between us, goes away." She crossed her arms. "I don't want to hear rumors from people who have seen you with someone else if we're supposed to be together. I don't forgive cheaters."

Jace knew that wouldn't happen, but if he said so, it would seem like he didn't care about her worries. He did. Claire was his one. However, if she decided after a year or two of them being together, she wasn't happy and left him, he'd didn't think he'd recover. It was why his actions had to show her they would be great as a team.

"I get that," he said after a beat. "I also know saying that would never happen wouldn't ease your fears."

"So you think we wouldn't last? That you won't be faithful?"

"Oh, I believe if you give us a chance, we'll be together until our last breath. I never cheated on Leah. That's not how I was raised. You know deep down that's true." He raked his fingers through his hair to gather his thoughts. "However, you need proof. That can't come after talking for an hour."

He made his way to her, taking her hand. "Buttercup, outside of my family, you are the only one who sees the real me. That won't change when we add kissing to the mix." He flashed a wink.

Claire rolled her eyes. "Silly."

"Truthful. I haven't been with a woman since I realized I wanted you. Ask Izzy or anyone in town. I also don't miss it."

He sucked in a deep breath at the realization. He and Noah still went to the bar once a month to shoot pool and have a beer, but that was all he did. It was easy to maintain his reputation when he stayed at the firehouse with his single friends. He had different priorities now. One being the dark hair beauty who contemplated stealing Luna's siblings from her former owners.

Jace mentally slapped himself to return to the conversation at hand.

"All I can do is ask for a chance to show you I'm serious about us," he said. "I've learned words don't mean a thing unless I back it up."

"I'm not fast like those other women."

It took Jace a moment to grasp what she said. He shook his head. "I know that and wouldn't ask you to do anything you weren't comfortable with. This relationship will go at your speed."

"I also don't see me jogging these five hundred plus acres with you." Claire nibbled her bottom lip, dropping her gaze to the ground. "I will never be a size six."

"Okay. Your body is perfect the way it is. I would never ask you to be someone you aren't." He gently cupped her chin to look at him. "Before you say something about your scars, I've seen them. They don't bother me. I also know what happens when you overuse your hand. I'll make sure you rest."

Claire exhaled and studied him for a moment. Jace watched a myriad of emotions dance in her eyes, but never rushed her. He meant it when he said she would control the pace of their relationship. Claire meant a lot to him, his family, and to Hawkins Ridge. Stability meant a lot to her. If he thought for a moment, it wouldn't work out or he wasn't ready for a committed relationship, he would be happy staying friends.

But he was ready to share a life she deserved.

"Okay." Claire nodded. "Let's take a chance."

Jace's loud whoop of joy startled both dogs. Luna let loose a series of hearty barks before forcing her way in front of Claire. She immediately stroked the dog's head and mumbled calming words. Oriole took the opportunity and gave Luna a sloppy kiss. The boxer took that as a cue for a spirited game of chase.

Jace wrapped his arm around her shoulder as they watched the two dogs burn their built-up energy.

"So now what? Do we go on a date? Are we official?" Claire asked.

He chuckled, dropping a kiss on top of her head. "I'm not sure if we need to go on a date to make it official. We are, though, going on a date. If we didn't already have plans, I'd say tonight. How about lunch tomorrow?"

"I can't. Your mom is supposed to help Naomi and I plant window boxes. I hope Luna doesn't destroy the greenhouse."

Jace didn't want to appear overly eager and suggest doing something afterwards. "Why don't I watch Luna so you can enjoy yourself? I can have Logan help me introduce her to all the dogs before dinner."

Claire watched Luna sitting in a patch of grass, sniffing the air. "If you're sure? I need her to get used to different people."

"Positive. We can do dinner during the week."

"Okay. Thank you." She squeezed his hand before checking her watch. "I need to head home and get things ready for Naomi and Fiona."

Jace lost track of time and still had to get his wings into a marinade. He could always do it at Logan's.

"Let me take everything in and grab the wings. I'll give you a ride home."

"I'll help."

The two made quick work of taking their snack dishes and dog bowls into the house. Luna followed Oriole indoors and sniffed every corner, paying special attention to Cammie's bed. Jace kept a watchful eye in case Luna decided to mark the fleece covered cushion. Claire remained close for the same reason, but the boxer simply sat near Jace's recliner.

"Are you telling your brothers about us?" Claire picked up a picture from his mantle. It was the one his father took of them with the Christmas trees they'd cut. Claire's smile was blinding.

"It's up to you." Jace slid the party size tray of wings into a bag. "We can wait."

She shook her head. "I'll probably freak out once it hits me we're together. I'm sure I'll say something to Naomi."

Jace placed the bag on the counter and closed the distance between them. The last thing he wanted was for her to have doubts. He'd feel like a heel if she felt pressured.

"Are you sure about this? We can wait and have another discussion in a week or two if you need more time."

Claire chuckled and rested her hand on his chest. "I'm not having doubts. At least not the doubts you think. I wonder about the hateful glances when it becomes public and telling Garrett. Not about my decision. As you said before, I am known for 'what ifs'. Nothing you can say or do will change that. It's okay, though. A beer and some of Josie's dip. I'll be fine."

Jace saw the certainty in her green eyes and nodded. He wouldn't push the subject and gave her hand a final squeeze. He couldn't wait to tell his brothers over poker. Her concern about the hateful stares was an issue. Jace was a catch. No baby mama drama, a body that rivaled Alan Ritchson's, homeowner, and an easy charming smile.

Claire didn't have the sharp tongue like Izzy in case someone said something mean. She had Naomi. His sister-in-law dealt with those same mumbles and held her head high. It eased Jace's concerns she had someone to talk to. He also knew his mother would stand up for Claire if she heard anything negative. But it would take Claire to ignore them when it happened. All Jace could do was be there for her when it did.

He grabbed his phone and slipped it into his pocket before picking up the wings. Claire, Luna, and Oriole met him on the porch. The sun peeked from behind the trees, causing a stunning orange sky. The temperature would drop in the thirties overnight.

He led them to his UTV. It was larger than his mother's and Oriole scurried to the back seat. Jace helped Luna get situated before guiding Claire to the passenger side. He gently grasped her arm before she fastened the seatbelt.

"Thank you for giving us a chance." The setting sun did nothing to hide the flush in her cheeks.

"Thank you for not giving up on me."

He pressed his lips to her cheek before closing her half door. "I had no intention of giving up on us."

And he meant it.

Chapter Twelve

Claire tossed another log onto the fire and closed the chain link screen. The calendar said March, but spring was still ten days away. Nighttime on the mountain was a stark reminder. Winter wasn't finished yet.

Luna lay on her side in front of the corner fireplace. She graced Claire with a rump wag but made no attempt to leave her spot. Claire didn't blame her.

"I hope you're more social when Naomi gets here," she playfully admonished.

Her friend sent a text Fiona wouldn't be joining them for their movie night. Instead, she was spending the night at a friend's. Claire would miss the tween's commentary, but she didn't mind. It would give her and Naomi a chance to talk freely.

She'd yet to freak out, and it surprised her.

Why she expected everything would feel different made no sense. She wasn't sixteen. This wasn't her first relationship. Though they may not have gone on an official date, she'd spent time alone with Jace. What changed?

Absolutely nothing.

She cared deeply for Jace. He checked all the boxes on her checklist of what she wanted in a partner. His explanation for not committing to another relationship fell in line with his brothers. Whereas Caden and Noah threw themselves into their work to avoid dating, Jace went the opposite direction. There was the simple fact that the single female population in Oak Mountain wasn't large. They couldn't risk dating the same woman and cause a strife. The men would never take that chance.

Claire mentally cleared her wayward thoughts. Naomi was due any minute. She strolled to the kitchen area to check the stuffed mushroom caps in the oven. They stuck to finger foods for their monthly movie nights. A moment after closing the oven door, a rapid knock echoed in the space.

Luna scrambled to her feet and let out a couple of barks.

"It's just Naomi," she said. "You know her."

She swung the door open to a bag laden friend. Claire hurried to take one of the canvas totes. She then noticed Logan at the end of her walkway and tossed up a wave.

"What did you bring?" Claire stepped to the side to let her in. Luna sniffed each bag.

"Josie sent stuff." Naomi shrugged off her fleece jacket. "Logan and I stopped past their place since my mom and Harold were there. They sent cookies, chicken salad sandwiches, toast points for the cream cheese dip, deviled eggs, and cherry tomatoes. Logan took the mac and cheese and red beans and rice."

"How can they eat all that and still play games?"

Naomi followed her to the kitchen after placing her phone on the coffee table. "They're better at partying than we are. I'm hoping to finish two movies before I nod off."

Claire chuckled. Their last movie night, Fiona woke them up when the second movie ended.

"Since we don't have our alarm clock, you may want to send Logan a text to come get you if you're not home by eleven," Claire teased.

"That's a good idea."

The two unpacked the bag and arranged the containers on the limited counter and tiny kitchen table. Luna supervised from in front of the refrigerator.

"Do you want a beer?" Claire asked after giving Luna two tomatoes.

"Do you have tea?"

Claire nodded and pulled the pitcher of sweet tea. "I should probably leave beer alone with all this food."

Naomi gave a weak smile and focused on adding ice. Claire studied her friend for a moment. "Is everything okay?"

"Yep. We can talk once we make a plate."

"Okay," Claire drugged out the word. Before she could question her further, the oven dinged for the mushrooms. "I need to talk to you, anyway."

"Oh. How did Luna do with Oriole?"

"Really well." Claire placed the cookie sheet on the stove and turned off the oven. They two made their plates while she relayed Luna and Oriole's friendship. The boxer was not a beggar, but Claire wanted her to feel part of the evening and gave her a bully stick. Luna positioned herself near the fireplace and eagerly enjoyed her treat.

"So what's going on?" Claire asked once they settled on the couch and tuned the TV to the Hallmark Channel.

This time, the smile Naomi gave was bright and joyful. "I'm pregnant."

Claire's scream startled Luna, who barked and hurried over. She ran her hand along the dog's body to let her know everything was okay. The image of a chubby face little boy with dark hair and blue eyes popped into her mind. Way too soon to think about children with Jace. She needed to get through at least one date.

"Oh, my gosh! I'm so happy for you two. When did you find out? How far along are you? Who knows?" Claire cringed. "The tea has caffeine. I don't think I have decaf."

Naomi beamed and waved off the concern. "I can have it in moderation, but I will switch to decaf coffee." She took a sip before continuing. "I took an at home test three weeks ago. We didn't want to say anything until after we went to the doctor."

"That's why you left early yesterday. I didn't even think about you and Logan leaving early. I thought you were just having a date."

"We made it seem like that. Anyway, the doctor confirmed it and I'm due the first week in September. She wants me to be careful because of my age and weight, but she doesn't foresee me having difficulties. Blood work is normal and I'm healthy."

"What did Fiona say?"

"She said it was about time," Naomi said, rolling her eyes. "We had to bribe her to keep it secret today. She wanted to tell everyone."

"Is that why you went to Josie's?"

She nodded. "It saved us a trip to tell my mom. I swear Thomas cried before our mothers."

"You know, he sees you as a daughter." The patriarch of the Beckett clan took to Naomi within minutes of meeting her, and Claire suspected the feeling was mutual. "Fiona's going to be a great big sister."

"We think so. Logan wants to spend time with her when he picks her up tomorrow. Make sure she's okay with the pregnancy. She was the only grandchild for twelve years and now she'll have to share the attention. We told her she can have a say in the name."

"After planting, I'm thinking of making a quick stop past Izzy's if you want to go. We have a full schedule for Monday, and I want her excitement out before patients arrive. Will Luna be okay by herself? Izzy's dogs don't do well with new animals." Naomi reached for a deviled egg. "Oh yeah. Didn't you say you had to tell me something?"

It was the opening Claire needed. "Jace volunteered to watch Luna and introduce her to your dogs while we're at the greenhouse. He planned on asking Logan for help, but I'm sure Caden wouldn't mind."

"He's taking her to breakfast at the diner. They'll be back before we go."

Claire relaxed. Luna knew Logan from being at the clinic the past few days. If the meeting over stimulated her, Jace and Logan were familiar humans she trusted and she would have Oriole there. Claire took a deep breath and focused on her tea.

"Jace and I decided to see each other."

"What?!" Naomi screeched. "You let me go on about my peanut and you have huge news?"

Claire chuckled. "I think your pregnancy beats my dating life."

"Says you. Okay, tell me everything."

Claire gave her details about their conversation while they nibbled. Including her failed engagement. By the time she finished, the fire was low. Claire added two more logs before grabbing the glasses for refills.

"I think we're going to go on a date this coming week." Claire glanced over her shoulder. "Did you want more tea or water?"

"Water, please." Naomi stacked their empty plates. "So are you okay? You seem calmer than I expected."

"I know." She studied her friend for a moment. "Maybe I had time to come to terms with it beforehand. I think just explaining the cause of my hesitation and Jace offering an explanation settled my nerves."

"That's probably it. You've known the Becketts probably a month longer than I have. I just don't see any of them cheating."

"They know they'd have to answer to Josie," Claire teased, causing them both to laugh.

She handed Naomi a glass of water before topping off her tea. The two worked in harmony cleaning the kitchen. They'd lost track of the movie shortly after it started, but it was okay. Claire needed to talk.

Until Naomi and Izzy came into her life, the only female she felt comfortable talking to was Rue. She didn't share with her previous work friends. Naomi and Izzy accepted her immediately. She cherished their friendship.

"You know there will be a period of mourning when word gets out about you two," Naomi commented before biting into a celery stick. She spoke around her bite. "There also will be snide comments."

"I know. I'm not looking forward to it. It can't be worse than what my classmates said." She knew it could, but wouldn't let the thought ruin her good mood. At least not that night.

"Always remember, you're the one he chose. Not them. Jace wants a partner, not a freeloader." Naomi rested her hand on Claire's arm.

Claire nodded, squeezing her hand. Naomi's words helped. She needed time to tell Garrett before he heard it through the grapevine. His overprotectiveness might hinder him from being happy for her, but she'd cross that bridge when she came to it.

"We talked through the first movie. Which means we should stay awake for the second one," Claire said, taking the container of cookies into the living room.

It was enough chatter for the night. It was time to watch a cheesy rom-com and stay inside her happy bubble for one night.

Chapter Thirteen

"Today is going to be different. There will be people you aren't used to, and I need you to be on your best behavior," Claire said to Luna as she snapped the doggie cape on. "Shorty will be there, but not the rest of your friends."

Luna's large, dark eyes sparkled with understanding. At least Claire hoped she understood. She kissed the dog's forehead and rose to her feet. Naomi's practice was open today after being closed the week before. Her friends had a full schedule and random people and pets would be in and out. She hoped it wouldn't overstimulate Luna.

According to Jace, yesterday's introduction to the other dogs went well. Claire saw the benefits firsthand during the family dinner. Luna kept Claire in her sights all evening, but she still played and napped in the living room with the other dogs. It eased Claire's concerns about bringing her to work. Last week, with just Izzy and Naomi, Luna became comfortable with the office and the decompress room for the sanctuary. She hoped Shorty would show Luna how to interact with other humans not part of the property.

Claire slipped her phone and keys into her scrub top pockets before shrugging on her fleece jacket. She chuckled when Luna snagged her stuffed banana and sat by the door.

"I'm coming."

She lifted the tote that held a four dozen fresh treats, checked to make sure everything was off, and hurried out the door. Luna took off like a light while Claire locked the door.

"Wait! Let me put your leash on."

"I don't think she'll need it," the new and familiar voice said.

She turned to find Jace giving her baby lots of loving. The boxer's bum wagged a mile a minute.

"What are you doing here?" Claire asked, joining them at the end of her walkway.

"Since I couldn't walk you home last night, I figured I'd walk you to work."

Her office was across the gravel road and another two hundred feet. She wouldn't complain. During dinner last night, a goat handler called Noah to say the livestock dogs chased off two predators. The brothers left to see if they could find the wolves. The last thing they wanted was for them to go to the stables. Meanwhile, Claire, Naomi, and Thomas headed to the goat barn to check for any injuries to the livestock and the guard dogs. Fiona eagerly volunteered to watch the pets.

Claire gave his hand a squeeze. "Thank you. You didn't need to."

Jace plucked Luna's leash from her hand and snapped it onto her collar. "I wanted to share a cup of coffee with you, but Caden asked if I could help this morning. A worker called in sick. So I had to change."

"You still look handsome."

Jace's cheeks pinked, bolstering Claire's confidence. The two fell into step, letting Luna sniff her way to their destination. She noticed his UTV parked beside his parents' house.

"Do you have plans for dinner?" Jace asked out of the blue. They hadn't set a firm day for their first date.

"No. I still have a few leftovers from movie night."

"Let me cook for you."

Claire stopped in her tracks. No man ever cooked a meal for her. Garrett didn't count. Would this be their first date? She'd be okay if it was. She was a homebody person. Jace enjoyed staying home—now. She wasn't ready to make a show to the town that they were dating. If they went to the steakhouse or even the diner, it would get back to Sara before Claire could tell Garrett.

"Dinner sounds nice. Let me know what I can bring and the time."

Jace shook his head. "I want to cook at your place. I need an outlet for the air fryer and a knife to cut the vegetables."

"You're serious?"

"Yes. I want our first date to be just us. Something low-key because you're not one to have a lot of attention. Believe me, that will happen when we go out to the movies or something." He took her hand and stepped into her personal space. "I want candles, maybe a movie, and just be together."

Swoon.

Claire fell into his blue eyes. He understood her nerves would prevent them from having a relaxing date in town. The family dinner was stressful enough, with congratulatory hugs from Josie and Thomas and teasing from his brothers. Dealing with stares and whispers while trying to eat a meal would be too much.

Claire gave him a warm smile. "I'm sure I can make space for the fryer. You'll bring Oriole and Cammie?"

"Of course."

"I didn't think you two could be any cuter, but I was wrong," Izzy called out from the path leading to the clinic. Claire didn't know how long her friend was there.

"I should go." Claire stood on her tiptoes and pressed a kiss to his cheek. "I'll text you later."

Jace nodded before giving Izzy a wave. He waited until Claire was close to the front door before turning to walk away.

"So, an early morning date." Izzy winked, causing Claire to flush.

"Nothing like that. He just walked me to work. Caden asked him to help this morning."

The two stepped into the clinic and shrugged off their jackets. Claire went into the interruption of the family dinner while they prepared both practices. Luna sniffed the area behind the front desk before making her way to the pile of toys in the decompress area. Her stuffed banana long forgotten on Claire's chair. By the time she finished the story, Logan and Naomi strolled in with an excited Shorty.

"Good morning!" Logan said, a wide smile on his face. Naomi, however, scowled at her husband.

"You're sleeping in the guest bedroom. Better yet, sleep at Caden's."

Claire and Izzy exchanged glances. Rare did Naomi and Logan argue or if they did, it wasn't in front of people. Logan ignored her mood and pressed a kiss to her temple.

"You have to watch your caffeine intake. You chose iced tea over coffee. I'm just trying to support you."

Naomi rolled her eyes. "You act like I asked for an entire pot. One sip of your coffee was all I wanted."

Logan snorted, slipping his arm around her shoulder. "Darlin', I know your sips. They turn into guzzles. You had two cups of decaf and a large glass of iced tea."

"I feel I earned it, giving I got little sleep." Naomi stomped to the small refrigerator and pulled out a bottled water. She turned her attention to Izzy. "Why am I getting morning sickness in the middle of the night?"

"No clue. I got sick whenever the mood of the child hit." Izzy shrugged. "I hate to agree with Logan, but adding caffeine will dehydrate you. Call your doctor."

"I already left a message," Logan added as he walked to Claire, who focused on adding treats to a glass jar. "While my beautiful wife is working on forgiving me, we need to talk to you before patients arrive."

Claire frowned. "Me? What did I do?" Did they want to talk about her and Jace? Did they see them together from a window? Naomi sat in the extra chair behind the desk and smiled.

"It's nothing like that. We wanted to bring it up last night, but the call pushed it out of our minds."

"Two people called Dad yesterday asking where they can buy the treats," Logan said.

"When he told me the names, I knew they were patients," Naomi added. "They thought it was something they could get, like the goat cheese."

"Okay?" Claire glanced between the two. "I don't mind making them a batch, if that's what you're asking."

Claire enjoyed making the homemade treats. It was easy since most of the ingredients came from the Beckett's greenhouse and chicken coop. Bananas weren't expensive and the large tub of peanut butter Garrett could get from the feed store. She made ten dozen once for the stand the family had at the Farmer's Market. It surprised her when it sold out and Thomas handed her the profit.

"I know my hellhounds like them and they're picky eaters," Izzy commented.

"What we're saying is, would you consider selling them for Hawkins Ridge?" Logan stopped her before she could answer. "Nothing big like what we're doing with the goat milk soaps. Just for the county vets, local farms and the feed store."

"We would all pitch in to help," Naomi piped in. "The stove and ovens at the stable house are commercial grade, since we use it to make the dog food."

Logan nodded. "It would be a sixty/forty partnership, with you getting the sixty percent. Something we'd put in writing. We would have Noah run the numbers."

Claire slowly sat in her chair. Their words battled her emotions in her mind. Everything sounded wonderful, but she wondered if this was because of her and Jace dating. If they didn't last, what then? Would they take everything? She'd have to find a lawyer to cover herself. Naomi did the same thing when she moved her practice to the property before she married Logan. It's not like they could take her recipes. She and Rue came up with them when they couldn't afford the quality brand. The cheap ones were nothing but fillers and ultra-processed. She'd have to talk it over with Rue. And Jace.

Naomi rested her hand on hers to pull her out of her thoughts. Concern shown in her brown eyes.

"No one is expecting an answer right now. It's a big decision."

"She's right," Logan added.

Claire moved her gaze to Logan. "I'd have to talk to Rue. She helped me create the recipes for the dog she had before Balty." Before she could stop herself, she blurted a concern. "This isn't because I'm dating Jace now, is it?" Logan's response was instant.

"Not at all. We've been thinking about it for a few weeks. At first, we figured it would be something we'd sell at the practice. Expanding it to the different locations came when we were trying to settle Naomi's tummy last night."

Claire's gut told her to agree, but she really wanted to talk to Rue. The small profit would help supplement her aunt's disability checks. It may also be a selling point for her to move to Oak Mountain.

"I'll talk to Rue," Claire finally said. "She wanted to see the property this weekend."

"Great." Logan clapped his hands just as a car pulled into the lot across the gravel road. "We can talk more then. The offer still stands about her staying in the suite at the main house if she wants to stay the weekend."

Claire's tiny home was fine for a dinner, but with extended guests, and two medium-sized dogs, it would be a tight fit. She also had a full-size bed.

"Okay. Thank you."

He tapped the desk. "Oh, we can do Luna's spaying after Duke tomorrow. Can you also put together my bag? I'm heading out to the Norris' farm to check on the calves."

"Bring back jerky," Izzy chimed in.

"The mesquite and teriyaki, please," Naomi added.

The Norris' ran the butcher shop in town and supplied the meat for the dog food they made for the sanctuary, including the family. Their jerky was tender, mouthwatering, and addictive. The wife, Ophelia, was part of Josie's crew.

"Garlic and pepper for me," Claire said just as Naomi's patient strolled in.

Luna followed Shorty as they greeted the visitor. The cat in the carrier hissed, causing both dogs to back up. Izzy went about checking the patient in while Claire moved towards the hallway that led to Naomi and Logan's offices and exam rooms. Luna followed, sniffing along the way. She punched in the code for the medication and supply room and propped the door open.

The offer Logan and Naomi made was still in the front of her mind. She didn't think Rue would be against doing it. It would benefit them both. She could even use the same lawyer as Naomi. Claire hoped it wasn't expensive. The biggest sticking point would be if things didn't work with Jace, how she could protect herself and Rue. It would be something she'd talk to Jace tonight and call Rue during lunch.

Maybe this would be her way to stay a part of Hawkins Ridge.

Denise Stephens scrunched her nose as she slowly spun the pot of blossoming buttercups on the counter. "Have you thought about roses?" the town florist asked Jace when he requested a bouquet of buttercups and daffodils. "Most women prefer them. Or tulips."

He shook his head and pushed the cluster of stems with the mature yellow flowers towards her. "Not this woman. Buttercups are her favorite flower, and she has this cute scrub top that has them on it. Daffodils are her second."

"As romantic as that sounds, Jace Beckett, your mother would skin me alive if she knew I put together a cheap-looking bouquet for you to give to a young woman. It's also boring."

He fought the urge to roll his eyes. Instead, he tapped into the charm that his mother's friends adored. "Ms. Denise. Claire isn't like other women. She—"

"Claire Everson? Logan's assistant?"

Crap, he thought. "Yes, ma'am."

A blinding smile enveloped the woman's brown face. Her dark eyes sparkled with joy. "She is an absolute delight. You know she helps Naomi at the nursing home, checking the residents' pets. Izzy, bless her heart, has her hands full with that household of boys so she can't help on the weekends. You know her cousin manages the feed store, right? I had my doubts about him when he came back with little Sara four years ago, but he is a good man and husband." Denise studied the flowers again. "You're right about her not being like other women. She has a kind heart. She still deserves better than this. Unlike the fast girls you used to spend your time with. They were only looking for the next husband. Didn't care a lick about who the man was."

Jace politely nodded. There were advantages and disadvantages to living in a small town. Especially one that knew everyone's business and hung out with your mother. When he asked women out in the past, he knew they weren't the right one. Most he grew up with. He wasn't perfect, not by a long shot, but he was always honest with them when he asked them out.

Another disadvantage of a small town at that moment is the limited options of flower shops. Denise was the only florist in town. She also won first place at the county fair for the past five years for her floral arrangements.

She was also Noah's aunt.

"Claire mentioned she didn't understand why people would spend a lot of money on roses when wildflower bouquets were more colorful and last just as long." Jace leaned on the counter. "Maybe if we wrap it in a pink ribbon, it will be colorful."

The look the older woman graced him with was one of pity. The gentle patting of his cheek brought home the look. He'd hang his head in shame if she said 'bless your heart.'

"You poor thing. A simple pink ribbon won't help." She strolled to her refrigerator and rested her hands on her full hips. "The problem is buttercups are small and would get lost against daffodils. I use them in wreaths and headpieces. You want something to make that young lady know you're serious about getting to know her."

"We've been friends for close to a year."

"But you're trying to step out of the friend zone, right?"

Jace exhaled. "Yes, ma'am."

"Then giving her a bunch of buttercups is a step up from a bunch of weeds. Why don't you plant her some buttercups? It will be something she sees every day and will remind her of you. Getting back to your bouquet. You said she likes wildflowers?"

Jace hadn't thought about planting her the flower. He nodded and joined her in front of the offerings. "She'd like them more than roses."

Denise clapped. "Well then. Give me twenty minutes and I'll have something colorful she'll absolutely love."

"That sounds great." He checked his watch as he followed her back to the register. "That'll give me time to get something from the bakery."

Denise spoke while studying a drawer full of ribbon. "So…how long have you two been dating? Your mother mentioned nothing at Friday's luncheon."

Jace wasn't embarrassed about dating Claire. He just wanted a date or two before the town knew.

"This is our first date. I'm making her dinner. Can you keep it to yourself for now? I know she hasn't told Garrett yet, and I'd hate for him to hear it from a customer before she tells him."

Denise mimicked zipping her lips. "Not a problem. Can I make a suggestion for dessert?" He nodded. "Don't get a pie or a regular cake. What they have are leftovers from the weekend. Ask them for a shortcake. If you have some of the strawberry preserves your mother canned, use that. Their pastries are also fresh."

Her suggestion is the advantage of a small town. Jace thanked her and hurried out the door. The bakery was at the end of the block. He would miss the lunch rush of the shop's workers stopping in for a sugar fix to go with the sandwiches the bakery offered. Jace heard his name called from across the street. A low groan escaped when he saw Tinsley crossing the road to meet him.

The bottled blonde worked at the diner. Her family purchased the town's favorite eating hole when the original owner retired ten years ago. They kept the same recipes and added a few of their own.

Jace had one date with the woman. He realized they had nothing in common and never called her for a second. Tinsley, however, interpreted the date differently and didn't understand why he hadn't called her in a year for a second. She would be the one to give Claire a hard time.

"Afternoon, Tinsley," he said in greeting when she stepped in his path.

"Hey, Jace. How have you been? We don't get to talk much when you come into the diner, and I haven't seen you at the bar lately."

Jace went to the diner for late lunches because she never worked the shift, and when he went with Noah to deliver their order. She had two kids and had to pick them up from school if her ex-husband couldn't.

He shoved his hands in his pockets when she reached for them. "I've been busy with drumming up business for Hawkins Ridge."

"I know. My uncle said you have a meeting with him in a couple of weeks. Something about putting the goat cheese and soaps in all of his stores." She stepped closer. "You know

I could put in a good word for you." He immediately shook his head.

"No, thank you. Our products speak for themselves. I'd rather have him taste what we offer, then decide." His phone pinged with a text. He smiled, seeing it was from Claire. It was a picture of Luna and Shorty sleeping head-to-head.

"Cute dogs," Tinsley said, looking over his arm. He slipped the phone back in his pocket.

"It was good seeing you. I have to run." Jace stepped to his left, but Tinsley cut him off.

"I was wondering if you'd like to grab a cup of coffee this week. Maybe the next time you're in the diner, I can take my break."

Before he could respectfully decline, a large hand clapped his shoulder. He breathed a sigh of relief as he met Logan's smirk.

"If you don't mind. My brother and I have to be somewhere. I'm sure he'll call if he wants." Logan shoved his brother down the sidewalk. Jace glanced over his shoulder and met Tinsley's gaze before she turned to cross the street.

"It's not what it looks like," he said. The last thing he wanted was for Logan to think he was spending time with the woman.

"I know. I was getting out of the truck when you left the florist. She called out to you before I could. I laughed when she almost got hit trying to get to you." He followed Jace into the bakery. "When she stopped you from moving, I knew I had to step in."

"One date a year ago." Jace rubbed the back of his neck and waited for his turn. "She was the one that asked me out. I only said yes to get her off my back. I didn't even kiss her good night."

Logan barked out a laugh, drawing the stares of the few customers. "She has asked each of us, except Noah."

Jace scowled because he knew why. Tinsley announced she couldn't date a man with a gay father, and that was why she hadn't pursued Noah. Jace cut the evening short and just ignored her rooster laying eggs comment. He never told Noah the real reason, but he knew it didn't matter. Tinsley was not his best friend's type.

"He wouldn't give her the time of day." Jace stepped up to the counter and placed his order for four shortcakes without the topping. He faced his brother while they boxed his treat. "Why are you in town?"

"Same as you. Getting flowers for Naomi. I didn't share my coffee this morning, and it hurt her feelings. She's fine now, but I want to make sure she doesn't smother me in my sleep."

Jace choked on a laugh. "I'd be worried she'd tell Shorty to take a bite out of your ankle."

Logan shuddered. "That too. Getting flowers for your date?"

He didn't need to ask how he knew. He was sure the grapevine of Claire, Naomi, and Izzy made it back to his brother.

"Ms. Denise gave me a good talking-to about my choice of a buttercup bouquet. Needless to say, I'm not getting one."

Logan nodded. "I tried to buy carnations once and I swear she wanted to backslap me."

"She gave me the cheek pat and 'you poor thing' response." Jace ran his card over the screen and waited for the receipt. "She knows who it's for."

"She's not as bad as Mom's other friends and won't blab your business around town. I think it helps she's considered family."

Jace thanked the worker, taking the red box. He waited until they were outside to respond.

"I don't mind people knowing about Claire. I just want to get one date under our belt first. Oh, and for her to tell Garrett. She swears he will try to talk her out of us dating because of my reputation."

Logan agreed. "Naomi said he told her to stay away from you."

Jace raked his fingers through his hair. "She's an adult and capable of making her own decision."

"But they were raised like siblings instead of cousins. We'd be the same way if we had a sister and wanted to date someone with your past."

His brother had a point. He would be exactly the same. Jace didn't think it would be a big deal to date casually. His reputation didn't bother him at first because the women understood he wasn't looking for anything more than a couple of good times. He didn't expect to meet a woman who would have him consider opening his heart again. If he could go back in time, he'd take the path his brothers took and just focus on Hawkins Ridge. Jace wondered if he hadn't followed Logan's advice to be friends with Claire first, if he'd ever be buying her flowers.

He worried about Garrett. Did he have enough sway over Claire to make her second guess giving him a chance? Should he be the one to talk to him first? Could Garrett talk Rue into doing his dirty work?

Jace mentally shook his head and pulled the door open for the florist. It was something he would talk to Claire about later. His focus now was to give her a memorable first date.

Chapter Fourteen

C laire twirled in front of the mirror, pleased with her outfit. Though they were eating in, she wanted to look nice for their first date. After deep consideration, she decided on a knee length black skirt and a green spring sweater. Shoes weren't necessary.

The date and Logan's offer volleyed for attention all day. She reminded herself it was just another dinner with Jace. The only difference is she would look nice instead of her usual yoga pants. Once she settled her mind on that subject, the other came roaring to the front.

During lunch, she went home and called Rue. After the pleasantries, she jumped into telling about the offer. Rue thought it was a wonderful idea, just as long as Claire had a lawyer look at any contracts first. Her aunt also agreed to spend the weekend at Hawkins Ridge. Once Josie heard, she planned a family dinner for Friday. Claire invited herself to spend the first night with Rue at the main house. She wanted to make sure Rue was comfortable being with everyone.

After speaking with her aunt, she made plans to have lunch with Garrett later in the week. If her second date with Jace was in town, her cousin would get wind of it the next morning. Claire couldn't figure out why she dreaded telling him. He had no control over her life. Garrett wouldn't risk losing the

Beckett family's business with the feed store. They might not be their largest customer, but they were definitely in the top five. But would he stop talking to her? It was another case of her 'what ifs.'

She couldn't or wouldn't let it stop her from seeing where things went with Jace. He sounded like he wanted long-term. Claire wouldn't have agreed to give it a chance if he didn't. She harbored strong feelings for him and was positive they would become deeper.

A rhythmic knock pulled Claire from her musings. Luna led the short distance to the door. A hearty butt wiggle confirmed the visitor. She swung open the door with a firm hand on Luna's collar. The last thing she'd want was for Jace to trip as he stepped across the threshold. One look at the man sucked the moisture from her throat.

The only time Claire saw Jace in a tie was at Logan and Naomi's wedding. Tonight was the second. Dressed in a white button-down shirt with a charcoal gray tie to match the color of his vest. He finished his look with a simple pair of dark jeans and casual loafers. He slicked back his dark blond hair, letting it curl at the end. The man looked good.

"You're a vision, Buttercup."

Heat surged up her face. "I could say the same for you."

He leaned forward, pressing his pillow soft lips against the corner of her mouth. Claire sent thanks for the door, keeping her up.

"Compliments will get you everywhere." He then dropped a kiss on her forehead and stepped into the room. "I hope you don't mind me bringing this in."

It was then Claire noticed a tote wagon behind him. Oriole finished marking his territory and trotted in. Luna instantly dropped to her front paws before leading Oriole in a game of chase around the coffee table.

"Where's Cammie?" she asked, following him to the kitchen area.

"I left her at Logan's." He nodded towards the playful dogs. "They would have stepped on her at least once by now. Not on purpose, but it would happen. She also would need supervision to keep her from knocking into things. She hasn't been here in a few months, so it would take time to remember."

Claire didn't think of that. She made a mental note to have Jace and the dogs spend more time at her house. Luna needed to build a bond with Cammie, too.

Jace opened the lid and handed her a kaleidoscope of color bouquet. Different wildflowers perfectly arranged and wrapped in a white floral ribbon. She blinked back tears when she noticed the floral print was a variety of buttercups.

Jace's lips turned down as he tilted her chin. "Please tell me those are happy tears?"

Claire flung her arms around his waist. No one, not even her ex-fiancé had given her flowers. Jace closed the embrace. After a moment, she found her voice.

"The flowers are perfect." She rested her chin on his chest, meeting his worried blue eyes. "Thank you."

Time stood still as Jace closed the distance with her lips. For almost a year, Claire had wondered what it would be like to kiss Jace. Now she would know.

The world exploded behind her lids the moment his lips touched hers. Soft, gentle pressure of his full lips almost had her knees buckling. The friend zone was no more.

Too soon of a moment later, Jace ended the kiss. He closed his eyes and rested his forehead against hers.

"I didn't think it could be better than I imagined. I was so wrong." He opened his eyes, his gaze slightly unfocused. "Wow."

"You're telling me. I'm glad we can kiss now."

Jace flashed a crooked grin. "You and me both."

Before Claire could dazzle him with more of her flirting, Luna and Oriole wedged their way between them. The blazing spark between them turned to an ember. He cleared his throat, taking another step back.

"I should get dinner going."

Claire gave each of the dogs a loving scratch before heading to the linen closet to grab a vase.

"Let me put these in water and I can help. Do you want something to drink?" Claire kicked herself for forgetting her manners.

"Water is fine for now. I have two of your favorite beer for later." He handed her bottles of a state IPA from the tote. Claire wasn't a wine drinker and only liked a few beer brands. The only one she could stomach over two bottles was that brand.

"Thank you."

She sat them in the fridge and poured him a glass of water. While he finished unpacking his ingredients, she made quick work of the flowers.

"How was your day?" he asked, before plugging the air fryer into the outlet next to the microwave.

"It was interesting." She didn't know if Logan told him about the offer, or if he knew his brother was considering it for a few weeks. "Luna is being spayed tomorrow after Duke."

"I'm meeting with a potential supplier for the wrappers we use for soap tomorrow. I can stay with her in recovery afterwards if you need me to."

"Thank you. I'll let you know in the morning. Logan isn't sure if we have another farm to visit in the afternoon." She set the square vase on the small kitchen table. She'd move it to her nightstand before bed. "What can I help you with?"

Her kitchen area was compact and would be hard to navigate if he needed the stove. Jace shook his head and stacked the containers holding the ingredients on the counter.

"I got it. I pre-chopped the veggies at home. The only thing I need is a big spoon."

Claire handed him a spoon from a drawer by the stove before taking a seat on a kitchen chair. She waited a moment while Jace became comfortable in her kitchen before she brought up the other subject.

"I also spoke with Logan and Naomi about an offer."

"What kind of offer? I saw him in town earlier and he mentioned nothing." He scooped the chopped peppers and onions into an air fryer basket. "Does he want you to work more hours when Naomi gets closer to her due date?"

Claire hadn't thought about that. She would help however they needed. Now that she thought of doing the treats, she would work more.

"More hours, yes, but not what you are thinking."

She went into telling him about the offer and her conversation with Rue. Jace quietly listened while starting the air fryer and cleaning his mess. By the time she was done, he leaned against the counter with his arms crossed. She stared at him, expecting a response. She didn't have to wait long.

"That's a good idea." He tapped the rim of his glass against his chin. A tell for when he was thinking. "Every farm in the county has dogs. We can deliver a week's worth if they can't make it to the feed store. The Norris' would let us display it at the butcher shop."

"Oh, there's peppered jerky in the cabinet if you want something to nibble on."

Jace spun around and grabbed the three-pound bag. He tore off a piece for Luna and Oriole before tilting the bag in her direction. She declined. The aroma of the garlic marinade he used on the chicken filled the air. If she started on the jerky, it would ruin her appetite. He popped a piece of the dehydrated meat into his mouth and spoke around the bite.

"What do you want to do? You know I would support any decision you make."

She knew that. "I told Logan I wanted to run it by a lawyer."

"That's smart. My parents have been friends with Owen for over forty years. When they pulled him out of retirement to take over the managing of the property fifteen years ago and added him and Noah to the business, they made sure a lawyer reviewed everything. No one would stop you from doing it."

"I know. Logan agreed when I told him." Claire nibbled her bottom lip, debating on telling him about her first thought. She wanted an open and honest relationship and went for it. "I also asked if they made the offer because we're dating now."

Jace immediately started shaking his head and squatted in front of her. "I know they didn't. I remembered last month when we tossed the idea around of what else we can offer. Caden brought up the treats because of how quick the pack goes through them." He reached for her hand. "I think it would be a great opportunity for you. I don't want you to overdo it and cause more damage to your hand."

Warmth washed over her as she pushed up her glasses. The amount of work to meet the demands they expected would do a number on her hand. Being a vet tech was her job. If making treats interfered with her doing her job, Claire would have to decline.

She squeezed his hand. "Naomi said they would help. At least at the initial start. If it is too much, then Logan said they can hire more staff. I just don't want to overwork my hand so that I can't do my job."

"I agree. If we do it on the weekend, we can get Fiona and a couple of her friends to help. Toss them a couple of bucks as long as it's okay with their parents."

The more she thought about it, the more her heart raced. She would be a business owner. Knowing that the Becketts wanted to keep Hawkins Ridge regional and small helped her realize this was doable. She would be in a better position to give back to the community. Maybe she could help Rue find a nice apartment or single-story home to rent. The thought of Claire buying her own home brought a smile to her face.

Even if things work with Jace, she would want to help with bills. Did he own it outright or did he have a mortgage? What about property taxes? Those were questions she'd have to ask later down the road. For now, she wanted to focus on having a wonderful date.

"I'll think hard on it. I wanted everyone to meet Rue first before I decide."

Jace stood to his full height and pulled her along with him. He rested his hands on her shoulder and held her in place with his gaze. "This is a wonderful opportunity for you. No one is going to pressure you, though. Take as much time as you need."

She rolled to her tiptoes and gave him a quick peck. "Thank you for listening and supporting me."

"Of course. Business arrangement between friends and even family can have moments of doubt."

Claire nodded, putting space between them. It was Luna's dinner time, and they had ten more minutes for their food.

"I know Naomi was worried about the practice on the property before her and Logan were married." She picked up Luna's dish and pulled the fresh food from the fridge door. "Do you want to feed Oriole? I have an extra dish."

Jace pulled a silver bowl from the wagon tote. "I thought ahead. This will help cut down on the begging."

Claire worked on feeding the dogs while Jace heated the tortillas for their fajitas. A sense of normalcy washed over her, working side by side with him. The heavy conversation about the offer was out of the way. No awkwardness hung in the air. Being with Jace was natural. It was just as she hoped—easy.

Falling more in love with him was inevitable.

"I'll be right back," Claire said, then quickly shuffled to her bedroom.

Jace couldn't stop his smile as he watched the door close. If he didn't already love her, their date solidified his feelings. Claire was easy to talk to. She laughed at his corny jokes and always found a reason to hold his hand across the table. They didn't get in each other's way when cleaning the dishes.

Then there were her kisses.

Their first kiss after he gave her the flowers ruined him for other women. Until then, Leah was the last woman that created a spark when they kissed. Claire's caused an inferno. No woman between the two women caused his heart to race from a simple touch of the lips.

Jace lifted Luna's leash from the hook by the door. They were taking the dogs for a walk before calling it a night. Claire wanted to change since the temperature dropped, and being bare-legged in a skirt wouldn't keep her warm. He pulled Oriole's lead from the bottom of the tote and clipped it on.

"We should take Cammie," Claire said as she slipped a pink hoodie over a long sleeve tee. Thick leggings and sneakers finished her outfit.

"That's a good idea." He typed a quick text to Logan to bring Cammie to the back door. In the meantime, Claire fastened a doggie cape on Luna and had both leashes in her hand.

"Logan is meeting us at the back door. We'll put the tote in the back of the UTV first."

They weren't going far, and Claire opted not to lock her door.

"Are you planning anything special for Rue's visit?" Jace asked as they hit her walkway. The sun had set and the lampposts along the gravel roadway lit up the silhouettes of the nighttime insects.

"I want to show her the greenhouse and stables. I hope to have time to let Balty and Luna get to know each other before the family and dogs arrive for dinner." Claire stopped to let Luna sniff a bush while Jace continued the few feet to his UTV. "I want to get some baking done with her. I hope Naomi will let us use the oven in the main house."

Jace wanted to get to know Rue. He and Claire had a future together and knew Rue would be a part of it, but he didn't want to horde in on their quiet time together. However, he knew his mother. Just a family dinner wouldn't be enough and figured a Sunday breakfast would be called.

"If you want help baking, count me in, or perhaps the three of us could have dinner Saturday evening at my place. I'll grill steaks." Jace cringed at how desperate he sounded. Before Claire could answer, Logan stepped out with a wiggly Cammie.

The Pomeranian smelled Jace and let out a little yip as he came closer. He tucked her in his arm, letting her get a good amount of licks in.

"Thank you for watching her."

Logan waved off his gratitude. "Between the dogs and Fiona, they love when Cammie visits. Did you enjoy your dinner?"

The glow of the street lamps highlighted the blush on Claire's cheeks. "It was nice. Your brother is an excellent cook."

Jace set Cammie on the grass. Oriole and Luna gave her sniffs and kisses. "I'm not sure using an air fryer counts as cooking."

"You made the marinade for the chicken and the seasoning for the veggies. They were cooked perfectly, and you did a heck of a job heating the tortillas." Claire snickered, ducking her face. Jace wrapped his arm around her, tucking her into his side.

"I was believing you until you joked about the tortillas."

"I was being serious."

Logan shook his head, backing away from them. "You're going to be one of those sappy cute couples, aren't you?"

"Maybe." Claire gave a comical, toothy grin, causing them all to laugh. They said their goodbyes to Logan and picked up the leashes. Jace handed her Cammie before wrapping the leads for the larger dogs in one hand.

"Do you like public displays of affection?" Claire asked when they resumed their walk.

"I draw the line at public groping, but I like hand holding and a few quick kisses."

The worry in her eyes vanished. Jace wanted to let Oak Mountain know they were a couple. He'd hold Claire's hand every chance he could. To prove his point, he linked his fingers with her weak hand.

"I wasn't saying that to make you hold my hand." He gently tightened his grip when she tried to pull her hand away.

"I know. I planned on doing this, anyway. You just asked before I could." They stopped when Cammie found her spot. "You didn't answer my question about dinner with Rue."

"Oh. I think that's a great idea." Claire pulled a baggie from her pocket and cleaned up after the tiny dog.

"I could have done that," Jace said, taking the baggie and putting it in the communal trash can along the road.

"This way you're free to get the big dogs," Claire teased, side stepping his fingers aimed for her ribs. "I was hoping to have breakfast at my place Saturday morning with Rue, but I don't want to be rude and not have it with Logan and Naomi."

"They won't think it's rude and would understand." They stopped for Luna and Oriole. Jace finished while they waited. "Remember your first family dinner? For someone that isn't used to that much noise, she'll need the break."

"It was an eye opener. A lot of love."

Jace's thoughts drifted back to the moment. Claire was a deer caught in headlights the first half hour of the dinner. By the end of the evening, she relaxed and opened up. Now, she teased them all and helped his mother and Naomi gang up on the men. It warmed his heart how much his family took Claire in and made her feel like one of their own.

Jace took the extra bag from Claire and spoke while he picked up. "It is a lot of love. It's also loud. Did Garrett have a lot of guys hang out at your place growing up?"

Claire shook her head. "Garrett preferred to be outside. He also had a friend who had a gaming system, so he spent more time there. When we were older, Rue switched to third shift at the fulfillment center, so she was usually sleeping when we came home from school."

Jace noted the yawn she tried to hide. It was late and though he wanted to spend more time with her, she would need to get up early.

"Why don't we head back? Luna's going to need her rest for tomorrow."

"Are you sure? It's only eight-thirty?" Claire glanced at her watch. "Never mind. I didn't know it was after nine."

"Thought so." He clasped her hand and led her the way they'd come. "We're usually in bed by now."

"When did we become old?" Claire couldn't hide the yawn that followed. "Sorry."

His answering yawn had them laughing.

"I don't know if it is us getting old or the realization we start our day at five o'clock during the week."

"Let's stick with the time excuse."

Jace walked her to the door and handed her Luna's leash. He waited until she unlocked the door and unclipped the dog.

"Thank you for a wonderful first date." He tucked a strand of her soft hair behind her ear.

"I should thank you. I love my flowers."

"I'm glad. Call me in the morning and let me know if you need me to sit with Luna. I think Dad is picking up Cammie."

Oriole went with either Noah or Caden if he had meetings and someone babysat Cammie. Being with the goats or in the stable wasn't safe for her. Naomi offered to let Cammie stay at the clinic. Now that he was dating Claire, maybe he would take her up on it.

"I will." She wrapped her arms around his waist. Jace went soft with her open affection. "Good night."

He lowered himself, then pressed his lips to hers. A content sigh escaped them both. The world faded momentarily, and all Jace wanted was her kisses. A hard nudge against his thigh brought him back to the present. He took a step back, allowing Oriole to wedge his way between them. He scratched behind his ears.

"I guess that's my cue. I'll text you when I get home."

They said their goodbyes. Jace scooped up Cammie from the edge of the step and waited until he heard the click of her lock. He whistled for Oriole to follow and made his way to the UTV. He tucked Cammie into his vest and waited until Oriole settled before starting the engine.

That night solidified Claire was his future. He may have developed a reputation, but Jace was thankful he had never settled. Leah, breaking his heart, showed him what he wanted in a relationship, and Claire had it in spades. Now he hoped Rue approved of him.

Chapter Fifteen

"You didn't need to go through all this trouble," Claire said to Josie's back as the older woman plugged in the single serve coffeemaker. A basket holding a variety of tea pods sat next to a glass jar of honey sticks on the granite countertop.

Josie ran her hand across the tea towel to remove the buckle of fabric.

"I told you it's no trouble. We want your aunt to be comfortable. That means making the suite a place she can find a moment of peace. Besides, you're going to be here too. What if you both want a cup of tea while you're talking? You shouldn't have to walk all the way into the kitchen."

"The kitchen is down the hall from the suite. You make it sound like we'd have to go to the next building."

Josie giggled. "This is an addition, so technically, it is the next building."

Claire rolled her eyes but couldn't help but laugh. Jace told her about the history of the space. When Josie's mother became a widower and could no longer walk up the stairs of the main house, they built a six hundred square foot suite to the lower level. The cozy space included a full-size bath and a sitting area with a pull-out loveseat and recliner. When Owen and Sam lived in the suite, they added a hot plate to the kitchenette area. The separate bedroom was large enough for a king-size bed and walk-in closet.

Josie closed the short distance between them and wrapped an arm around her shoulders. "It will be okay."

Claire nodded, leaning into the contact. Rue would arrive in thirty minutes. Logan let her leave an hour early so she could move what she needed to the main house. After a quick shower, Claire packed a small overnight bag and brought over one of Luna's dog beds. Balty usually slept with Rue, but she wanted to bring his bed just in case the Becketts didn't want him on the guest bed.

Speaking of Luna, her girl was recovering well from her operation. She wasn't a fan of the fabric cone. True to his word, Jace arrived shortly after her surgery. Claire and Logan went to a farm in the next town to exam two horses the owner recently purchased. Jace stayed with Duke and Luna, helping them move around to ensure there were no complications and that they could use the bathroom without any issues. He moved Luna home shortly before Claire returned. They shared a pizza she picked up before he went home to answer emails. The last of Luna's stitches dissolved that morning and Claire would remove the cone before Rue arrived. She pushed aside the worry of not being able to talk with Garrett and placed the dog bed next to the small entertainment center.

Her cousin canceled on her because of a huge delivery error. The more she thought about it, the more she would rather Rue met Jace first. It's like bringing your boyfriend home to meet the folks. Except her folk are spending the weekend with her boyfriend's family.

"I don't know why I'm nervous," Claire eventually said. "Rue will like everyone."

"And we will like her, too." Josie gave her shoulder another squeeze. "You could have invited Garrett and Sara to dinner."

"I thought about it, but figured they would enjoy a night to themselves." Claire sighed. "I also haven't spoken to him about Jace or the offer. Sara would text her mother and friends before we had dessert."

"That is very true. Sara is a nice girl, but she's friends with women who wanted what you have."

Claire smiled and followed Josie out of the room. "I remember going out with them once when I first came to town. It was a flashback of high school."

"Those same girls never liked Sara. She was a grade behind them and part of the debate team. They thought she wasn't popular enough for them." Josie scowled. "They didn't give her the time of day until she came back from college and Garrett showed up months later."

Interesting, she thought. Claire didn't think the women were her real friends, but it wasn't her place to say anything. She shared a love of books with her cousin-in-law, but they weren't "secret sharing" close. With Garrett being friends with the women's brothers or husbands, Claire knew they wouldn't be her tribe. She found her community at Hawkins Ridge.

"It's another reason I want Rue to meet everyone. She has tried to do things with Sara's mother, and they don't have similar interests." Claire tugged on a stack of napkins from the package and set them on a tray. "I think if Garrett is serious about Rue moving here, Sara's mom is not the way to go."

Josie chuckled. "I agree. You know, she brought cilantro seeds to the exchange last spring and got mad when no one would do a swap. No one wants that in their flower garden or as part of a crop. Don't get me wrong. I like a little in my salsa or maybe on a taco, but it's not a substitute for onions or garlic."

Claire laughed at Josie's indignation. "Rue's been doing most of the cooking to avoid the excess of the herb."

"Another reason your aunt needs this weekend."

The buzz of the oven timer interrupted their conversation. Josie slid on an oven mitt and pulled out two sheets of walnut chocolate chip cookies. The intoxicating aroma of chocolate and cinnamon had Claire's mouth watering.

"I'm thinking a taste test is in order," Claire teased, reaching for a cookie. Josie slid the cooling rack towards her.

"Only one. I'm hoping to have them in a container be-fore—"

The opening of the back door interrupted Josie. A second later, Luna galloped into the kitchen with Jace close on her heels. The dog greeted Claire with excited butt wiggles and kisses on her hands. Josie laughed, crumpling up the parch-ment paper.

"What I was going to say is before the boys get a whiff of the cookies."

"I have a sixth sense for food," Jace commented. He dropped a kiss on Claire's forehead. "I missed you."

Heat rose to her cheeks as she gave her pup a scratch. "I missed you too. How did Luna do today?"

Jace snagged a cookie from the rack and took a bite. "She did better than I thought. The gardeners loved her."

Claire wanted to get Luna used to other areas of the property for the days she and Logan spent hours making house calls. Jace volunteered that day to babysit while he ran errands and helped move plants in the greenhouse. Claire hoped to send her to the stables with Naomi and Logan's dogs one day next week.

"When is Rue getting here?" Jace asked, taking another cookie. Josie smacked his hand.

"Any minute. I'm heading outside to wait for her."

"Go." Josie moved a plastic container to her. "I'll put these away and meet you out there."

Instead of having the entire Beckett calvary converge on Rue the second she parked the car, she figured Josie and Jace would be an easy start. Logan and Naomi would be there a few minutes later. The last thing Claire wanted was for her aunt to feel overwhelmed.

"How did Luna do on the car ride?" Claire asked as the dog in question trotted past them and chased a bird. Jace led her to the bench, which had a great view of the gate leading to the sanctuary.

"Again, better than I thought. Since we don't know how the previous owner took her to the shelter, I was worried she would be anxious. That's why we started at Maeve and Harold. They're close in case I needed to bring her back. But she did well."

"I'm glad. Maybe we can take the dogs on a car ride next weekend. They have that nice park in the next town." Claire smiled at Luna, who lay on her side, taking in the sun. Thankfully, she still wore her shirt to protect her skin.

"That's a great idea. Pack a few snacks and toys and grab take out on the way back. We can make a day of it."

It sounded perfect to Claire. Spending the day with the dogs and Jace—what more could a woman ask? Before Claire could respond, Rue's pickup truck pulled up to the open gate. She jogged to the road, waving her arms to signal her to keep going. Jace quickly secured Luna's leash, and moments later, Rue pulled into the spot next to the main house. Claire rushed to the driver's side.

"You made it!" Claire yelled in greeting. She helped Rue climb out before getting a good grasp on Balty's collar when he tried to dart past. Rue gave an awkward hug around a spastic Balty.

"I can see why you prefer to stay out here. The drive up was breathtaking. I can't wait to get a peek in that greenhouse." Rue reached for her cane before closing the door. "Is it okay to park here?"

"It's fine. We'll take your bags in shortly." Claire guided her to the other side of the truck, where Josie had joined Jace. Luna bounced, tail wagging, as she tried to get to Balty.

"I'll help your aunt," Josie said, hurrying over. "I'm Josie Beckett. Welcome to Hawkins Ridge."

"Nice to meet you. Claire, his leash is in the truck." Rue attempted to turn around, but a masculine voice stopped her in her tracks.

"On the passenger side?" Logan said, moving to the other side of the truck.

Naomi moved past her husband and joined the group. Logan saddled up beside Claire, who fought the pull of the forty-pound mixed breed. Logan clipped the leash on and took over. Claire thanked him before returning to her aunt.

"Sorry about that, Rue." Claire rested her hand on her shoulder. "You've met Josie. This is Naomi. The man holding Balty is Logan, Naomi's husband. Jace is the one with Luna."

Everyone said hello in unison while the brothers worked on introducing the dogs.

"We got this. Why don't you get Rue settled? We'll be there in a sec." Jace squatted next to Luna and let Balty sniff his hand.

"Why don't I take Luna?" Naomi offered. "We'll help the dogs get their excitement out."

Claire hesitated for a moment, then turned to grab Rue's bags. Jace quickly fell into step with her.

"I think Luna has a way with other animals."

She looked past him to Luna and Balty frantically sniffing each other. Both tails whipping in the wind. Claire handed Jace her aunt's suitcase while she clutched Rue's purse and doggie bed, closing the door with her hip.

"Balty is friendly and even-tempered. When Rue first adopted him, I didn't think she'd be able to handle his energy." She let him link his fingers with hers as they strolled up the walkway. "But I think he's the reason she's as active as she is."

"I don't think he'll have a problem getting along with the pets."

Laughter greeted them as they stepped through the back door. Rue leaned against the counter, holding a cookie while Josie poured a glass of sweet tea. Her aunt shoved a finger at Claire.

"Remember the first time you called yourself making cookies? What did you use instead of the cookie dough roll?"

Claire laughed as the memory washed over her. "I thought I could put chocolate chips on biscuit dough. I even sprinkled sugar on it and everything."

"Dumped. She dumped sugar on them. Garrett ended up eating all of them." Rue thanked Josie for the tea. "I made him double brush his teeth for days."

Josie chuckled and patted Jace on the arm. "This one tried to bake mud pies. Didn't understand why it wouldn't come out of the pie tin."

"To be fair, Logan told me I could. He was the one who heated the oven for me."

"It's a good thing your cooking has improved," Claire teased. Jace flashed a wink, causing butterflies to take flight in her stomach. "We'll take these to your room."

"I haven't shown her where she's staying," Josie said. "Why don't you two relax? Jace can help me get the lasagna ready for the oven."

Claire and Rue offered to help but were shooed away. Josie agreed to let them help with the salad. Claire led her aunt down the hall to the suite. She closed the door behind them when they stepped in.

"This house is beautiful." Rue strolled to the bedroom and checked out the bathroom. "I may extend my visit."

"You're more than welcome to. This isn't being used, and I'm sure Logan and Naomi won't mind. Balty will have dogs to play with." Claire moved to the kitchenette area. "Josie stocked pods of tea. There are snacks in the cabinet, and I think bottled water in the mini fridge."

Rue rested her cane against the loveseat and motioned for Claire to take a seat in the companion chair. Her aunt glanced out the window, her gaze settling on the view of her truck and the roadway.

"I hope Josie didn't go through too much trouble. She didn't have to do all this."

"I told her the same thing, but that's how she is. What you see with the Becketts is what you get." Claire slipped off her sneakers and wiggled her toes. "I can take you past my house after dinner. If you angle yourself, you can see the oak tree in my yard from the window."

"All the family lives on the property?"

"Immediate family, yes. Josie and Thomas used to live here but switched houses with Logan after Christmas." Claire cleared her throat and plucked invisible lint from her jeans. "What do you think of Jace?"

"I just met the young man, and I don't think I said over five words to him. I have the entire weekend to get to know him. Why are you worried about what I think? You're an adult and this is your relationship."

"I know." Claire met her aunt's gaze. "We've only been official for a week, but I was expecting this big change between us."

"What were you expecting?"

Claire rapidly blinked. What was she expecting? Her heartbeat increased when he winked at her. She noticed his cheeks pinking when she fixed his hair. She turned to goo when he babied Cammie. They were adults, not teenagers experiencing their first love. There wouldn't be woodland creatures breaking out into song or their pupils turning into hearts.

Realization slapped her like a wind. Things had changed. She never had a reaction to Andy. With Jace, she wanted to find ways to make him blush. She looked forward to his soft touches to her lower back if she walked in front of him. Rue's knowing laugh pulled her out of her reverie.

"That goofy smile tells me you noticed some changes."

Claire's cheeks heated. "I did. Guess I'm looking for something to worry about when I shouldn't have."

Rue chuckled and grabbed her purse from the floor. "It's good that things feel the same. It shows the man you cared about as a friend is the same one you'll care about as a partner. Don't go looking for something to worry about. Enjoy being together."

Claire had the same feeling playing on a loop in her brain. Being with Jace made her happy. If there was another side to him, it would have shown by now.

It wasn't just Jace she wanted Rue to like. It was the entire Beckett family. They would be partners, after all. Claire decided the day before to accept Logan and Naomi's offer. She wanted to tell them once everyone left. Not that the rest of the family wouldn't know by the following day. No, Claire wanted to have the discussion with the friends who extended the offer. She also wanted Rue to be part of the conversation. Any concerns her aunt might have, she could express them easier without eleven other people staring at her.

A knock on the door interrupted their conversation.

"Come in," Rue called out.

The door opened, allowing Balty and Luna to trot in. Jace crossed the threshold with a bright grin gracing his lips.

"It seems they are fast friends. Once they came in, they started looking for you two." Jace walked to the wall with a few switches. "Did they show you the blinds? This middle one lowers and the one on the right raises them." He flicked the switch to demonstrate. "The one in the bedroom are manual."

"Can I get that at my place?" Claire played with the blind control, laughing. "This is so cool."

He linked his pinky with hers and kissed the top of her head. "Yes, Buttercup. I'll check my schedule next week and install them."

"I was kidding." Claire didn't know how expensive the blinds were and would need to budget for them.

"I wasn't." Jace wrapped his arm around her waist. "We have them in storage. Caden planned to use them for his windows but decided on the remote tinting instead."

Claire nibbled her bottom lip. She opened her mouth to say no, but Rue cut her off.

"Girl. Let him put the blinds in. It sounds like they are just sitting there collecting dust. Just say thank you."

A warm memory of Rue saying something similar washed over Claire. When Medicaid approved to pay for her plastic surgery, Claire thought they would drop her afterwards because of the cost. Her aunt told her not to worry about that and just say thank you. It was the same with the blinds.

"Thank you. I want to help install them."

"It's a date."

Rue clapped her hands and rose to her feet. "Now that's taken care of, let's go help Josie."

Claire smiled as the dogs led the way. This was her family, blood and found.

CHAPTER SIXTEEN

Jace ran his hands over his full belly. He should have stopped after two servings of lasagna, but the crispy corner piece called his name. Now he fought a food coma as he waited for Claire and Rue to return from Claire's house.

After cleaning the kitchen, everyone said their goodbyes and returned to their homes. Jace, Logan, and Naomi took all the dogs outside for the nighttime potty breaks. Claire asked his brother if they could talk when she returned. She told Jace about her decision that morning when he picked up Luna. She wanted him with her for support. It meant more to him than he could describe.

Jace didn't worry Claire had feelings for him. She showed it when she wasn't even trying. But to want him by her side when she and Rue spoke to Logan said she saw him as a partner. At least that's how Jace saw it. Claire was happy, and that's all that matters.

"I really like Rue," Naomi said as they herded the dogs inside. "If she stays, she'll get along with Josie's crew."

"I'm sure Mom is going to do everything in her power to make it happen." Logan closed the door behind them. "We can make room for her here, or we have that empty house near Owen and Sam. Something until she can find a place."

"I'd have a babysitter for Cammie if she stays." Jace's little baby fell in love with Rue as soon as the older woman held her. She stayed on Rue's lap throughout dinner and even went with them on the tour of Claire's home.

Logan nodded. "She's good with animals. I see where Claire gets it from."

Jace used a napkin to grab three cookies before taking a seat on an island stool. "It would mean a lot to Claire if she stays. Mom plans to invite her to lunch with Winnie and Maeve."

"Having my mother there would be good for Rue," Naomi commented. "She can share her experience as a retiree who moved less than two years ago. Rue can see how welcoming the town is for older residents."

Jace spoke around a bite of cookie. "I know Garrett is close to his in laws, and no offense to Sara's folks, but—"

"They aren't down to earth like Rue and Claire," Logan interrupted. "I wonder if Garrett hadn't landed managing the biggest feed store in the county if they would have been as *welcoming.*"

Jace tilted his water to his brother. "I wonder the same thing." The locals praised the improvements Garrett made to the store, including the informed and helpful staff. Jace remembered Logan said it was one reason he agreed to interview Claire, expecting her to have the same work ethics. Which she did.

Giggling drew their attention to the back door where Claire and Rue entered with an excited Cammie. All the dogs went to greet the women. Luna and Balty gave extra-long sniffs of their owners before pressing their bodies against them.

"I just love that house," Rue said, making her way to the island. Logan pulled a dining room chair over so she could sit. "It is the perfect size for a single person."

Claire ran her fingers across Jace's arm. He ignored the instant goosebumps. "We can look for a small piece of land and build you something similar. You only need half an acre."

"Before she heads back to Garrett's, show her Owen and Sam's place," Logan suggested. "It's larger than Claire's, but it's a modular and comes partially assembled. The builder has smaller square footage."

Rue shook her head. "That's something I would need to think about later, but it would be good to see during our tour of the property."

Claire hopped up on the stool Jace vacated. She reached for a bottled water still in the bucket of ice on the counter. She shared a glance with Jace before clearing her throat.

"I know it's late, but thank you for staying up," she said to Logan and Naomi.

"It's sad when eight thirty is our bedtime," Naomi teased, but there was truth in the statement. Jace barely made it to ten o'clock. Claire continued.

"I wanted to tell you, I would like to accept your offer about the dog treats provided we can include Rue. The base of all the treats is her recipe, and the demand for them wouldn't be there without her."

Rue waved her hands in front of her, dismissing Claire's condition. "Nope. I planned on telling you this weekend. This is your thing and something you alone should be part of. I planned on putting anything you gave me from it to an account for Garrett's baby and any future children you may have." She winked at Jace. "I'm comfortable. I have my disability check and the settlement from the fulfillment center. I know you wanted to look out for me, and I love you for it, but you have my blessing to use the recipe."

Claire opened her mouth to argue, but Jace gave her shoulder a squeeze. "I'm sure we can work something so that you get the proper recognition you deserve."

Logan nodded in agreement. "Definitely. It's something we can work out over the next few days." He stood and pulled Naomi to her feet. "That being said, I think we're turning in. Call us if you need anything you can't find."

"You're having breakfast at your place?" Naomi asked.

"That's the plan and start baking around eleven. I should be back from the store and greenhouse." Claire gave Naomi and Logan a hug. "Thank you."

Logan's face softened. "You're welcome. Can you lock the back door on your way out, Jace? Fiona is staying with the folks."

They said their good night and made their way to the stairs at the front of the house. Their six dogs were on their heels. Luna, Oriole, and Balty lay down at the archway, watching their friends leave. Rue rose to her feet and passed a sleeping Cammie to Claire.

"I think I'm going to turn in myself. Maybe make a cup of chamomile tea." Rue gave Jace a hug. "I'm glad we met. You're good for my niece, your entire family."

He returned the embrace. "We all feel the same way. I'll see you in the morning."

"I'll be there in a minute." Claire patted Balty on the head. Luna swung her dark eyes to her owner before lying next to Oriole.

Jace wrapped his arms around Claire when the door to the suite closed. She rested her head on his chest and blew out a deep breath.

"Thank you for stopping me with Rue. I figured she would fight me on this."

"She wants what's best for you. We can write it so she may not be part of the partnership, but she will still get her share of the profit. What she does with it is her decision."

"I know. It's just she sacrificed so much for me and my recovery, I want to make sure she's taken care of." She tilted her head back and met his eyes. "Does that make sense?"

"It makes perfect sense, Buttercup." He pressed his lips to her forehead. "Besides, I'm sure you're going to have your hands full trying to talk her into letting you help her find a place and getting settled here."

"Do you really think she's going to stay?"

He nodded and took a step back. He could hold Claire until the end of time. "I do. At her age, knowing she has an established community will make it easier for her. You saw how much she and my mother talked and laughed. Add Izzy and Naomi's mothers into the mix, and your aunt will celebrate the fall festival as a new resident."

"I hope so." She rolled on her tiptoes and planted a playful kiss to his chin. "Thank you for being an amazing boyfriend."

"You make it easy." He returned the affection to her nose and ran his fingers through her hair. "We need to say good night. We have an early start."

After breakfast, Jace volunteered to take Claire to the box store forty-five minutes away for silicone molds or cookie cutters. They planned to make five hundred treats so Jace could give samples at his meetings next week.

"I know. I should check on Rue and make sure she found everything for her tea."

"Go. I'll turn off the lights." He dropped a quick kiss to her lips. "Night."

"Night."

She called Luna, who followed her down the hallway. Jace scooped up Cammie before killing the lights, plunging the lower level into darkness. The glow of the streetlight cast shadows on the kitchen flooring. Jace sighed as he stepped into the cool temperatures and locked the back door.

Watching Claire and her aunt interact, opened his eyes to why Claire was the woman she was. Rue was a spitfire. Jace knew Sara's family. Though Sara and her sister were down-to-earth people, the parents expected their daughters to marry well. Both married blue-collar men who knew the value of hard work. Rue didn't strike him as the type who would enjoy golfing at the country club in Stark Valley. Neither did Claire. A lively home cooked meal with family and loved ones were their speed.

Seeing his family welcome Rue with open arms warmed his heart. Jace knew they would do what was necessary to make Claire happy. Turns out, they only needed to be themselves. It was what made him fall more in love with her.

The corners of his lips ticked up, thinking back to a statement Rue made. Claire and her future children. He and Claire talked about kids when they were friends. Nothing deep, but both wanted a family. It was too soon in their romantic relationship to bring it up now. The thought of a little girl with dark pigtails helping Claire measure ingredients for a cake popped into his mind. Even a little boy. Jace didn't believe in antiquated gender roles. Heck, he loved cooking and wouldn't have a problem having dinner ready for Claire when she came home from work. The idea washed over him before settling in his soul.

The love he had for Leah was one of a young man who considered turning his back on this life. Her leaving allowed him to find what he was looking for. Claire would give him the relationship he always wanted. Her love for the life of Hawkins Ridge meant more than even he had five years ago. He could see them growing deeper in love, like his parents.

No matter what people threw at them.

Chapter Seventeen

The scent of pine and oak mixed with the calm, early spring breeze. Claire leaned her head against the seat rest and sighed. The morning was off to a great start.

She and Rue woke early. They passed Logan scrolling through his phone at the kitchen island on their way to Claire's house for breakfast. All the dogs were in a row, enjoying their meal. Claire apologized again for not eating with them, but he waved it off. Naomi had a case of morning sickness and wouldn't have been much company.

Breakfast was simple toast and boiled eggs. Neither were early breakfast eaters, but didn't want to bake on an empty stomach. It gave them time to talk. Rue admitted to feeling as if she'd worn out her welcome at Garrett's. Claire invited her aunt to extend her stay at the sanctuary for the full week. If it wasn't okay with Logan and Naomi, Claire would give up her bed so Rue could enjoy the property.

Jace met them at Logan's when they finished eating. Rue declined going and gave a list of a few things she needed. Claire believed in shopping local or online shopping. When she made the trip to the big box store, it was to stock up on toiletries, dry goods, and paper products.

"Have you ever made a large quantity of treats?" Jace asked from the driver's seat.

"Ten dozen is the most I've baked in a day. You've seen my oven. I think I've pushed it to handle that." Claire didn't want to mention that she had to let the oven cool after baking four dozen, as it ran hot from extensive use. She'd bet a dollar that if she brought it up, he'd either have a new stove installed or suggest she use his. The break didn't bother her and gave her hand a chance to rest. A new stove wasn't a necessity.

Traffic increased the closer they came to the city. Its population peaked at roughly sixty thousand; by metropolitan standards, that's a town. Compared to Oak Mountain population of fifteen thousand, Stark Valley was huge.

"Have you thought about making cat treats?" Jace asked as they took the exit for the store.

"I have. I would need to experiment and ask Josie or Noah to let me test them with their cats. Your mom has pots of fresh catnip, so I would want to try something with that first before I move to a protein flavor." Claire sat straight in the seat when the store came into view. "Has Logan thought about making his dog food available to the town, or like the mail order fresh stuff you see advertised?"

Jace shook his head. "He knows it would take more of his time and expenses. I think if he didn't have the pack and the family pets, he would use one of the mail order companies. They're organic, which he likes. Like you, I think it's a way for him to decompress and he can guarantee the quality of the ingredients."

The sanctuary also used quality dry kibble for the dogs whose tummy couldn't handle the richness of the homemade soft food.

He pulled into a parking spot at the end of the aisle. The sanctuary truck wasn't small and parking closer to the building would increase the chance of getting dinged or people parking too close to climb back in. Jace helped her climb out and pressed the fob to lock the door. He linked his fingers with hers and walked up the sidewalk.

"Do you think your brother would have a problem with Rue staying the week?" Claire blurted. "I want to ask before we bake. I know Josie said it wouldn't be a problem, but I don't want to assume. If not, I can move her to my place tomorrow."

Jace pulled a cart from the corral and pushed it with one hand through the automatic gate at the entrance.

"I'm sure he won't mind. He and Naomi will be out of the house all day during the week. Mom will keep her busy during the day and probably plan a few dinners, but Rue can have dinner with you or us. Did she say she wanted to stay?"

Claire shared Rue's concerns about Garrett and Sara. She nudged him towards the pain relief section and picked up the acetaminophen for her and Rue.

"She has two more weeks left of her visit and she doesn't want to leave them dreading her next visit. I think it's more Sara than Garrett, but she'll never say."

"That makes sense. I don't see Rue spending her days with Sara's mother."

Claire's snort caused a few heads to turn their way. She ducked her face in Jace's chest as heat rose to her cheeks. His body shook with silent laughter.

"Are they finished looking?" she said into his shirt.

"Yes, but I'm sure another snort would draw their attention again."

She shook her head and focused on the next item on Rue's list before answering.

"Rue is a simple woman. Not in a bad way, but she's laid back and down to earth. Chicken just needs four seasonings and barbeque sauce on special occasions. Water doesn't need cucumber and mint to taste good. As long as it's filtered, she's fine."

"And Sara's family is not like that," Jace finished her thought. "That explains why she gets along well with my mom."

"She adores Josie." Claire tossed the arthritis cream into the cart, then motioned towards the bakeware. "She heard so much about the Becketts, she assumed y'all would be like Sara's family. Do you know how much she enjoyed Caden and Thomas out burp each other?"

"I liked when Mom cuffed both of them." Jace laughed. Claire choked on her sweet tea when Josie did it.

"I think Rue needed to meet your family to know I'm okay, and she'll have support if she moves." It made it easier for Claire knowing she had her cousin.

The couple selected molds shaped like animals, balls, and vegetables. Josie was adamant Hawkins Ridge would pay for everything needed for baking, so she didn't stop Jace from tossing in dog shape cutters, cookie sheets, and cooling racks. His theory of better to have it and not need it than to need it and not have it made sense. She still couldn't wrap her head around the cost they were spending.

"Stop worrying, Buttercup. Everything we're getting, we're going to use." He pressed a kiss to the top of her head. "Now, let's buy a ton of bananas and the seasoning I'm going to need for dinner."

Claire turned to continue down the aisle and met the hateful glare of the server from the diner, Tinsley. Thanks to Izzy, she knew the woman scowling went on a date with Jace over a year ago. According to Noah, Tinsley couldn't accept Jace wasn't into her. That was her problem, and Claire couldn't allow herself to get upset. She knew his colorful past. She'd have to leave the county if she didn't want to run into a woman who knew Jace. The stare down lasted maybe five seconds before an adorable little boy with curly blond hair ran up to her with a toy in his hand. The scowl instantly turned to a smile for the child. Claire looked over her shoulder to see Jace staring at the same interaction. His face was unreadable. When he linked their fingers together and guided her to walk, Claire fought the urge to stick her tongue out at the woman.

Growing up, Claire never got the school hottie. Even as an adult, the few men she went on a date with were considered average by society's standards. That included Andy. On paper, Jace should be with Tinsley. Both were attractive and came from upper middle-class families. But Jace chose her. Tinsley had her entire life to snag Jace. That thought alone had Claire lifting her chin higher.

No one said anything when they crossed paths. There wasn't a reason to. They were adults, after all. Was Jace even aware that Claire knew who Tinsley was? It wasn't a subject that needed to be discussed. His past was his past. They were in a committed relationship and laid their issues on the table weeks ago. Claire had to put her what ifs and insecurities behind her if she expected their relationship to last.

She gave him a sincere smile and squeezed his hand. "I may need a toy for Luna." Jace's hearty laugh warmed her soul.

"Let's go spoil our children."

Our children? The thought took root in her heart. Yes, he meant the dogs, but she imagined bringing a little boy or girl shopping to pick out a toy for their puppy or a new backpack for their first day of school. Her heart warmed thinking of a pigtailed girl running around a yard chasing a butterfly. Being able to give that to her child would make all the sacrifices Rue and she had made worthwhile.

One can hope.

Jace washed two ibuprofens down with a gulp of lemonade. His back screamed after hours of baking and house cleaning. Only the feeling after giving all the dogs a bath and mucking the stalls was worse.

He pressed his fist into his lower back and leaned back. He welcomed the popping of bones.

"Be glad you aren't human," he said to Oriole. The dog barely acknowledged him as he played with his new oversize stuffed snake. Cammie simply fell asleep on her stuffed monkey.

Jace chuckled and pulled the extra steaks from the fridge. They would be for the dogs without seasoning. The ones for the humans were marinating. Claire and Rue would be there in ten minutes. He'd cooked dinner for Claire before, but Rue had him upping his game.

He and Rue were both Baltimore Orioles fans. Hence the name Balty. She laughed, learning he named Cammie after

Camden Yards, the baseball team's home stadium. They made plans to watch the season opener before she headed home.

Rue was a sarcastic woman who loved and was protective of her niece. It was a concern if Claire knew who Tinsley was and if she told her aunt.

Jace saw the other woman when he gave Claire a kiss. Their relationship wasn't common knowledge, but was only a matter of time before the town knew. It didn't embarrass him. He just didn't want the store subjected to a bitter, scorned woman. What had him breathing a sigh of relief was Tinsley's son. Jace felt confident if her son wasn't with her, she would have made a scene. It was who Tinsley was. Jace wasn't naïve to think the other woman wouldn't approach Claire if she saw her in town. Did he need to warn her of the possibility? How would he even broach the subject? Would Tinsley now try to manipulate her uncle and the deal Hawkins Ridge wanted to make with his four co-ops?

Jace took a deep, calming breath to center himself. This was something Tinsley had to deal with. He had no intention of jeopardizing his relationship with Claire to make a deal. He also told Claire during their talk that there would be upset women. Something told him Izzy and Naomi already gave her a heads-up.

Claire was his future. Period. If anyone had a problem, they could take it up with him and leave Claire alone. He waited almost a year to have this chance with her and he won't let any random woman come between them, no matter her connections.

The crunch of tires on gravel drew Jace and Oriole's attention. He wiped his hands on a towel before lifting Cammie, who woke when she heard the noise. Oriole led the way to meet the visitors just as Claire parked his UTV. Jace let her borrow his because he didn't want Rue walking the distance, and the drive was less than two minutes if you cut through the trees.

The setting sun brought cooler temperatures. He planned on eating on the back patio and turning on the heat lamp. Claire's flushed face and hysterical laughter told him she had taken the path through the trees. Claire hurried to the passenger seat to open the door before taking two dishes from her aunt.

"That was amazing!" Rue held onto the frame of the UTV roof for balance as she stood. "I want to drive going back."

Claire shook her head. "We'll see."

Once Rue was out, Luna and Balty clambered over each other to greet Oriole. The three took off in a spirited game of chase. Cammie tried to follow, but nature called. Jace pressed a kiss to Claire's cheek and gave Rue a hug.

"I thought you were just making a salad." He took the dishes from Claire. The top one was a pie tin.

"I made a pie," Rue replied. "Your mother had the pie crusts in the freezer and apples she canned. I just added the little things to make it a filling."

"She was supposed to be resting." Claire playfully glared at her aunt.

"I lay down for about thirty minutes. Talking to Josie and Naomi wasn't strenuous."

That didn't surprise him. "I can't wait to try it." He whistled for the dogs while Claire picked up Cammie. "If you have time tomorrow, I can take you on the ATV around the property."

"That sounds like something I want to make time for." Rue took in his single-story home and the surrounding trees. "I like this. You have privacy, but close enough to sponge food off your mother."

Jace laughed. "I think you're the only one that figured that out."

He motioned for them to go forward. Claire hurried and opened the screen door for her aunt. The dogs zipped by before she could cross, causing Rue to stumble. Claire's quick reflexes grabbed her elbow.

"Sorry about that," Jace said. He couldn't fuss at the dogs because they didn't understand what they did. He made a mental note to clear the path of animals if Rue was moving about.

"I've always loved open floor plans," Rue said, shrugging off her light cardigan. "It's airy and you're mindful of clutter."

"It's also good for when you have company," Claire added.

Jace walked past them and placed the dishes on the island separating the living space from the eat-in kitchen.

"Let me give you a tour. I figured we could eat outside? I have the grill heated."

Claire went about getting sweet tea for her and her aunt while Jace showed Rue, and Balty, his home. When he built the home, he wanted space for company or to add if he had over two children. Now that he and Claire were in their thirties, Jace would be thankful if they had one child or perhaps adopt. Given the appreciative comments from Rue, he would have to make sure there was a space for her, whether or not she lived in Oak Mountain.

Jace wondered if Claire liked his house, or if she would want to make changes. Their relationship was new, and she may not even think about marriage and sharing a home with him in the future. He hoped she did. He put a pin on the subject to talk about later.

They caught up with Claire at the sliding back door. She'd let Luna and Oriole into the fenced backyard, while Cammie sat on the mat. Jace led them to the patio table and checked the grill temperature.

"I have a heat lamp in case you get cold. I'll be back with the meat and potatoes."

"Let me help," Claire offered, but Jace motioned for her to stay seated.

"Everything is on a tray. Just make sure I don't trip over a dog."

She gave a thumbs up and giggled. Rue pointed to the spikes in the back corner of the yard they used for horseshoes when he stepped back inside. Maybe he could plan another evening where they could play a game or two.

Jace noticed the relief on Rue's face earlier when Logan and Naomi eagerly agreed to let her stay the rest of the week. Keeping her busy on the property wouldn't be a problem. He didn't want to monopolize all of Claire's time after work so she could spend it with her aunt. He hoped they would still keep their drive for the following Saturday.

Jace quickly gathered the tray of plates, napkins, utensils, condiments, and dinner. He placed the salad container on top of the napkins and headed outside. Claire and Rue entertained him while he grilled with stories of Claire's childhood and her mother, Dot. He shared his experiences of growing up with his brothers on the property.

By the time he finished, the temperature had dropped more, and the moon was out. Stars dotted the sky, creating a relaxing glow. Claire flipped on the switch for the lights on her way to grab the pitchers of tea and lemonade. The dogs pranced around, waiting for their treat. When Jace set their bowls on the floor, he barely moved his hands before they dug in.

After fixing their plates, they took a few minutes to sample everything. The garlic and herb roasted potatoes were perfectly creamy and crispy. Mesquite rub gave the steaks a smoky hearty flavor. Jace sent a silent prayer of thanks Rue didn't need steak sauce. He never used it and would have to go to the stable house to borrow a bottle. No one in his family used the stuff.

Rue took a sip of her tea and broke the silence.

"Can I be blunt, Jace?" she asked, wiping her lips. He didn't know what she was about to say, but he braced himself for the worst.

"Please don't," Claire pleaded. Rue patted her hand and held Jace's gaze.

"I know about your reputation in town, and the string of broken hearts left in your wake. I want to know my niece is safe from these women." Rue held up her hand when he went to speak. "It is obvious you care deeply for Claire. I know the feeling is mutual. What I don't want is for her to live in a real *Lifetime* movie. Can you assure me she will be safe?"

Maybe Claire knew who Tinsley was, after all, he thought. He gave Claire what he hoped was a comforting smile and focused on Rue.

"I can assure you I will do everything in my power to keep her safe. One or two of my past dates may say something rude to her. I wish I could call each one and tell them to stay away from her, but I'm a realist. Most are already in committed relationships. Some may still want something, but I made it clear to every person at the beginning. I just wanted to keep it casual.

"Claire is the person I want to build a future with," he continued. "No one will turn my head or tempt me into throwing away something I waited almost a year to have. That I can assure you."

Rue studied him for a long moment before a smile formed on her lips. "I needed to hear you realize you have no control over a scorned woman. You're a handsome man from a re-spected and close family. According to your mother, women have lost their minds over not being the person you picked to build a life with. Claire can handle herself. There is a lot of snark behind the glasses."

They all chuckled, breaking the seriousness of the conver-sation.

Jace respected Rue for looking out for Claire. Not that he had a doubt, but she went straight to the source and confront-ed him. He wished he could say no one would be rude to Claire, but it would be a lie. All he could do was stand by Claire's side and be the man she deserved.

Chapter Eighteen

"You need to be on your best behavior today," Claire admonished Luna while she rubbed her special sunblock on the bare spots of her fur. "You may also need to keep an eye on Cammie in case some other dog tries to harass her."

Luna replied with a gentle lick on her cheek, causing Claire to giggle. She wrapped her arms around the boxer's neck. "Who's a good girl?" Luna's stubby tail wagged frantically in response.

Claire secured Luna's lightweight dog coat around her neck and chest. With a final kiss to her forehead, Claire rose to her feet, pushing up her glasses. Glancing at her watch, she had five minutes before Jace would be there to pick them up.

Claire worried after Rue brought up the subject of Jace's past female friends. She'd confided in her aunt about seeing Tinsley at the store and the hateful look she gave them. Rue wanted to find the woman and have a talk. It brought back memories of her aunt confronting the parents of the kids that teased Claire about her burns. Though it may have impressed Izzy and Thomas, bailing her aunt out of jail was not the impression she wanted to give the rest of the Beckett clan.

It didn't matter. Jace said the right words. There was nothing he could do about the feelings of others. If they had a problem with Claire because she was in a relationship with Jace, then that was on them. They are supposed to be adults.

Once they were past the subject, the rest of the evening was uneventful. Jace put on music, and they played cards.

She looked forward to their time with the dogs all week. They both needed the break and to spend alone time together. After their dinner with Rue, Claire and her aunt had a girls' day with Naomi, Josie, Fiona, and Maeve, watching cheesy movies, doing facials, and manicures. It helped prepare for a bear of a work week. Three farms required Logan and Claire to make emergency visits. When they weren't checking on their outside patients, the Hawkins Ridge goats were going into labor. There were also three new rescues to add to the chaos.

Rue stayed busy during the day, either helping Josie take care of the cats, planting flowers in the greenhouse, or answering phones at the clinic.

When Claire wasn't working, there were Beckett family dinners or quiet ones with Rue and Jace. Claire loved having her aunt with her. It gave Garrett and Sara time together.

But today was her day to spend a few hours with her dogs and Jace.

Instead of going for a drive as planned, Jace mentioned an art crawl and live music in Stark Valley. That had their names written all over it. Since it was outside, they could bring the dogs. Jace promised to take the back roads so they could enjoy the beauty of the mountains in the spring. Claire's grin was wide, and she didn't care.

She slipped her crossbody purse on before tugging her ponytail through the back of her Baltimore Orioles baseball cap. Technically, it was Jace's, but it looked cute on her, so she took it. Dressed in a pink T-shirt and jeans, she was ready for the day.

Claire guided Luna out the front door. Jace pulled up just as they made it to the end of her walkway. Oriole barked loudly from the open window. Luna returned the greeting with a bark of her own. Jace hurried out and helped her secure Luna in the back. Cammie looked adorable in her seat between the two larger dogs.

"Morning," he said before giving her a toe-curling kiss. She could get used to starting her morning this way. She fisted his shirt to maintain her balance. Her breathless voice caused her cheeks to heat.

"Morning. I'm really glad we added kissing to this relationship."

Jace barked out a laugh before pressing his lips to her forehead. "That makes two of us, Buttercup. Ready?"

She nodded. He led her to the passenger side and helped her into the seat. He closed the door once she fastened her seatbelt. Luna and Oriole had their muzzles out of their respective window, saying hello to the world. Their tails wagging up a storm. Jace folded himself behind the wheel and eased the car down the road. They waved to Noah, Owen, and Sam, who were climbing into Noah's truck. The trio made plans with Noah's mother for her birthday. Claire met his mother a handful of times and liked the woman's caring nature.

"Have you ever been to this art crawl?" Claire asked. Jace answered as they turned out of the property.

"Three years ago. Mom wanted to find something for the living room. She didn't find anything, but ended up with hand painted note cards." Jace tilted his head. "You know, I think she ended up putting them in frames around the house."

"That's a great idea. I love repurposing things." A memory brought a smile to her face. "My first year on my own, I found a studio apartment above a store and had nothing for artwork. Rue and I spent a weekend going through thrift stores and yard sales for anything. One store had a box of assorted buttons and fabric. We stayed up all night gluing the buttons onto colored cardstock and the fabric onto cardboard and framing them. We ended up spending like twelve bucks and came away with ten eight by ten artwork."

To that day, Claire still found joy in going to the second-hand stores and discovering hidden gems. Maybe she could plan a craft day with Naomi soon.

"Caden got the artistic talent in our family," Jace commented, guiding the truck down a country road. "I can follow directions if someone wanted me to glue something, but coming up with what you describe is not in my brain."

"I doubt that. Didn't you make popsicle stick houses and frames in elementary school?"

"Sure, but I followed the teacher. Oh, I can darn a sock." He turned and flashed a toothy grin, causing her to laugh.

"Sewing is an art, so I won't discount your ability to mend a hole in a sock. Though something tells me you would just get a new pair."

"You know me well."

Claire shook her head at his silliness. It strengthened her love for him. He felt comfortable being himself around her. Few in town saw him with his guard down. She glanced over her shoulder to check on the dogs. Cammie was curled tight on her cushion while Oriole and Luna sniffed the early spring air. Her worry about Luna handling a car ride was unwarranted. The boxer's tongue lolled while she cataloged everything.

Jace hummed a slow rock ballad, one of his favorite songs. Claire pulled her hand brace from her purse and slipped it on. Work wreaked havoc on her hand and wrist nerves that week and she found herself taking more ibuprofen than usual. She took her nerve spasm medication before leaving. The last thing she wanted was a flare up to ruin their date.

"Can I ask about your hand?" Jace's voice held a nervous tone.

"Of course."

"Is there an operation that can help so you don't have to wear the brace all the time?"

Was he embarrassed about being seen with her wearing it? They'd been in public with her wearing it. Did it bother him then? Would he prefer people to see the scars instead? Claire immediately tapped down on the bout of insecurity. His question was out of curiosity, nothing more.

She shifted in her seat to face him. "There is a surgery, but only a forty percent chance it would heal it and a twenty percent chance it would do more damage. I prefer the medication and brace for now."

"I don't blame you," he replied. "The odds aren't that great."

"Rest and doing my hand exercise is the best thing for it. I pushed it this week for sure."

"Do you want to turn around?" Jace spared a glance at her. "We can just take it easy."

She rested her hand on his arm to calm him. "Unless I have to walk on my hands, today will be easy. I took my medication and I have ibuprofen just in case. I'll be fine."

"If you're sure. If you don't mind carrying Cammie in her holder when we walk around, I'll handle Luna and Oriole's leashes."

Claire agreed. The Pomeranian used something similar to a baby carrier that the human wore, like a backpack. Cammie weighed five pounds. She didn't think it would be a hardship.

They drove across a bridge over a fast-flowing creek. People stood on the banks fishing. Claire didn't have a clue what fish made the creek their home and didn't want to find out. She liked seafood as much as the next person, but she preferred it cleaned, beheaded, and boned.

"You said you were a server after high school. How did you do it with your hand?" Jace asked out of the blue. Claire mentally shook the thought of hooking a worm and answered.

"It wasn't as bad fourteen years ago. I think carrying trays helped advance the damage. When it became a problem, the manager had me working the counter so I could just spin from the pick-up window to the customer. Eventually, I knew I needed to find something else. I lasted six months."

"My senior year of college, I was a bartender."

"I can see that," Claire teased. "I bet you made a lot of tips."

"Kinda. It was at a dive bar that laughed at people who ordered wine. Beer, whiskey, and deep-fried bar food were the only options they had. It helped me with gas money because my allowance went to food and dates with Leah." Jace chuckled as he took the exit for Stark Valley. "I broke up a fight every night I worked. I lasted three months."

"Did Josie and Thomas know?"

"Yep. They thought it was a good experience. It surprised everyone I lasted that long."

It impressed Claire that Jace tried his hand at bartending. He wasn't afraid of getting his hands dirty. None of the Becketts were. It's why she felt at home with the family. Not once did they look down on her upbringing. She was more embarrassed about her spasms than growing up scraping by. It helped her to appreciate a dollar, the value of hard work and gratitude when given an opportunity like Hawkins Ridge gave her.

The opening cords of an upbeat classic rock song started on the radio. Claire and Jace bopped and sang along as the traffic grew heavy, crossing into Stark Valley. Luna and Oriole barked hello to passing cars.

The older section of the city showcased a bright, artistic feel and a perfect area for the art crawl. Jace fell in line with cars headed towards the public parking garage. Row houses converted into storefronts, painted in vibrant, bright colors. Street performers sang and danced for strolling shoppers. A magician amazed children with simple parlor tricks.

"I love this," Claire said in awe as a couple dressed in traditional flamingo outfits performed the difficult dance.

"I knew you would. There's a fusion taco restaurant a couple of blocks over. They have a patio. Maybe we can go there for lunch."

Jace pulled into the three-story garage, took a ticket from the attendant, then found a corner spot on the middle level. It took five minutes to get the dogs situated. Luna, Oriole, and Cammie marked their territory despite Jace telling them to wait. Once that was taken care of and Cammie secured in her carrier strapped to Claire's front, they made their way to the street level.

"I hope the crowds aren't too much for Luna?" Claire worried as her pooch kept in step with Oriole. Jace kept both dogs in front of him and the leashes taut in one hand.

"If she shows signs of anxiety or aggression, we'll move to a less populated area and work our way back to the truck."

Claire nodded and laced her fingers with his. The streets were closed for a two-block radius. Tables and booths lined the curbs with offerings of everything imaginable. Jace led them to the middle of the road so they could glance at the displays on both sides. A police officer near a blockade strolled towards them. A welcoming grin appeared on his face.

"Jace Beckett as I live and breathe." The dark-skinned man, who was around their age and just as muscular as Jace, clapped him on his shoulder. "How have you been?"

"You act like I haven't seen you in decades. We had lunch three months ago when I visited the shelter here." Jace pulled Claire closer. "I've been good. I wanted to bring my girlfriend to see this. Claire, this is Deacon Smallwood. Noah's cousin."

"The infamous Claire," Deacon teased before giving her a quick hug. "Noah and Uncle Owen have been talking about you for a while. It's great to meet you."

Claire hoped the talk was good. "Nice to meet you, too."

"Noah's mother and his father are siblings," Jace explained. "His family moved to Stark Valley when Deacon started high school."

"My mother had hopes I would get a football scholarship by going to a bigger school." Deacon shrugged. "Blew out my knee in the opening game my senior year. Decided to be a cop instead."

Jace chuckled. "Knee injury didn't stop you from tackling me at the charity flag football game seven years ago."

"I thought you couldn't tackle in flag football." Claire looked between the two. She knew a little about sports, thanks to Rue and Garrett.

"Tell that to Logan, who lovingly flattened my brother first," Deacon quipped.

The men threw their heads back and laughed, causing a few heads to turn. Meanwhile, Luna and Oriole drew the attention of a small mix breed using a doggie wheelchair. Claire went on alert. She noticed Jace still spoke with Deacon, but his eyes were on their interaction in case he needed to rein in their dogs. The owners of the new friend cooed and asked about the discoloration on Luna. Claire explained about her condition and how Luna's adoption came to be. Vindication had her tilting her chin when the women voiced the same anger she had. Cammie's tiny bark asked for recognition.

"Oh. My. Gosh. How adorable is she?" one woman commented.

"Please tell me her story isn't traumatic," her partner said, letting Cammie sniff her hand.

"I wish I could." Claire pointed her thumb at Jace. "My boyfriend was a firefighter and noticed her chained and walking in circles in the backyard. He stopped the fire truck and asked the young people to surrender her. She's been his ever since."

It broke Claire's heart when Jace first brought Cammie to Hawkins Ridge. Cammie weighed less than two pounds and desperately needed a bath and food. The usual suspects eagerly helped nurse her to health.

"Good for him. I would have done the same thing and gave them a good swift kick in the shin if they said no." The older of the two was someone Claire could be friends with. She unzipped her bag and pulled out a business card.

"I'm not sure if you've heard of Hawkins Ridge, but we rescue animals who've been at the shelter for a long time or have disabilities. Most we keep, but we also offer some for adoption. We're looking for homes that can help us foster to prepare them for their forever home. Maybe think about it."

Claire handed the older woman the card. "We've been talking about doing that since I work from home. We're afraid of foster failures."

She laughed with the women. "My best friend fostered two terrier siblings and knew it was a fail within the first twenty-four hours."

"She even took my brother off our hands," Jace teased. Logan saw Naomi with Mika and Tam and fell in love with her passion for animals.

They said their goodbyes with the promise to call with their decision the following week.

"We better get going, too." Jace gave a smile before sticking his hand out for his friend. "You going to be here all day?"

Deacon nodded. "Until three. There's a food truck at the end of the block with the best smoothies. They have free pup cups with purchase for your furry friends."

They nodded their thanks and started walking again. It felt good to see Jace interact with someone outside their close circle. It was obvious the two were friends and probably grew up together.

"I don't think I've seen Deacon at the property." Claire took his offered hand when Jace replied.

"He doesn't get to Oak Mountain much. He and his wife recently moved back to Stark Valley because they have a special needs daughter, and their family is here to help them. Noah drives down about once a month with cheeses." Jace nodded towards a table with decorative flowerpots. "Thank you for giving them our card. They would make great foster parents."

Claire agreed. Their disabled dog was happy and well taken care of. Even the best animal people didn't have the time or resources to help an animal who required extra attention.

The couple went back to enjoying their date. Their dogs drew the attention of children and animal lovers throughout the day. They waved to a few Oak Mountain residents who made the short drive. People would know they were dating and drove the need for Claire to talk to Garrett soon. She didn't want him to hear of their relationship from the rumor mill.

She hoped he was supportive as Rue.

Chapter Nineteen

Spring had officially hit Oak Mountain. The town's land-scape workers planted new bushes in the square and edged the cobblestone walkway surrounding the city hall. Claire embraced the smile that formed on her lips. This was her favorite time of year.

She pulled into the parking lot shared by the downtown businesses when street parking wasn't available. This was her second spring in Oak Mountain. She loved the energy of the people milling around the window displays and taking advantage of enjoying their meals on the benches. Maybe she'll bring Luna for a walk one day.

For now, she had a lunch date to get to.

Claire climbed out of her car and shut the door behind her before stealing a quick glance at her reflection in the driver's side window. It was just lunch with Garrett; she wasn't sure why her hair even mattered.

Rue returned to her cousin's three days ago. Jace took Rue four-wheeling hours before she left. During her time at Hawkins Ridge, her aunt seemed more energetic and happier. Josie invited her to spend her days at the property if she wanted. Something told her Rue would.

While Josie kept her aunt busy, Claire and Jace spent quality time together. She helped him install her motorized blinds, give Luna and Oriole baths, and created a detailed question-naire with Noah for potential foster homes. The activities weren't anything special, but the normalcy meant more than a dozen fancy dates.

It was a taste of what life would be like with Jace.

A life she wanted.

Hence, when Garrett called to see if she was free for lunch, she jumped on the opportunity. Claire slipped her crossbody bag on and headed towards the Oak Mountain Burger Joint in the next block. The town council and the citizens of Oak Mountain made sure fast-food chains didn't litter every corner in town. They had regional franchises, but Oak Mountain firmly believed in supporting family-owned businesses.

A short honk drew Claire's attention. She waved to Izzy's husband as he drove by in his police cruiser just as she saw Garrett sitting on the bench outside the restaurant. His light brown hair needed a trim, but he maintained his clean-cut persona. Dressed in an Oak Mountain Feed collar shirt and a pair of jeans, her cousin drew looks of two women when they walked by. Garrett didn't give them the time of day. Once he caught sight of Claire, he stood and gave her a tight hug.

"What's up, cuz?" He flashed a crooked grin. Claire shook her head and laughed.

"Please don't tell me you're practicing 'dad slang' already? Don't be one of those fathers that try to be hip with his kid's friends."

"My kid and his friends are going to think I'm cool." Garrett stepped back and gave her a once over. "You look good."

"Thank you. Showering can make a tremendous differ-ence," she teased.

The aroma of grilled meat and fresh onions greeted Claire as she opened the door, causing her mouth to water. They placed their order at the counter, but a server would bring their meal. While Claire filled her cup with raspberry tea, she thought of how she wanted to tell Garrett about Jace. Could his call out of the blue mean he already knew? Sara and Tinsley's sister were friends. Could Tinsley have complained to her sister? Did she even know who Claire was? Perhaps Garrett just wanted to make up for canceling on her last week?

It didn't matter. People on the property knew about their relationship. They didn't hide it. Oak Mountain was her home now and if other people's lives were so boring that their relationship was the subject of gossip, so be it. Claire was happy, and that's all that mattered.

Claire chose a table in the back with a view of the library grounds. She sat their number at the edge of the table for the server to see. Garrett slid in across from her and placed his phone on the table.

For a moment, they made small talk about work. Thomas and Jace were having lunch with the owner of the feed store the next day to talk about the treats. Claire sent the contract for the partnership to Naomi's lawyer that morning. She didn't want to bring it up with Garrett in case the owner said no. Until she heard from him; she was keeping her lips sealed.

The server brought their order of bacon cheeseburgers, and a large basket of hand cut fries to split. Flavorful juice squirted in Claire's mouth when she took her first bite. The crispy salty bacon and perfectly seasoned beef had her swallowing a moan.

"Thank you for letting Mom stay at Hawkins Ridge," Garrett said after taking his own bite. A speck of avocado from his bacon burger dotted his lips. "She mentioned Josie gave her an open invitation during the rest of her visit. Can you give her my thanks?"

Claire held up a finger and spoke after taking a sip of tea. "Sure. Rue had a blast. Josie and Owen kept her busy. She spent a lot of time in the greenhouse. Balty was like a puppy again."

"I'm glad. It sounds like she's going to move."

Rue mentioned to Claire the day she left over breakfast she wanted to look at rentals in town. She hoped they could find something her aunt liked and in her price range.

Claire nodded. "I think so. Josie has taken her to meet a few women, even though Rue is a little younger."

"I had hoped she would get along with Sara's mother." Garrett shrugged. "I should have known better."

"They're different people, but it's not like Rue doesn't like her or anything."

"Oh, I know. Mom likes to stay busy. My mother-in-law's definition of busy is career advancement or making contacts."

Sara's family wanted her to date a boy from college, not the supervisor of the college's grounds crew. It took Garrett moving to Oak Mountain and buying Sara a house for her family to approve of him. Sara didn't care about any of that. She just wanted to be with Garrett.

"Maybe with Rue here full time and the baby coming, they will find more common ground," Claire suggested. Her cousin rolled his eyes.

"I'm sure the baby will be the only common ground. I like the Becketts a lot. They're good down-to-earth people and who I can see Mom being friends with."

This was the opening Claire needed. She sipped her tea to settle her nerves.

"Speaking of the Becketts, I wanted to let you know before you hear it from someone else in town. I'm seeing Jace."

Garrett's burger stopped inches from his mouth as he stared at her. "Seeing him? What does that mean?"

"We're dating."

He returned his burger to his plate and sat back in his chair. "Dating? His definition of dating is a few dinners followed by a weekend or two of *playing house*." Garrett said the last two words with obvious judgement. "You're not his type and deserve to be treated better. What about your job when he ends it after he gets what he wants? You're building something here in Oak Mountain. Don't throw it away hoping Jace will want the same things you do."

Claire shoved three fries in her mouth to stop the immediate retort. She needed to use calming words. His concerns were the same ones she used as an argument for the past months. If it was two months into her time in Oak Mountain, they would have merit. It's been a year. She knew Jace's heart. Garrett relied on town gossip and what his friends told him. He didn't know Jace as a person. Something Claire would have to change later.

"I understand what you're saying, but you're wrong. Jace has changed." She held up her hand to stop his response. "I listened to what you had to say. Now listen to me. I've gotten to know him this past year. Yes, he had a reputation of someone that wasn't looking for a relationship, but if you ask around, he hasn't been out with anyone in ten months. Want to know why? Because he wanted something more and knew keeping on that path wouldn't get it for him."

"So now he's this reformed man? How long do you think that will last?"

She wouldn't tell Garrett about Jace's college girlfriend; it wasn't his business. Claire had to approach it from another angle.

"I'm an adult. I know Jace better than you and the people spreading rumors about him. We've liked each other for a while but wanted to be friends first. I wanted to get myself settled at the sanctuary, and he needed to get a handle on his role at Hawkins Ridge. At Logan's wedding, he said he wanted more with me, but gave me time to think without pressure.

"A few weeks ago, I took a chance," she continued. "Jace is still the same caring man I was friends with, but now we're more. Rue even sees how he cares about me. She saw what I went through with Andy firsthand and still gave her blessings on our relationship."

Garrett dropped his head in his hands, groaning loudly. Luckily, no customers sat near them to hear their conversation. Claire took another bite of her burger while her cousin worked through his issues.

"What about when it ends?" Garrett said a few moments later. "Have you thought about that? Do you honestly think the Becketts would keep you on? You'd have to start over, again. I won't be able to help you get another job in another town."

"You got me an interview. I was the one that got the job. Me." Claire patted her chest before taking a breath. "Don't you think I've already considered that? If it doesn't work out and I have to leave Hawkins Ridge, then I'll find a job at a medical practice or maybe go back to school for something else."

Realization hit Claire as she said the words. Hawkins Ridge was a dream job, but she had options if the worst happened. She had the qualification to be a medical assistant. Heck, she could be a school nurse or work at a shelter. Starting over wasn't scary. Her gut said she wouldn't have to.

Jace proved he wanted their relationship to last. Claire definitely did. Nothing Garrett could say would change how she felt about Jace.

She rested her hand on his arm, drawing his gaze. "I love that you've always looked out for me and had my back. But I'm thirty-two and can make my own mistakes if it turns out to be one. Jace and I make each other happy. The reason I told you is so you wouldn't hear it from someone else."

Garrett squeezed her hand. "I hope you're right about him."

There was nothing more Claire could say or do. Garrett had his opinion, and she respected him for it. She knew it came from a place of love. Only time would prove him wrong. Something she hoped she and Jace had plenty of.

Maybe it was time to plan a dinner.

"I can't believe you talked me into clothes shopping," Noah said as he pulled a pair of jeans in his size from the display table. "Don't you have enough dress pants?"

"I need another pair of pants in beige or brown," Jace replied. He shoved hangers on the rack to the side until he saw the color he was looking for. "Besides, it will help the wings we inhaled digest."

"I told you to stop at ten. I don't know why I have to suffer through shopping." Noah draped the jeans and a T-shirt over his arm. "But I am getting these."

Jace laughed and held the pants in front of him. He would try them on at home and return them if they didn't fit.

Noah was right. Jace had enough pants he wore for meetings, but the two haven't had one-on-one time in two weeks, so he invited him to lunch. The last thing Jace wanted was for Noah to feel neglected because he was dating Claire. Jace helped with the care of the goats or making the milk products when he wasn't doing his own work, but it wasn't the same.

"Pops said Rue is thinking of moving," Noah said, moving to the display of belts. "That will be good for Claire."

"It will. It also gives Mom another cohort," Jace teased.

"That goes without saying."

Jace moved past his friend to the display of costume jewelry. The department store sold men's and women's clothing. He never had a reason to look for an item for a girlfriend, but now he wondered what she may like. Jace wanted to spoil her, but she made it clear when they were friends she liked things simple. He understood it came from growing up watching every penny. He respected her for making it on her own, but it made it hard when he wanted to do something nice.

A set of floral hair combs caught his attention. "Would Claire wear these?"

Noah stepped beside him and twisted his lips. "I don't know. She uses one of those hair thingies when she puts her hair in a ponytail. Maybe for a special occasion. Wait." Noah went to another display and lifted a piece of cardboard that held six scrunchies, two of them in a floral print. "What about these?"

"That works." Jace added the hair ties to his items, but kept the combs as well.

On their way to the cashier, Jace's phone rang. The screen displayed the name of the county co-op owner he scheduled to meet with the following week. He motioned for Noah to wait a minute. He did a brief glance around, thankful the section was empty of shoppers. If the man wanted to meet earlier or reschedule, Jace would agree. The co-op would be a tremendous boost to their goals and would help them with the expansions planned.

"This is Jace Beckett."

"Jace, Ethan Sanders here."

"Mr. Sanders. It's good to hear from you. Are you calling to confirm our meeting on Tuesday?"

The older man cleared his throat, triggering a red flag in Jace's mind. "Well, I spoke with my store managers. I don't feel now is a good time to bring new products into our stores. Online shopping has put a hit on our revenue and our customers are happy with the selection we have. I'm not sure they would be interested in something new."

"With all due respect, sir. The reason residents in the four counties shop at co-ops and regional grocers is because they offer local products from names that they've grown to trust.

Hawkins Ridge has offered quality organic produce, goat's milk, and cheeses for fifteen years. Communities trust us to deliver the best products. The top three steak houses in the county use our cheese for their menu."

Jace had a gut feeling why Ethan was passing on a deal with their business. He met Noah's concerned gaze and gave a slight head shake.

"That may be the case," Ethan's gruff voice argued, "but right now is not the best time for us. Perhaps in a year or two, we can revisit the possibility. Good luck."

The man hung up before Jace could respond. He let a string of curse words fly just as a salesperson walked by. After apologizing, he slipped his phone into his jean pocket. Jace summarized the other side of the conversation for Noah as they walked to the register.

"This came out of the blue. No one in this area orders milk and cheese online." Noah handed his clothes to the cashier before pulling out his wallet. "What do you really think is the reason?"

"Tinsley. She saw Claire and I kissing at the box store. I was worried about her saying something to Claire. Apparently, she went the other way."

"Do you really think that's the reason? You don't think she'd have her father pull the eggs and cheese orders from the diner, do you?"

Jace hadn't thought about that possibility. "We just renewed the contract a few months ago. I don't think they can, but renewing may be an issue. Regarding her squashing this po-tential deal, most definitely. The excuses he gave were weak."

"Ethan sees Tinsley as a daughter, so I guess it's not a surprise," Noah pointed out. "Selling the treats will help make up for losing the deal."

"I guess."

Jace paid for his clothes and Claire's gift, but his mind raced. The treats were to help finance the therapy dog training expansion. The rest of the expansion financing relied in part on that co-op deal. Now he would need to think of another avenue to pursue.

He thanked the cashier and stepped out into the sunny afternoon. Jace couldn't wrap his head around why Tinsley would purposely kill the deal before it even happened. For what reason? Did she think he would end things with Claire? Maybe ask her out again to get the contract with her uncle? Did she think manipulation would spark his interest? If so, then she truly was not the woman for him and he dodged a bullet, keeping it to one date.

Noah pressed the fob to unlock the truck's doors. They tossed their bags in the extended cab section before climbing in.

"Don't stress over this," Noah said, starting the engine. "We always figure out something. That's what this family does."

Noah and Owen may not be blood, but they were family in every sense of the word. He was right, as always. No matter what, Hawkins Ridge would meet the goals they set, and they would do it as a family.

Chapter Twenty

Hues of deep orange and vibrant red colored the skies as the sun disappeared behind the tall oak trees. Claire tilted her head and took in the glorious sight. The view was a perk of living in the foothills. She let her smile form to take her mind off her stressful lunch.

She wasn't angry with Garrett. Love fueled his concerns about her relationship with Jace, and he had a right to his opinion. As wrong as it was. She would give him time to come around, maybe invite him and Sara to dinner.

Claire clutched the tote bag that held ingredients for her dinner. She raided the greenhouse for romaine lettuce, radishes, and tomatoes. When she suggested a salad to Jace and Rue for dinner, both eagerly agreed. It seemed they all had big lunches and wanted something light.

Her aunt accepted Josie's invitation to spend the day at Hawkins Ridge. They worked with the cats and had lunch with friends. When Josie lined up two rentals for the next morning, Rue opted to spend the night. Balty was beside himself and spent his time playing with any dogs that crossed his path. Claire didn't know how he would adjust when they returned to Rue's small apartment at the end of the following week.

Josie planned another family dinner for the following night. Claire wanted to take advantage of having something low key with her favorite people. Instead of eating at Jace's, he set up a table and chairs on her side lawn that afternoon for them to eat on. Trying to fit three adults and three large dogs inside her house wouldn't be comfortable. Poor Cammie might have been stepped on.

She strolled through the gate leading to the sanctuary and caught sight of Jace leaning against a tree next to the chicken area. Luna, Oriole, and Balty stared into the tightly woven chicken wire, attempting to taunt the feather creatures. The four large roosters strutted in a protective mode. Claire was positive all three dogs would turn tail and run if the barrier wasn't in the way. Cammie, however, rolled in the grass enjoying the weather.

A blinding smile lit his face when he saw her, causing the butterflies in her stomach to take flight. Her usual reaction when she was around him. The dogs abandoned their game of intimidation and ran to meet her. She gave them all scratches while Jace closed the distance. He greeted her with a kiss.

"I was on my way to meet you but as you can see, chicken moment." Jace whistled, then clicked his tongue for Cammie to find them. When she was close, Claire picked her up and gave her a kiss.

"I'm glad I saved you some steps. How did you end up with Balty?" She knew he picked Luna, Oriole, and Cammie from Thomas, but Balty was with Naomi.

"I ran into Rue on her way to your place." Jace collected the leashes for the large dogs and guided them to walk. "I was hoping we could walk and chat."

Claire set Cammie down and wrapped her lead around her wrist so she could hold his hand. When they spoke earlier, he said he wanted to talk about something that happened. She planned to tell him about her talk with Garrett, but this sounded important. She figured something was up when she saw the Beckett brothers converged into their parents' house after lunch.

"Is everything okay?"

Jace told her about his conversation with Ethan Sanders and his suspicion it was because of Tinsley. Claire wanted to find the woman and yank her hair out. This was a woman in her thirties, a mother to boot, who still played high school games. A person who thought one date meant commitment. Claire wondered what sort of message she would tell her child when he had his first heartbreak.

"Are you going to talk to her about this?" Claire knew girls like Tinsley in high school who played games to get Garrett's attention. It wouldn't work as an adult.

Jace shook his head. "No. Dad made a good point. Did we really want to be in a business deal with someone easily manipulated over something childish? Things happen for a reason."

"Your father's a wise man."

"Don't let him hear you say that," Jace quipped.

Making business deals meant a lot for Hawkins Ridge to expand the sanctuary and get the therapy dog program really going. Jace felt the pressure to make them happen. His guilt laden eyes said this was eating him inside. Not just because of the deal falling through. It was because of his past. No wonder he wanted a quiet night.

"What else did your family say? What about the diner?" Claire mentally cringed at the thought of Hawkins Ridge losing them as a customer. They stopped for the dogs to sniff bushes.

"The contract states they can cancel if they go out of business, change ownership or the quality of our product drops. No one is worried about them." Jace shrugged. "I just have to research where we can put our products. We want to stick with small business and within a two-hour drive so we can deliver fresh. Ethan was the last co-op in the three counties."

Ideas popped into her mind, but she would bring them up at a better time. Now he needed to get this off his chest. He gently tugged for the dogs to walk again and finished speaking.

"While I'm coming up with different avenues to get more customers, I'm going to help Owen more. Did you hear we've narrowed the list of potential managers down to two? We want to bring them out for their final interview."

Claire nodded. "Logan mentioned it after lunch. I know Owen wanted to have someone by now."

"He did. The people we found willing to move from larger ranches and farms to someplace smaller were in their fifties and ready to retire in five years. That's why we had to go out of state."

Claire sat in on the initial virtual interviews. She understood why the Becketts expanded their search.

She nudged Cammie, who became obsessed smelling a bush. "You know I can help with whatever research you need for potential business opportunities."

He pressed a kiss to their joined hands. "I know. Thank you. Mom volunteered to help wherever we need her. I feel bad because they are supposed to be retired."

"But it's what we do. We back up those we love."

He stopped and held her in his gaze. Did she say something wrong? Should she not have volunteered to help? Maybe he wanted to solve the problem on his own? The worried lines that creased his forehead softened. She held her breath.

"I love you," he blurted. "For months I kept how I felt quiet because I didn't want to scare you off. But each day I'm with you, I can't keep quiet any longer. You have such a warm and caring heart. Thank you for giving me a chance to open up my heart again."

She didn't stop her feelings from rushing forward. She fell in love with Jace months ago when he took her to three different Christmas lots to find a tree that would fit in her house to decorate. He had more patience than her when she wanted to give up after the first lot. But they found one. She knew then how much he meant to her.

"I love you, too," she quietly replied. "I'm glad you let me see and get to know the real you. You make it easy to open my heart to you."

He leaned closer, brushing his lips against hers. He met her gaze. Feelings bottled up for months flowed freely when they deepened the kiss. This was her future. Jace, his family, Hawkins Ridge, her job. All of her dreams realized with a simple kiss.

Jace could kiss Claire for hours. It was actually his goal until Cammie bumped into his leg, followed by the other three dogs wanting to get in on the loving. He rested his forehead against hers and sighed.

"Our children and their cousin apparently want attention."

Claire giggled before kissing his cheek and taking a step back. "We should probably get back. I don't want Rue to worry."

It was a twenty-minute walk to and from the greenhouse. Jace was positive Rue would understand if they took longer, but she was right. Besides, they had her dog and he wouldn't want her to think something happened. They nudged the dogs to start walking again.

Jace hadn't planned to tell Claire he loved her. He definitely wasn't ready for her to return the sentiment. He meant it, though. Before Claire, when he thought of having a relationship like his parents, he didn't think it was possible. At least not for him.

But he was wrong.

A voluptuous beauty who wore glasses with a sharp tongue and a love for animals slayed his bachelor days. He couldn't be happier.

Claire listened when he told her about what happened. Like his brothers, no one blamed him. He blamed himself, but there was nothing he could do. He couldn't control Tinsley's feelings or how she interpreted their date. That part was all on her.

What he felt guilty about was what if he hadn't asked her out just to stop her endless flirting? Would she still have killed the deal? Could his past come back to bite Hawkins Ridge in the future? His father's words from earlier resurfaced in his mind.

"We can't change the past, Jace. All we can do is work for the now and future. No one expected this, but things happen for a reason. Something better will come along when you least expect it."

He was right. Getting caught up in the past and what ifs solves nothing. Jace had to find another deal, and he would. First, he had to focus on taking over part of Owen's management of the property and staff for the next month or two.

Also, to be a great boyfriend.

"Tell me about your lunch with Garrett."

Claire rolled her eyes. "He's just worried that I'm going to get hurt. He listens to gossip. I told him he has to get to know you. I figured once Rue returns home, we could have dinner with him and Sara."

"That's a great idea. He knows my parents and Owen better than he knows the rest of us. We say hi and all, but now that I think about it, he's never been out here."

She tapped her chin with the hand that held Cammie's leash. "You're right. Except for the day he helped me move in, he hasn't been out here. You were at the firehouse that day, so he only spent time with Logan."

"Then it's settled. Not a family dinner, just the four of us."

Claire flashed a smile that cemented his love. "Thank you."

"You're welcome."

She didn't need to thank him. Rue and Garrett were the only family Claire had left. Jace planned on spending the rest of his life with her, meaning they would one day be his family. He wasn't naïve to think he and Garrett would be best friends. But he knew what Garrett had heard, because he heard the same whispers. The only way to change his mind was to show him how much he cared about Claire. Something he didn't have a problem doing.

"Did you talk to Rue when you took Balty?" Claire asked as they rounded the slight bend, and her house came into view. He shook his head. "Izzy's mom knows of a house available next month. She's taking Rue to look at it tomorrow. It's near the high school. An old caretaker place the owners renovated a few years ago for their son and his wife."

Jace nodded. He knew the house and the owners. It was on a former plantation they'd converted into a bed-and-breakfast. Last he heard, the couple planned on renting it as a cottage for guests who wanted privacy. However, they changed their mind thinking a long-term renter would mean extra income. The home was away from the main house and the guests wouldn't bother her. It would be perfect for Rue and Balty.

"I know where it is. There's plenty of room for Balty to run around. We can go down to help her pack and move." Jace, at least, would make himself available if she asked.

"I'm sure she'd appreciate it."

Jace dropped the leashes when they passed the large oak in Claire's front yard. Luna and Oriole guided Cammie up Claire's walkway. Rue sat on the porch with a book in her hand. She greeted the dogs with a lot of loving words.

"I thought you got lost," she teased.

Claire apologized and gave her aunt a side hug. "Sorry. We got to talking. Let me get these cleaned and chopped, then we can eat."

"Let me help," Rue said, but Jace gently rested his hand on her shoulder.

"We got this. I'll bring out food and water for the dogs," Jace volunteered. "If you wouldn't mind making sure Cammie doesn't get stuck somewhere."

The dog in question sat beside Oriole with her tiny muzzle tilted to the sky. It was her way of cataloging scents in case she ever became lost on the property. Something he was sure Oriole wouldn't let happen.

Rue grasped his hand to stop him as Claire stepped inside. Jace hoped he wasn't in trouble.

"I know Claire talked to you about Garrett. Don't let him put a wedge between you two."

Jace squatted to be eye level with the woman. "I have no intention of letting that happen. You're right, she told me about their lunch. We realized he doesn't know me and plan to invite him and Sara to dinner in a couple of weeks. Give him time to come to terms with the news and for him to see how much I care about her."

She patted his hand. "I told him he was wrong, and I've seen you two together. Garrett loves Claire like a sister. He protected her in school from the bullies, including that snake in the grass, Andy. Had to stop Garrett from coming back to Virginia to kick his butt."

Jace laughed because he would do the same thing if he had a sister. "I understand why he is protective, and I don't blame him. The only way I can stop the rumors of my past is to show that I've changed. I've been doing that since I accepted Claire was the woman I wanted. It will take time and I'm okay with that. We have a lifetime to show Oak Mountain that she's my world. That includes your son."

"You have my support." Rue kissed his cheek. "You make her happy. That's all my sister and I ever wanted for her. Dot would approve."

That meant more to Jace than he could express. He gave a warm nod before rising to his full height. It was time to look forward. He and Claire couldn't live in the past. They were together, partners. Building a life together started now. Lost deals and concerned family members were things Jace could handle.

As long as he had Claire, he could achieve anything.

Chapter Twenty-One

Jace laughed silently as Claire peppered Luna, Oriole, and Cammie's faces with kisses. To say she loved their dogs was an understatement. When they planned dates, she always asked if the dogs were going. This would be their first one without them.

Jace couldn't wait until the first time she entrusted their child with a babysitter.

"Are you sure you don't mind watching them?" Claire asked Logan from her kneeling position. "We don't need to stay for the second movie if it's a problem."

"Yes, we do," Jace said as he helped her stand. "It's a double feature with an actor you love."

"But that's nine dogs," she argued.

"Who we've watched before," Logan added, a teasing smile on his lips. "Mom, Dad, and Caden are coming over to play board games. Fiona is at her friend for the night. Naomi should be up from her nap soon. It will be fine."

Jace heard the old drive-in outside of town was showing a double feature matinee starring Jimmy Stewart. Claire loved old black and white movies. She couldn't afford cable her first year after leaving home. Rue gave her two boxes of old DVDs she watched when she wasn't working. *Vertigo* and

Rear Window were her favorites and scheduled to start in ninety minutes.

"Buttercup, we have to go if we want time to stop past the grocery store."

Claire's mouth formed an O when she checked her watch. "Sorry. Thank you again. Whenever you need us to watch the dogs, let us know."

"Will do. Have fun." Logan shook his head when she said bye to every dog in the room. "She's going to be a wreck the day you don't have a babysitter."

"If I had known she'd be like this, I would have gone to the store after breakfast."

"But this is why you love her."

Jace's cheeks pinked. "Yeah, it is."

Claire apologized again as she gave Logan a quick hug and hurried out the door. Jace caught up with her on the walkway and clasped her hand.

"Are you okay?"

She shrugged. "Yep. I don't want her to think I'm abandoning her."

"She's not going to think that. You leave her during the day to check on patients."

"True. She's usually with the other dogs or in the office with Shorty."

Jace pressed the fob to unlock the doors. He guided her to the passenger side and helped her in. He finished the conversation when he climbed behind the wheel.

"I could see if we were leaving her with people we didn't know, but she loves everyone that will be there tonight. Plus, she'll be with her small pack."

She sighed. "I know I'm being irrational, but she's my baby."

"You may not know, but I was the same way with Cammie." He put the truck in drive and headed off the property. "After her surgery, I was worried sick she'd knock over something and hurt herself."

"Is that why you took her everywhere?"

"Yep. My parents stopped by one day and told me Cammie needed to learn how to be independent. So we worked with her and you see her now."

Claire's laugh lit up the cab. "She's better than some of the other dogs getting around."

"Right. But the only way she became the pocket-sized dynamo she is today is because I had to take a step back and let her learn. Luna is with people and animals she loves. She knows you're coming back, and she won't forget you."

"You're right." She gave his hand a squeeze as he turned onto the mountain road. "Thank you for talking me down."

"You'd do the same for me."

Jace knew she would, too. Claire was that person you vented to. The one who would just listen while you talk through whatever was bothering you. She dripped empathy. The animals always ran to meet her. Even the ornery buck goat, who purposely head butted everyone, nuzzled her.

"I've never been to a drive-in. Rue said my hometown used to have one when she moved to the area." Claire focused on the passing scenery. "It's going to be great seeing these movies on a big screen."

"I remember the first time you saw *Vertigo* on my eighty-inch TV."

She poked him in the shoulder, laughing. "It was perfect, but tonight may spoil it the next time I want to watch it at home."

"We could always get a projector, mount a retractable screen to the back of the house and watch movies that way."

"Not gonna lie. That sounds amazing. Even though I know you and your brothers would use it to watch sports."

The thought of watching baseball and football appealed to him. He made a mental note to mention it to them at breakfast.

Claire's eyes twinkled. "You're thinking about watching the Orioles now, aren't you?"

"Yep, and I'm sure I could talk everyone into helping me set it up." Jace pulled into the Oak Mountain Market parking lot and found a spot near the end. "Remind me to bring it up at breakfast."

"Only if you let me use it for our girls' movie night." He brought their joined hands to his lips and kissed her wrist.

"Deal."

Jace climbed out, pocketing his phone as he jogged around to the passenger side to help her out. He tried not to get too excited hearing her plan for a future that involved his house. He wanted her to think of his house as an extension of her home. Heck, Luna had a dog bed there already. It was only a matter of time anyway before Jace made it official. He wanted Rue in Oak Mountain first before he popped the question. He would bide his time until then.

Jace linked his fingers with hers and led her to the entrance. Usually, he enjoyed movie concessions, but the theater no longer had a stand. Instead, they allowed patrons to bring in outside food. When he heard of the drive-in feature, he placed an order for easy to eat foods. Pasta salad, salami, cheese, crackers, and carbonated flavored water. He packed her favorite bagged popcorn and a variety of candies in the lockbox of his truck before meeting her at Logan's.

The bustle of voices greeted them when the automatic doors opened. An older couple who knew his parents acknowledged them with a curious smile after taking in their joined hands. When Claire went to remove her hand, he held on tight.

"If the people who saw us at the art crawl haven't spread the news of us dating, this outing will," he mumbled in her ear. "People will stare. Nothing we can do about it. What we will do is ignore them and hold our heads high. Right?"

Claire rose to her tiptoes and kissed his cheek. "Right."

"That's my girl. Now, let's get our snack and go watch our movies."

The deli sat near the cash register. Unfortunately, one of his former dates was working the counter. He kept hold of Claire's hand and greeted the woman with a quick smile.

"Hey, Erica. Picking up an order?"

"Jace. I was wondering if this was for you. Let me get it." Erica gave Claire a look before turning towards the industrial refrigerators and pulling out a large canvas tote. "I heard you were dating Sara's cousin–in–law."

"Her name is Claire." Jace didn't mask his annoyance.

"Don't get snippy," Erica said around a chuckle. She handed him the ticket and bag. "I'm glad for you. I held no false illusion when we went out two years ago. Unlike a few women, I knew we would have fun, and that was it. I started dating Oscar three months ago. We're in love and talking about moving in together. Our kids get along and actually were the ones who set us up."

"Really?" Claire flashed a genuine smile. "How did they do that?"

"I should have known something was up when my daughter said her friend's father could fix the dishwasher." Erica rested a hip on the counter. "I think she used too much dish detergent on purpose, but I can't prove it. Anyway, Oscar shows up wearing a tight T-shirt that showed off his tattoos. Let me tell you, he was all kinds of yummy. I offered him a beer when he finished, and we've been together ever sense."

Claire rested her hand on her chest. "Aww, that's so romantic."

"Isn't it? He made me a prime rib for my birthday. My mother just loves him."

"That is so important." Claire nodded.

Jace knew if he didn't put an end to this instant friendship, they'd be here forever. Claire preferred animals over people. But when she met anyone with a kind smile who said hi first, she wanted to talk. Jace chalked it up to only having Garrett as a friend growing up.

"We really need to go or we're going to miss the beginning of the movie. I'm happy for you and Oscar."

"We'll have to double date sometime. Sara has my number," Erica called out as he led Claire away from the counter.

They quickly checked out and headed toward the truck. They waved to a couple who worked at the property before climbing in.

"We're not going to double date with them, are we?" Claire asked, humor in her voice.

"Not a chance. Erica is nice, but the guy she's with tried to bully Noah in high school."

"Tried?"

Jace laughed. "He forgot that messing with Noah is like messing with the Beckett brothers. We didn't have a problem reminding him and his friends."

"I can see that. By some chance, was Izzy part of your reminding crew? I heard from reliable sources she had a tendency to support putting people in their places."

"Was that reliable source Izzy?"

Claire chuckled as she adjusted her brace. "I promised full anonymity."

"That's what I thought. Izzy may have offered to handle any girls that showed up."

Jace shook his head, thinking of his lifelong friend. Izzy, like Claire, stood up for those who couldn't stand up for themselves. She chalked it up to having five brothers and being the only girl. Her family and friends knew underneath the tattoos was a woman with a heart the size of Alaska.

"There's a chance this Oscar person may have changed," Claire said when he took a back road to avoid taking the highway for one exit. "You changed and everyone sees that. Maybe he has too."

Jace thought about the statement. Not about Oscar, but about change. His initial reason for changing his playboy ways was for the woman sitting in the passenger seat. Then it turned into taking his role at Hawkins Ridge seriously. When did he change for himself? Could the two reasons be excuses he told himself to do what he knew he needed to do? Perhaps.

A memory surfaced when he told his parents and brothers he successfully negotiated the deal with the steakhouses. The feeling of seeing the pride on their faces was better than all his dates since college combined. That was when he knew he made the right decision. Logan asked him the night before his wedding; what would he do if Claire wanted to remain friends? Would he return to his old ways? Jace considered the question for a long minute. He eventually said no, he wouldn't. It would hurt, yes, but deep down, he didn't like the old version of himself. Jace recognized changing for himself was the only way it would last. Getting Claire was the icing on top.

"I agree there's a chance Oscar has changed," Jace said, continuing the conversation. "But don't you think it would be weird to double date with someone I've spent a weekend with?"

"Huh. I didn't think about it like that. You're right, no double date with them or anyone else you've *spent time* with."

Jace laughed when she used the air quotes. He turned on the road that led to their destination. The theater sat in a small clearing surrounded by mature trees with an extra thick canopy. It always sat in a shade. Though they started showing movies at three, the sun was never an issue.

"Speaking of change, have you talked to Garrett?" Jace worried he would have to have a conversation with her cousin. Claire sighed.

"No, but Sara and Rue have texted. They think he just needs time to see that you're serious."

"Does it bother you he isn't trusting your decision?"

She shrugged. "At first, but he knows you can't fool his mother. Rue likes you and sees our feelings are real and she told him. I think at this point it's a little pride."

Jace pulled up to the older man sitting underneath an umbrella behind a folding table. The grizzled man with wild white hair and overalls moseyed his way to the driver's window. He flashed a knowing grin and held out his hand.

"Thirty bucks for both movies. Sound is on FM 89.1. Pickup trucks park in the rear. Don't think about doing anything more than simple kissing or else you get kicked out." He lifted a brow. "I know your father, Jace Beckett. I have no problem giving him a call."

Jace handed him the cash. The old-timers still saw him as the snot-nosed teenager. "I know you would, Mr. Jones."

"Don't let him get fresh, young lady." The older man looked around him. "Oh, I know you. You work at Hawkins Ridge with Logan and little Izzy."

Claire leaned forward and gave a smile. "Yes, sir. Claire Everson."

"Good to meet you official like. Jace here will tell you I'm serious about only light kissing. We have families bringing their little ones. They don't need to see anything like that."

Claire winked. "I'll keep him in check."

Jace faced her, a crooked grin on his lips. "Really?"

Mr. Jones cackled and sent them on their way. Jace pulled into a spot in the back row and tuned the radio. He hopped out and grabbed the snacks from the lockbox.

"I like Mr. Jones," Claire said when he returned to the cab. "There are more people than I expected."

Jace counted ten other cars and trucks. He spoke as he handed her the bag. "This is on the Jones' property, and they only show movies in the spring and fall. They say it's too hot in the summer and cold in the winter. Rumor has it this is their last year having a theater."

"That's a shame. I'm glad I get to experience this with you."

Jace brought her hand to his lips and kissed the tip of her fingers. "Me too."

Change is good.

Chapter Twenty-Two

Steady pitter patter of raindrops bounced off the roof of the Oak Mountain community center. Residents splashed puddles as they darted from their cars for the dryness of the free-standing brick building. The gloominess of the weather outside didn't stop the excited voices and important tasks inside.

Claire smiled as she took a damp rag to a stackable chair before sliding it to the ones ready for placement in the largest room in the center.

"I was promised food," Izzy said, snapping a black trash bag and stuffing it into a metal garbage can.

"No, your mother threatened you with no more free babysitting if you didn't help," Naomi teased from beside Claire as she wiped long folding tables.

"She still promised to feed me," Izzy argued, then turned a pointed playful glare at her friend. "It didn't help that my boss agreed to close the practice today, so I couldn't use work as an excuse."

Naomi laughed. "You're the one that said we were going to be the biddies running the town in twenty or thirty years. We need to see what that entails."

Claire coughed out a laugh. "You eagerly agreed when Josie and Maeve asked because you didn't want to help Logan go through the boxes in your catch all room."

"That too," Naomi agreed, causing them all to double over in laughter.

The three were helping set up for the seed exchange and community flea market scheduled for the following day. The event allowed residents to share seeds and seedlings, mostly flowers and plants, with their neighbors. If you didn't have seeds but an old set of dishes you wanted to sell, you could sign up for a table to peddle your items or handmade crafts. Claire and Jace signed up for a table for their old items and the dog treats.

Three weeks had passed since the deal with Ethan Sanders fell through. Claire expected Jace to mope or run himself tired over finding new avenues for their products. But that wasn't the case. Her boyfriend grabbed the responsibility of helping Owen run the property with both hands. She wondered if he regretted not going the property management path after college. But he enjoyed meeting people and marketing. He was good at it. It was how they had the dog treats at the feed store and vet offices in the neighboring counties.

Claire signed the contract with Hawkins Ridge for the use of her recipes and the percentage of the profit. The offer was fair and would allow Claire to continue building a nest egg. The Becketts pushed back on the addendum the lawyer added to buy Claire out if she left Hawkins Ridge. Logan swore it would never happen. They considered her family, but Josie helped the men to understand anything could happen and

Claire was looking out for herself and any children she might have.

"Are you still taking the two days off at the end of the month?" Izzy asked as she picked up a rag to help wipe the furniture. Claire nodded.

"Jace rented rooms for us last night. Garrett will already be there to help pack. We want to be on the road the next day by noon."

"Josie has everyone meeting at the rental by three to help unpack," Naomi added.

Rue rented the house on the plantation the moment she saw it. She returned to Virginia last week. The management company allowed her to break the lease. She only had two months remaining and was a wonderful tenant. Her doctor referred her to two pain management clinics in Stark Valley, easing the major concern for her aunt. Excitement didn't describe how happy Claire was that her aunt would be near. She hoped there wouldn't be an issue with Garrett.

Claire invited her cousin and wife to dinner the following weekend. Jace was an important part of her life, and she wanted her cousin and him to get along. Rue planned to visit Hawkins Ridge regularly and wanted Garrett to come to terms with everything. He promised he would have an open mind.

Heavy footsteps in the hallway drew their attention. Thomas and Naomi's future stepfather, Harold, strolled into the cramp storage area. Both wore wide grins.

"Ladies, are these ready to go?" Thomas said, looking around the space.

"We just finished the last table." Naomi stood and stretched her back. "They have the hand carts to make it easier."

"Don't you even think about trying to carry something, Doc," Thomas fussed at his daughter-in-law. "There weren't chemicals in the wash water, was there?"

Naomi rolled her eyes at his over-protectiveness and went about stacking chairs. Thomas and Naomi had a special bond. Josie said it was because he always wanted a daughter and why he had spoiled Fiona since birth.

"Just plain soap and water," Claire answered. "Are they finished mopping the main room?"

Harold nodded and pushed a handcart underneath a stack. "Jace had to run Josie to the hardware store for more of that removable tape. The helpers are setting up refreshments."

"Please tell me it's more than veggie sticks." Hope danced in Izzy's eyes. Thomas chuckled.

"Ophelia's on her way with fried chicken, potato salad, and biscuits from the shop."

"And your mother picked up cupcakes from the bakery," Harold said, wrapping his thick arm around Naomi's shoulder. "We need to make sure the baby eats."

"The pea is eating just fine thanks to her father shoving apple slices on me." Naomi laughed warmly.

They quickly stacked the chairs and tables onto the various carts and rolled them into the next room. Colorful balloon clusters greeted them when they walked in. Handmade signs hung from the rafters to inform potential shoppers where they could find seeds, foods, and their next treasure. Izzy's brother and father hurried over to help set up the furniture.

Thomas let out a long growl upon hearing loud, pitch laughter. Everyone turned to see who had arrived. The rest of their small group groaned. Tinsley and two other women strolled in carrying boxes of supplies. The ladies glared at Claire and Naomi when they walked by. Claire laughed in response, carrying two chairs to the check-in area.

"I thought we were out of high school," she commented to Naomi.

"Please. Pettiness knows no age." Naomi grasped Thomas' arm. "You behave."

Thomas' eyes went wide. "I always behave."

Everyone in their small group snorted in unison.

"She better not give me heartburn," Izzy commented loudly as she helped her brother move a table to the opposite side of the room. "I get slappy when I get heartburn."

"Like you need an excuse to slap someone," her brother teased, causing pink to rise in Izzy's cheeks.

Claire loved her friends. The Becketts told their friends what happened with the deal and who was responsible. Josie wanted to kick Tinsley's mother off the planning committee, but Jace told her that would do more harm than good. It wasn't her mother's fault her daughter was manipulative, he said. Tinsley's father contacted Thomas to tell him not to worry about losing the diner as a customer. Either way, Ethan stuck to his guns about not doing business with Hawkins Ridge.

Ophelia Norris, the owner of the butcher shop, hurried in shaking water from her umbrella onto the mat. She pushed the hood on her slicker back. Little drops of water dotted her afro. She waved to Thomas and shuffled over.

"Is Jace here?"

"He should be back soon. He and Josie went to the store. Do you need help with the food?"

She handed the keys to Thomas. "Everything in the back seat. When you see Jace, tell him I need to talk to him about something." Thomas, Harold, and Izzy's father took off for the parking lot. Ophelia noticed Claire and gave a warm smile. "I'm glad you're here. I made a special mesquite jerky for you to say thank you. That batch of treats you made for Bruno that had his medicine in it worked wonders. He could always tell when we put it in his food. Smart old dog."

Claire squeezed the older woman's hand. "I'm glad it worked. Let me help you set up the food."

"No need. I got everything in serving trays. Just take off the lid and tell people to get in line. You finish what you need to do so you can make a plate."

Claire did as she was told and helped Naomi set up chairs behind tables. She turned to get another stack of two when someone bumped into her. Prepared to apologize, she scowled when she saw Tinsley and her minions. Apparently, the bump was not an accident. Claire shook her head and lifted the chairs from the cart.

"You know he's only with you out of pity." Tinsley sneered. "I mean, why would someone like Jace Beckett be with someone like you unless he felt sorry for you?"

"She's not even pretty," one of the other ladies commented.

"Pretty enough to get a relationship from him," Claire countered, sliding the chair under the table. Izzy and Naomi stood behind her. "From my understanding, you couldn't even get a second date."

Tinsley tilted her thin chin in the air, flipping her long bottle blonde hair over her shoulder. "I turned him down when he asked me out again."

Claire knew that was a lie, but it was Izzy who called her on it. "Please. You weren't smart enough for him to even consider a second date. Everyone knows the only reason he even asked you out was because he wanted to stop your pathetic flirting."

"That's a lie. He's been attracted to me since high school. Jace just waited until my divorce was final to ask me out." Tinsley gave Claire a once over. "You're delusional to think he would ever give you what you're looking for. It's only a matter of time before he moves to someone thinner who would look good on his arm. Jace doesn't care about you. You'll never be good enough for the Becketts to accept. You're just ugly, fat, trailer park trash."

A scathing comeback formed on Claire's lips when she noticed the background chatter came to an abrupt end. A quick glance over Tinsley's shoulder brought a smile to her lips. She didn't need anyone to fight her battles anymore. Claire wouldn't let bullies tell her she wasn't worthy anymore.

She pushed up her glasses and spoke with confidence. "Growing up, girls like you got off on picking on those you felt were beneath you. It's usually because you didn't have self-esteem or thought being easy was the only way you could get people, boys usually, to like you. When those same boys didn't give you the time of day, it was always their problem. It was never you.

"Now that you're an adult, nothing's change," Claire continued. "You're too busy working on your outer shell instead of working on your vile, bitter, and petty personality. Jace chose someone *you feel* isn't worthy, but let me tell you, I am worthy of his love and that of his family."

"Got that right!" Josie yelled, causing Tinsley to turn. The color drained from her face when she saw the audience. Jace and Josie were mere feet from her.

"I love Claire," Jace said with conviction. "Nothing you can do to me or our family's business will change that. If you have anything else you want to say about my relationship, come to me and say it."

"Or me," Josie added.

"Ditto for me too," Thomas piped up.

"You don't have the nerve to say anything to me," Izzy chimed in. "Now, if you don't mind, I am ready to eat, and your presence is making it difficult."

Claire glanced at her friend and laughed. Tinsley huffed and stormed from the room. Her girlfriends on her heels.

"You heard Izzy," Ophelia called out. "Let's eat."

Everyone spoke at once as they made their way to the food table. If the town had doubts about their relationship, Jace cleared any confusion with the simple professing of love. Jace took her hand and guided her off to the side.

"Are you okay?"

"I am. Did you hear everything she said?"

Jace nodded. "I'm glad you didn't believe her lies."

"I knew the truth. You show me every day how much you love me. Tinsley had this dream that you two would end up together and is just upset it didn't happen. She went back to her childish high school tactics, hoping it would change the outcome. You know, Naomi told Thomas to behave when she came into the room."

Jace laughed, pressing a kiss to her forehead. "I had to stop Mom from stepping in when she saw you two."

"People don't realize she can be worse than your dad." Claire linked her fingers with his. "Ms. Ophelia brought me some jerky I wouldn't mind sharing with you this evening. Oh, and she wants to talk to you about something."

"I hope she doesn't mind talking to me while I inhale some chicken."

The two walked towards the food line, hand in hand. People squeezed her arm or gave encouraging smiles as they passed. Love washed over Claire as she took in those in the room. These people accepted her for her. They didn't care where she grew up or if she had visible scars.

Claire's fear of losing this community nearly kept her from the love she deserved. She's thankful she took a chance.

Jace kept his hand on her lower back as he guided her towards the food line. The town knew they were dating a couple of weeks ago when they went grocery shopping. His declaration a few minutes ago should leave no doubts in anyone's mind about his seriousness for Claire.

He loved her and didn't care who knew.

Stepping into the main room at the community center and seeing Claire face to face with Tinsley had him seeing red. Thomas rested his hand on Jace's shoulder and shook his head. Claire had to let the haters know she wasn't one to be bullied. Granted, he saw Izzy at her back and knew his childhood friend would jump in if needed, but it wasn't necessary. When

Josie made a move to say something, they both told her the same thing. He moved closer, so she knew he was there, just in case. Whether that gave her confidence, he didn't know. But she stood straighter and held her own. Jace couldn't be prouder.

The succulent aroma of garlic, pepper, and paprika pulled Jace's attention to the steaming food in front of him. Mrs. Ophelia offered fresh fried chicken at the butcher shop once a month. No one knew which day until they received an email the day before, telling people to place orders. Since she was part of the planning committee, it was a treat. Jace loved his mother's and Owen's fried chicken, but something about Ophelia's almost brought tears to the eyes.

The woman in question stood behind the table, handing plates and utensils to everyone. She met him and Claire and gave them both a hug.

"Good to see you put that woman in her place." Ophelia shook her head. "I'm proud of you both. Make sure you get an extra piece of chicken, and Claire, I gave your jerky to Josie."

"You didn't need to do that, Mrs. Ophelia, but thank you."

The older woman waved her hand dismissively and return to her post. Jace spoke while he scooped potato salad onto Claire's plate, then his.

"I hear you wanted to talk to me," he said. "Did you need me to move or hang something?"

"Nothing like that. Go on and finish fixing your plate. I'll be over in a minute. Save me a seat."

Jace didn't know what was going on, but he hoped she didn't mind him chewing while he listened. He fished two waters from the cooler, tucked them in his pocket and led

Claire to the table his parents, Izzy, and Naomi were sitting. Izzy waved a drumstick in her hand while she talked to his parents.

"I'm just saying that woman has guts." Izzy shook her head. Her red ponytail whipped back and forth. "No clue what she was thinking, but she picked the wrong day to go against our girl."

Red tinted Claire's cheeks as she focused on the lunch. Josie reached over and patted his girlfriend's hand.

"I'm glad you know how much we love you."

"We all do," Naomi added.

Maeve, Naomi's mother, and Harold joined them with Ophelia. The older woman wasted no time, leaning forward so everyone could hear.

"We met with the new owner for the resort in Stark Valley. You know that local boy who made his money playing football and now wants to build tourism for the county?" Everyone nodded. Ophelia continued, "Anyway, he is determined to use as many local farms as possible. Well, we cooked him a few pieces of our beef, including a filet mignon with your goat cheese and a balsamic reduction. He fell in love and wants to put it on the menu. When he asked to taste the cheese separately, he said he wanted to know the farm so he can use them for their recipes."

Jace stopped in mid chew. Was she saying what he thought she was saying? His mother spoke for him.

"He wants to use our cheeses?"

Ophelia flashed a wide grin and slid a piece of paper to him. "I gave him your contact information, and he told me to give you his. He's expecting a call."

Wes Chambers went to high school in the neighboring town and was a year or two older than Logan. He grew up on a chicken farm that went under while Wes was in college. He purchased the land back once he signed his NFL contract, but his family didn't want to start the farm again. Instead, he built homes for himself and his parents. Wes understood the survival of the local farms meant helping each other. Getting a deal with the resort would surpass the profit they would have made with Ethan's co-ops.

Jace swallowed his bite and found his voice. "I don't know what to say, Ms. Ophelia. Thank you. I will call him once I'm done eating."

"No need to thank me. Our families have been friends since before Josie and I were born. You do your thing, and you'll have a deal in no time."

It was true. Jace's grandfather brokered a deal with Ophelia's in-laws almost eighty years ago. As one of the few Black farms still in a segregated time, the Hawkins clan paved the way for other White farms to take a chance on the Norris' beef. Now the butcher shop sells poultry and pork to the same farms who struck a deal two generations ago.

"I read he plans on making the resort dog-friendly starting this summer," Claire said, meeting everyone's gaze. "We can give samples of the treats for each guest with pets, then see if they will sell the larger packs in their gift shops."

"The soaps too," Naomi pointed at Jace. "We can put something on the label about donating, fostering or adopting from the shelter in Stark Valley or their local shelter. These are the people that treat their dogs like children if they're bringing them on a snow or hiking vacation."

Thomas agreed. "I think we need to invite him to Hawkins Ridge. Let him see the operation."

Jace hadn't heard about making the resort pet friendly. He did, however, have the same idea as his father. Ideas volleyed for prominence in his mind, and he made a mental list he would jot down on his phone when he finished eating.

Claire gave him a side hug and flashed a smile that shot through his heart.

"You got this, baby. Like Thomas said, things happen for a reason."

He pressed a kiss to her forehead. With the support of Claire, his family, and friends, Jace would make this work.

Chapter Twenty-Three

Wondrous smells of fresh baked good complemented the myriad sounds of laughter and excited chatter in the main room of the community center. Next to the winter festival, the seed swap and flea market brought the residents of Oak Mountain out in force. The weekend long event was not one to be missed.

Claire loved every minute.

Josie and Thomas manned the Beckett's seed selections. Tiny individual plastic bags held apple, green beans, kale, lettuces, and cucumbers seeds. A sampling of each fruit and vegetable was available for people to taste if they doubted the quality of the seeds.

Claire and Jace peddled the fresh batch of dog treats, along with the hidden treasures found in closets on the property. Claire claimed a set of dishes Josie forgot she had before it even hit the table. It would be her first matching set as an adult. She couldn't wait to serve a meal for her friends on them.

Claire spared a glance at Jace as he spoke with a couple she'd seen around town. He told a story of the hand crank ice cream maker they were interested in. He was in his element. Jace enjoyed engaging with people. It was why he did well negotiating deals. And the reason Wes Chambers scheduled a visit to Hawkins Ridge the following week.

True to his word, Jace contacted the resort owner after he finished eating the day before. The two spoke for over fifteen minutes. Mr. Chambers knew of Hawkins Ridge from growing up in the area but didn't know it had branched into selling products to businesses. He also expressed an interest in supporting the sanctuary and animal therapy project. Josie called a Sunday family dinner to go over his visit.

"Take a sample of the chicken and beef treats." Jace pressed a bag into the man's hand after slipping a five-dollar bill into his pocket. "If your dog likes them, they're on sale at the feed store or call me and I can deliver them to you."

"Thanks, Jace. Good seeing you again." The man smiled at Claire. "Congrats on settling down."

Jace wrapped his arm around Claire's shoulder. "Just waited for the right woman. Enjoy the ice cream maker."

Heat rose to her cheeks as she gave them a small wave. As with most small towns, gossip ran wild. News spread of Claire's confrontation with Tinsley and Jace's declaration. People offered well wishes on their relationship most of the morning. It was the sense of community and acceptance she associated with Oak Mountain.

"Claire?" a familiar voice called out.

She let her gaze roam the crowd until she met Sara's bright blue eyes. Garrett held hands with his wife while pulling a shopping tote with wheels. Her cousin-in-law had the adorable pregnancy glow. A white button-down shirt covered her tiny baby bump. Sara styled her shiny blonde hair into a thick braid that hung over her shoulder. The woman could model for any expectant mother's magazine.

Sara led Garrett as they weaved around a circle of teenage girls on their way to the table. Jace kept his arm around her. Claire prayed Garrett left his negativity at home.

"Hey, you two," Claire said in greeting and came around the table to offer a hug. "I thought you were doing the baby registry today."

Garrett held their embrace a moment longer than Claire expected. Was that his way of apologizing? He answered her statement when they took a step back.

"We just came back. Neither of us wanted to deal with the crowd at the box store." He stepped closer to the table and stuck out his hand. "Jace."

Her boyfriend shook his hand. "Nice to see you two. Picked up a few things I see."

Sara's smile was wide. "We found a few things for the baby's room. Mrs. Talbot had the cutest baby quilt."

"I bought one of her quilts a couple of months ago. I'm thinking about looking at her selection for a housewarming gift for Rue." Claire turned to stand beside Jace, but Garrett rested his hand on her arm.

"You got a minute?"

She made eye contact with Jace, who watched the inter-action from a distance. Sara's attention turned to the box of books on the table. He gave a quick nod before placing a second box of books for the expectant mother to peruse.

The last thing Claire wanted was to cause another scene if Garrett became rude or negative. She hated being the center of attention. They stepped into the hallway and faced each other. Garrett rubbed the back of his neck, glancing at the floor.

"I heard what happened yesterday. Are you okay?"

"I'm fine. It felt good to stand up to her." Claire didn't know how many people knew of Tinsley's actions with her uncle and didn't want to bring it up, just in case. "She's just like the bullies from school, but older."

"Her sister told Sara how embarrassed their mother was over everything and told Tinsley she needed to grow up."

"Maybe she'll listen."

"I heard Jace confessed his love for you in front of everyone. Seems I may have been wrong about his intention. Understand, I've been here three years longer than you. All I've heard was how he didn't believe in commitment. He dated a couple of Sara's friends, so I heard it firsthand. Then, to say you two were seeing each other, I figured it would leave to heartache in a matter of weeks."

They waved to a family, leaving the event. The husband worked at the stable with Caden. Claire thought of letting her cousin off easy. However, she still had things to say.

"I told you at lunch Jace cared for me. You thought it was an act. Rue even told you, and all that did was convince you to have dinner so you could see for yourself." Claire pushed up her glasses and sighed. She listened to the rumors also when she first moved to town. She couldn't hold that over her cousin. "I understand why you were skeptical. I judged him based on those same rumors. The difference is I got to know him and you didn't. You were still only hearing old tales."

"I'm sorry. You're right, I should have listened to you and Mom." Garrett's shoulders slumped.

Now that he explained it better, his reaction made sense at lunch. Claire thought he should have trusted her to make her own decision. Heck, at least trust his mother. Growing up, Garrett protected her. Now it was time he learned she could protect herself.

"I get that. Jace asked me out a month after I started, but I turned him down. Mostly because of what you told me about him, but also because I wanted to make the sanctuary work. Instead, we became friends. I got to know the real Jace while making a life for myself." Claire took her cousin's hand to hold his attention. "Jace wanted to prove to himself and his family he was serious about working the family business. That never stopped his feelings for me, but we both needed that time to grow and build a trust."

"I just wanted you to be happy with someone who deserves you."

"I am happy."

Garrett's smile was warm and full of love. "I can see that. So you don't need me to fight your battles anymore."

She wrapped her arms around his waist and gave him a hug. "I'll always need your love and support. I can fight my own battles now."

He kissed the top of her head before taking a step back. "Enough with the mushy stuff. We should go back. I shouldn't have left her alone with boxes of books."

Claire laughed. She'd gone through the boxes before they put them out and snagged a couple for herself. Sure enough, when they made their way to the table, Sara had five books in front of her and was reading the back of another one. Concern etched Jace's face. Claire closed the distance between them and hooked her arm with his, quietly letting him know she was okay. Garrett shook his head when he saw the books. He still grinned at his wife.

"You said I couldn't buy anymore *new* books this month. These are used," Sara argued. "Besides, Jace said I could take them, so I'm saving us at least twenty-five cents so far."

Jace chuckled. "Dad and Logan made me promise not to bring these boxes of books back at the end of the weekend. We were going to donate the ones we don't sell to the library."

"See, I'm helping Jace keep a promise." Sara held a book in front of Claire. "I just started reading the first book last night. I can't believe I can get the entire series for free."

Garrett gently ran his hand down her back. "She's been reading murder mystery to the baby."

"I want her to get a good start on appreciating the written word."

"You know the sex?" Claire looked between the two. Garrett shook his head.

"She says it feels like a girl." He pressed a kiss to her cheek. "I know we planned for dinner next weekend, but we're getting Chinese tonight if you want to join us."

Claire faced Jace, who nodded. "We'd love to."

They settled on a time, and Sara left with ten *'new to her'* books. Claire told Jace about her conversation in between customers. Relief washed over her, knowing she and Garrett fixed their relationship. The last thing she wanted was to force Rue to be in the middle of a useless squabble. Now they could focus on getting her aunt to Oak Mountain.

Jace held Claire's hand as he drove down his driveway. He wanted to smile at the worry on her face when she spared a last glance at his front window. It just deepened his love for her. It was her first time leaving Luna without a dog sitter. The dog had Oriole and Cammie to keep her company and didn't seem to mind as long as she had her friends.

"They'll be okay. I have a camera in the living room. We can check on them if you want throughout dinner."

Claire slowly exhaled and squeezed his hand. "No. I know she'll be okay. I'm just stressing for no reason."

Jace found it adorable. Their original plan was to watch a movie with tacos and popcorn. When he saw the smile on her face when she and Garrett returned, he knew it was a productive talk and things were back to normal between the two. It didn't surprise him Garrett heard the gossip. If he hadn't heard from Sara, his mother-in-law would make sure Garrett knew.

Until then, Claire avoided being the subject of the Oak Mountain gossip train. She hated being the center of attention. Thankfully, her first taste was positive. He couldn't guarantee it would always be that way, but he would do what he could to shield her. That's what you do for the woman you love.

Hopefully, when he proposed, the gossip would be positive. It was another reason he was happy Claire and Garrett talked. He wanted to ask his and Rue's blessing once she moved. That was weeks away. For now, he wanted to make the night enjoyable.

He turned out of the property and tried to take her mind off the unsupervised dog. "You know, this is the first time we've had Chinese food together."

"Really?" Claire tapped her chin in thought. "I think you're right. Even as friends, we would always cook, get pizza or BBQ. Why is that?"

He shrugged. "No clue. I know you've eaten there with Izzy and Naomi."

"Well, I'm glad we're doing it together."

"Me too."

Jace focused on the sharp curve in the road. The thick canopy blocked the setting sun, casting deep shadows on the pavement. As if reading his mind, the streetlights flickered on, illuminating the path. They rode in silence for a minute before Claire spoke.

"Can I ask you a question?"

"Always."

Claire twisted in her seat to face him slightly. "Do you feel differently now that we're together? Were you expecting us to act different towards one another? Am I making sense?"

"I know what you're trying to say. Honestly, I thought it would, but I'm glad it doesn't." Jace came to a stop, then turned left, taking them towards the middle of town. He finished his thought. "We didn't have to go through the awkwardness of getting to know each other. We already did that. I think that's why it wasn't a huge leap to start dating."

Claire eagerly nodded. "You said that you wanted a relationship like your parents. Everyone says your partner should be your best friend. Thomas and Josie clearly are best friends.

Heck, even Logan and Naomi finish each other's sentences now."

"Are you disappointed there wasn't a huge cosmic shift?"

"Cosmic shift?" Claire threw her head back and laughed. The melodic sound wrapped around his heart. "No, I'm not disappointed. I think that's why it was easy to say I love you so soon. I loved you before we started dating."

Jace pressed a kiss to her palm. "Same with me."

Claire was right; she was his best friend. If the evening wasn't important to her, he would suggest turning around, picking up tacos, and watching one of her favorite black and white movies. But he wanted Garrett to witness his love for Claire, not just hear from someone that he said it out loud.

They would still have time to enjoy a short movie when the evening was over.

Chapter Twenty-Four

*T*wo weeks later…

The familiar 'Welcome to Virginia' sign grew larger as Jace navigated the truck down the highway. Claire closed her eyes, taking a deep breath to settle her racing heartbeat. It was too late to make the drive by herself. Jace wouldn't have let her, anyway. He was a great boyfriend that way.

The bittersweet reality of the trip weighed on her heart. They were helping Rue move to Oak Mountain. Garrett arrived four days ago to help his mother pack up and clean her apartment. He called the morning before saying he hired a hauling company to take most of her furniture. Like Claire, Rue's furniture was secondhand. However, her aunt invested in a new bedroom set when she received her disability settlement. Her back required the support. Her rental in Oak Mountain came mostly furnished, so saying goodbye to the old pieces wouldn't be a hardship. She wanted to be there in case there was something she could use. Claire doubted it, but she'd kick herself if she didn't see for herself.

So Claire and Jace rolled out of Oak Mountain at five in the morning for the four-hour drive. Their dogs were staying with Logan and Naomi. Jace chuckled when she handed Naomi Luna's overnight bag and her friend handed it back.

They would only be gone forty hours, but she wanted to make sure her baby had comfort toys. Logan reminded her, if she wanted a particular toy, they could just cross the gravel road and get it from her house. It was a good point.

"Do you need to stop? The exit is fifteen miles away," Jace said as he pushed the button to turn off cruise control. Traffic had picked up with Friday commuters heading to work.

"We stopped an hour ago."

"Yes, but you also topped off your travel mug."

Claire grinned. The sign for a regional convenience store caught her attention. Next to Owen's special blend, they had the best coffee in West Virginia and Virginia. She wouldn't be a true Virginian if she didn't get some. Even Jace admitted how perfectly brewed it was.

The sign for a travel stop came into view, but she shook her head. "I'm good. We're almost there."

"What is your hometown like? You don't talk much about it."

Claire sneered. "There's a reason. Landing Post is stuck in the past with their beliefs. The warehouses, fulfillment center, and packing plant technically are part of town, but they aren't within the town limits. They pay enough for people to hit the bar on the weekends, but not enough for them to better themselves. We can drive through it on our way to Rue's so you can get a sense of why she pushed Garrett and I to leave."

"Wait. I thought Rue lived in the same trailer."

"No. I thought I told you. Sorry." Claire reached across the center console to squeeze his arm. "Rue moved to the next town about two months after I started at Hawkins Ridge. She'd been on a waiting list at a fifty-five and older apartment complex. I had just started and didn't want to ask for time off to help her move."

"You know, Logan would have given you time off."

"*Now* I do. Back then, I wanted to impress your brother and family. Asking for time off shortly after starting wouldn't look good."

Within the first month, Claire knew she wanted a career at Hawkins Ridge. She truly didn't think asking for time off to help an aunt move was smart. She was still on probation, after all. Rue wouldn't want her to risk the job. Garrett arranged for movers and used his days off to drive down. Claire didn't think she was needed.

"We don't have to if you don't want," Jace said as the GPS announced their exit approaching.

"I don't mind. It will be a good reminder I won't have to come here again. When you get to the end of the ramp, make a left instead of a right."

Jace turned off the GPS and took the exit. Claire practiced her yoga breathing. She hoped seeing her hometown wouldn't change Jace's feelings for her.

They drove ten miles with the music from the radio as the only noise in the truck. When they hit the Landing Post town limits, the sign on the library lawn was one of many in town. The library was in a converted home of one of the town's founders and took donations from citizens to control what was available. The sign summed up everything Claire hated about her town.

"Please tell me that sign didn't say to repeal the fourteenth amendment," Jace growled.

"They've had some version of that since I was a kid. The town funds the library since they've lost state and federal funding."

Jace drove three blocks before Claire pointed out the trailer park. Signs, flags, and the gathering of men at the corner store across the street were enough.

"Turn around, please," Claire whispered.

Jace did a perfect three-point turn and headed in the opposite direction. She wrung her hands in her lap until they were a few minutes out of town. Jace stayed quiet the entire time. After passing through the intersection and under the highway, Claire found her voice.

"Rue and Mom had a savings account. They didn't want Garrett and I to go to high school here and put any extra money they had into it. They saved on babysitting costs by working different shifts so the other could watch us." Claire sighed when they passed the building where her aunt and mother worked. "They would tell us dreams of having a yard to play in and having our own dog. Rue ended up using the money for my mother's funeral. My grandparents in West Virginia disowned them when they became pregnant out of wedlock and couldn't go home. They became stuck."

"That's why Rue pushed you two to leave." It wasn't a question. Jace reached for her hand. "Is that how you avoided the hate?"

"Partly. If Rue had a day off, we'd drive to the town she lives in now and go to the library. She would read James Baldwin and Nikki Giovani to us. We'd get a bag of chips at the dollar store and sit in the park watching kids play basketball. Granted, it was still low income, but there's diversity. They have a sense of community. It was the only place people didn't tease me because of my burns." She ran her hand over the puckered skin on her hand. "I hope you don't think less of me because of my upbringing."

Jace pulled the truck to the shoulder of the road and threw it in park. He faced her with a scowl on his handsome face.

"Don't even think that. Rue did an amazing job with you and Garrett. She did what she could so that you wouldn't have that prejudice those people have. It makes sense why you only talked about the good times with your family and not your town." He tucked a wild strand that escaped her ponytail behind her ear, cupping her chin. "I love you. Everything about you. Seeing that was a shock, not even going to lie. But like you said, it's a reminder that you don't have to come back here again. Ever. We have our whole life ahead of us. Our children will grow up surrounded by a myriad of different people who they will love, no matter their race, orientation or economic class. That I promise."

"I'm thinking five children, back-to-back since you're getting up there in age." Claire poked his rib. She'd seen Naomi and Sara and honestly thought she could only handle one pregnancy.

Jace tapped this chin in contemplation. Mirth danced in his eyes. "Five children mean they would each have to have their own pet. So, five more dogs."

"You had a chicken. Maybe we should get them a dog and a chicken."

Jace pulled her open palm to his lips and pressed a kiss. "Dog, chicken, and goat."

Claire wanted to give her children a different life than the one she had. If that meant a gaggle of animals, she was all for it. Building a life with Jace was her future. Oak Mountain was her home. By the end of the day tomorrow, her aunt would be a ten-minute drive away living in a house. At least one of the two sisters could fulfill their dreams.

"I love you." Claire leaned as far as the seatbelt would allow and gave him a kiss. "Thank you for being awesome."

"I'm taping you saying how awesome I am next time, so I can play it back for my brothers." Jace pecked the tip of her nose and settled back into the seat.

As they drove closer to Rue, the pressure in her head eased. Claire would never forget where she came from. It was her motivation. Her chance to share the love her mother and aunt showed her.

Jace stacked the last box from the kitchen into the organized pile Garrett created in the almost empty living room. The junk removers were there when he and Claire arrived. To avoid being in the way, they offered to take Balty and check-in early at their hotel just off the highway. He understood why Claire insisted they get a room there instead of the motel on the outskirts of town.

He still tried to process what he witnessed in Claire's hometown. His initial reaction was shock. That quickly gave way to anger. When she mentioned her hometown held on to old beliefs, he thought no drinking on Sunday or rock music was evil. Nothing prepared him for the signs and homemade flags he saw on some lawns. He figured it was to keep the people in Rue's current town from visiting.

Oak Mountain wasn't perfect. Some showed their true side when Owen came out. Sadly, they tossed slurs at Noah because it was easier to taunt a kid instead of the adult. It took pillars of the community, his parents and families like Ms. Ophelia's and Izzy's, to stand with Owen. There were far more supportive people than not. Eventually, love and acceptance won.

Landing Post would never be that way.

Though he didn't know Garrett well, he knew the people he and Sara called friends. Snooty as they may be, it was a diverse group. However, he knew Claire. There wasn't a hateful bone in her body. He mentally chuckled. She had a deep loathing for people who abused or neglected animals, enough to want to shove toothpicks under their nails. But he took comfort in knowing that if one of them ever needed help, she wouldn't turn away.

He applauded Rue for showing Claire and Garrett the reality of the world.

"I think that's it, Mom," Garrett said, standing in the entrance to the living room with his hands on his hips. "We just need to break down your bed in the morning."

"Thank you for doing all that," Rue said from her recliner. She and Claire were packing up her DVDs and CDs. Balty snored in his bed. "I can't believe we got it all done."

"It helped we downsized when you moved last time." Garrett pulled his keys from his pocket. "We need to get the rental trailer."

Because Garrett and Jace drove large, crew-cab trucks, Rue only needed a cargo trailer to move her furniture, which Jace would haul. Garrett figured it would be safe at the hotel. Jace agreed, since Garrett was sleeping on an air mattress at Rue's. They would divide the boxes between the trucks. Claire planned to drive Rue's small truck with her and Balty.

"We'll pick up dinner while we're out." Jace looked at Garrett, who nodded.

He gave Claire and kiss and strolled out of the apartment. Garrett locked the door behind them.

"Thanks for coming with Claire," Garrett said as they jogged down the stairs instead of the slow elevator.

"I'd do anything for her and Rue. Even if we weren't dating, I would be here. Her hand wouldn't let her do that much, and it would be too much for you to do on your own."

"Claire would try, though."

They pushed through the door into the lobby. Garrett waved to the worker in the office before stepping outside. The temperature dropped a few degrees with the setting sun. People around the complex scrambled in or out of cars. A hard day of work, starting or ending. The difference between the two towns was clear. People smiled and greeted each other, no matter the race. The trailer park across the street was bright and cheery. The homes were older and some in need of repair, but the lawns were tidy.

"Claire said you drove through our old hometown," Garrett said as they climbed into his truck.

"Yeah. I'm glad Rue got out of there when she did."

"You and me both. I tried to get her to move to Oak Mountain when I first got there. She was just starting her disability claim and getting treatment for her back. She didn't want to start the process over in Maryland."

Jace followed Garrett's direction out of the neighborhood to the main street. The cargo trailer rental was two miles down the road. He spoke as they drove.

"Claire told me what Rue did, bringing you two up here when she could."

"Mom switched to the night shift when Claire turned twelve because it was more money. She usually slept on her days off, but once a month she would have a weekend off. That's when we'd drive up. You wouldn't think twenty miles would make a difference, but it does." Garrett pointed to the rental sign in the distance. "The messed-up thing is that most of these citizens work side by side in the same warehouses and packing plants as the people from Landing Post. They rely on the other for staying safe at work, but would never sit down and share a coffee with them."

Jace couldn't comprehend that logic. It wasn't how Thomas and Josie raised him. That was the difference. As he told Claire, children have no control over their upbringing. They could only make the changes when they became older and thought for themselves. Despite the environment, Rue taught Garrett and Claire the world operated differently than the hate signs they saw on their way to school. Jace thanked the Universe for his future aunt-in-law.

Jace pulled into the lot. He and Garrett made quick work of renting the trailer and hitching it to his truck. They were back on the road twenty minutes later and headed to a pizza place a quarter of a mile past the trailer rental. He wanted to change the subject from talking about the area while they waited for the two pizzas.

"Are you and Sara planning for more than one child?"

Garrett chuckled. "We wanted three. She's saying this pregnancy is making her reconsider the number to one."

"I wanted at least two. Now that I'm in my mid-thirties, I'm happy with one. With Naomi expecting, our kid would have someone close in age."

"Claire always wanted two kids and four dogs."

"Well, we have three dogs. We just need a child and another dog."

Garrett rested his arms on his thighs and held Jace in his gaze. "I thought I wanted Claire with someone like me. Someone with similar backgrounds. Then I met Sara. I realized if you love someone, it didn't matter if they grew up with or without money. Then I just wanted her with someone who can see the amazing, loving and kind woman that she is. You know I didn't think that was you. You've proven me wrong. Seeing you and her together, show how much you two love each other."

Jace matched Garrett's pose. He didn't know if Claire shared his past, but he wanted to lay everything out for him.

"My college girlfriend is the reason I let my reputation become what it was. She tore my heart in two. Add seeing my brothers go through hard divorces to the mix, and I thought it was the best way to protect my heart. It was a mistake. I could blame youth, but I willingly chose that path. I was wrong on so many levels. Then Claire came into my life. I knew I needed to change to even have half a chance. Then Logan met Naomi. I saw despite heartache, you can find the one you were meant to be with." He raked his fingers through his hair. "Claire is my one. I knew it a year ago and I'm certain now. I plan on asking her to marry me soon and hope I could have your blessings."

Garrett slapped him on the back just as their to-go order was ready. "You got it."

Jace gave a tight nod and lifted the bag containing paper plates, breadsticks, and salad. He asked Rue earlier when Garrett and Claire took bags of trash to the dumpster. They planned on ring shopping the following week.

As they headed back to Rue's, Jace was grateful he came with Claire. He fell even more in love with her and understood her need to fight for those who couldn't fight for themselves. Rue raised two incredible people in difficult circumstances. Jace was proud to call them all family.

Chapter Twenty-Five

Songs of crickets filled the evening sky, mixed with the gentle rustle of oak leaves. Hints of a new moon played peek-a-boo between the branches as it rose to brighten the night.

Balty sniffed every corner of his new fenced-in yard. His first. She couldn't wait to bring Luna over to play. Claire closed her eyes, letting her head fall back, taking it all in. She opened and closed her hand into a fist in hopes the numbness would subside. A sign she overdid it that day.

Rue moved into the cozy cottage on the old plantation land hours ago. Her aunt maintained a genuine grin throughout the drive from Virginia and while she supervised where she wanted her boxes. Rue's landlord rented the home furnished, minus the bedroom. It made moving easier. Rue wanted to make a fresh start. Claire didn't blame her.

Jace and Garrett worked in harmony, loading the small U-Haul van and their trucks. The dinner two weeks before was exactly what the two men needed to move forward in a friendly relationship. Garrett saw how attentive Jace was with Claire. Would they form a bromance? She doubted it. But they would be friends. It was all she wanted.

Claire used the tip of her sneakers to set the swing in motion. The porch was large enough for the wooden swing, two garden chairs, and a table. Visions of her and Rue enjoying a glass of sweet tea and playing cards popped into her mind.

The creak of the screen door had Claire opening her eyes. Josie stepped out carrying two bottled waters. The older woman welcomed Rue the only way she knew—with food. She supplied a deli tray and bread for everyone to make sandwiches along with individual size chips and homemade cookies. Winnie, Izzy's mother, and Maeve arrived forty-five minutes into the move with grocery staples, so Rue wouldn't have to worry about shopping for a couple of days. It showed the neighborly acts of the Oak Mountain residents.

"I figured you could use one of these." Josie joined her on the swing. Claire eagerly took the drink.

"Thank you." She twisted the lid and took a long sip. "Thank you also for everything you did today."

Josie waved dismissively. "No need to thank me. I like Rue a lot. I figured the move would be hard on her back and she would need to rest tomorrow. Going out to pick up food should be the least of her worries. Logan texted. They're on their way back."

Logan rode with Jace to return the cargo trailer to the U-Haul store in Stark Valley. Naomi had a craving for peanut butter cups from a specific candy store near the return spot. Logan wanted to surprise her. Thomas and Garrett stayed to put together Rue's bed and help unpack the big things. Claire hoped they would head home once they returned. She missed her baby.

"I can't wait to sleep in my bed."

Josie chuckled. "I always have to take my pillow and linen when we travel. It's the only way I can sleep."

"I didn't even think about taking my pillow. Next time."

The two sat in comfortable silence for a few moments. The moon cleared the top of the trees, highlighting the myriads of stars. Josie spoke after taking a drink.

"We haven't had a moment, just the two of us, since the incident to talk. I just wanted to say, I'm happy you know how much we care about you." Josie sighed. "Jace told me last year he found his one person. Before he told me it was you, I worried it was one of those women he'd been running around with."

Claire couldn't swallow her snicker fast enough. The disdain in Josie's tone about another woman was funny.

"I denied my feelings for him for too long."

"You did the right thing by waiting. Jace is my baby, always will be. But he wasn't the man you needed when you first came to Hawkins Ridge. He had to find his place. Heck, all my boys, including Noah, needed to find their place. It's part of the reason Thomas, Owen, and myself took a step back." Josie scratched Balty's head when he joined them on the porch before speaking again.

"Logan needed to get out of Thomas' shadow as the vet for the farms. That allowed him to open up his heart for Naomi. The town is finally seeing Noah as a man, not the boy whose family ended because his father came out of the closet. Caden…" Josie shook her head. "His heart is big. The other boys won't admit it, but they want the expansion to succeed so Caden can make his dream of a support animal program come true. Wes Chambers is an enormous step towards that."

Two days before Claire and Jace left to help Rue, the resort owner visited Hawkins Ridge for the day. The charming man was the epitome of *"you can take the man from the farm, but you can't take the farm from the man."* Wes and his assistant spent time with each brother, learning and actually helping the workers with their daily tasks. From milking the goats to transplanting flowers, feeding the chickens, even helping feed and pick up after the pack.

When he made his way to the stables and learned of the plans for the animal support program, he wanted to be involved. His nephew used a support dog to help with his anxiety and knew the benefits of having one. It was also Josie's cue to cook a spread using ingredients from the property. Wes told them to have their lawyer send the contract so they could start negotiations.

Loud laughter from inside brought a smile to Claire's lips. She returned her attention to Josie. Unclear where the woman was going with the conversation, she went back to the first statement.

"Your family made me feel welcomed from the first day. I remember you and Owen coming to my house while I was unpacking with bags of food and meals I just needed to heat." She played with the label on the bottle. "Jace and I agreed we wouldn't have worked if I said yes my first month. I guess I was also finding my place."

Josie patted her hand. "I'm glad you found it with us and am happy for you and Jace. I pray my other two boys find the love Jace and Logan have."

Claire chuckled. "You just want a reason to keep having family dinners."

Josie's throaty laugh said Claire hit the nail on the head. "And grandchildren. Though Noah's would be honorary, but I'd still love them like my own."

"Shame Izzy's already happily married."

"Girl, she had the biggest crush on Logan in elementary school." Josie's smile was warm. "Since I'm good friends with her mother, she'd always bring Izzy to the property to play with the boys. I think she was eight and Logan was eleven or twelve. She told him they would get married one day. Logan said he didn't like girls with freckles. She punched him in the stomach before throwing a rock at him. Killed any childish crush."

Claire choked on her water, using her arm to wipe her mouth. She could see her friend doing that and planned to tease her on Monday. Their boisterous commotion brought Rue, Thomas, and Garrett from the house. All looked tired and ready to call it a day once Logan and Jace returned.

Everyone took a seat and spoke of what still needed to be done with plans for them to return the next day to finish. Claire looked at the people on the porch. Her blood family embracing her heart family.

She looked forward to the day she could officially call herself a Beckett.

"I should be home in about ninety minutes, maybe less," Logan spoke into his phone as Jace climbed into his truck. "Don't wait for me. You and Fiona go ahead and eat. I'll make a hot dog when I get there."

Jace rested his head on the back of the seat and exhaled. He asked Logan to drive because he didn't think he had it in him. Muscles he forgot he had screamed. He popped the top off the bottle of ibuprofen he kept in the center console and dry swallowed two pills. A long, hot shower was in his future. Logan ended his call with Naomi and connected the phone to the car system.

"Everything okay?" Logan asked, putting the car in drive.

"Yep. I returned the trailer, and Rue's receipt is in my pocket. I am ready for a nap."

The oldest Beckett brother laughed and pulled out of the lot. Traffic was heavy in the city. People bustling to dinner out or maybe heading to a movie, perhaps visiting loved ones. Jace wished them well, but ached for the quiet of Oak Mountain.

"Overall, how was the trip?"

Jace ran his fingers through his hair, making a mental note to get a haircut. "It was better than I expected. Claire and I didn't fight over music. We only stopped once, going down to top off the tank. I'm not sure what I expected, but she surprised me."

"Enjoy it now. Traveling with children will test your love and patience."

Jace chuckled. "I am looking forward to having a little Claire. Knowing the universe, I'll probably have a carbon copy of me."

"Have you two talked about kids?" Logan asked as he pulled onto the highway.

"No, but I know she wants at least one."

"I thought we could have two. I want to see how she does with this pregnancy." Logan tapped his fingers on the steering wheel. "I just want her and the baby to be healthy."

Logan mentioned last week that Naomi's doctor had strongly emphasized the importance of her taking it easy. Convincing his sister-in-law to accept help was proving to be a challenge for the independent woman. Thomas suggested they either find another veterinarian so Logan could assist with Naomi's workload, or, given the brothers' vision for Hawkins Ridge in two years, bring on a new vet now.

"Things will work themselves out. Whatever you need, just ask. Dad said he was going to help a couple of days a week."

"Yeah, and I appreciate it," Logan said. "Tell me about Claire's hometown."

Jace let his brother switch topics. His concern for Naomi and their unborn child was obvious. If talking about something mundane as his trip helped, Jace didn't have a problem.

"Let's just say I see why Claire loves Oak Mountain as much as she does."

"That bad?"

He nodded. "First, I thought Rue still lived in the trailer she grew up in. However, she moved shortly after Claire came to Oak Mountain to a fifty-five and older complex in the next town. When we exited the highway, we drove through where she grew up. I think the sign said a population of about thirteen hundred." Jace took a moment to organize his thoughts. "It was a town you could see people taking pride in their homes and business. They know hard work and don't shy away from it. But, based on signs and items in people's yards, let's just say I don't think they would be as open to your marriage."

It took his brother a moment to understand what he meant. Logan didn't see his wife's skin color. He loved her for her. "Oh. But Rue didn't raise her and Garrett that way."

"No, she didn't, and I'm thankful for that. The only thing she said was she's happy she'll never have to go back to visit." Jace lowered the window slightly before speaking again. "I get we've lived a privileged life. But Mom and Dad made sure we valued hard work, sent us to schools that exposed us to all walks of life."

"In Caden's case, sadly, the images of war," Logan interrupted. They took time to think about the images their middle brother may have seen. Jace continued the conversation when Logan took the exit for Oak Mountain.

"I want to give Claire the life she deserves, to take away that fear she has of losing all she's worked so hard to achieve."

"I get that. What you have to realize is Claire is independent. She won't let you swoop in and take care of everything. Support and encourage her, definitely. Saying she doesn't have to worry about her bills because you'll pay them—you're asking for a fight." Logan shook his head. "Trust me. I know."

"If we're married, why can't I?" Jace argued.

"Wait. You're already talking marriage?"

Jace shrugged and focused on the quiet neighborhood streets. "We've talked about the future. Luna already has a bed at my place. When we aren't working, we're together. We were also close friends for almost a year."

Logan raised his hands in surrender at a stop sign. "I wasn't criticizing the decision. It's not like I can talk. I proposed to

Naomi after dating for four months, then married her two months later. You knew Claire was your one before she even gave you the time of day. I'm just asking if you think she'll say yes."

"I do. I asked Rue for her blessing this morning. She wants to help me pick out the ring."

His brother pointed a finger. "Smart. It's why I took Maeve and Mom with me. I was going for flashy and they both called me an idiot in the middle of the store."

Jace barked out a laugh. "You never told us that."

"Oh yeah. They told me to just be prepared to hand over my card. They found the perfect ring at the second store."

Jace had considered asking Josie to go with them. Unlike his brother, Jace knew Claire was not a woman who'd want a big ring. Simple with an antique feel was her speed. He didn't, however, know what stores to go to or her ring size. It was why he eagerly accepted Rue's help.

They turned into the driveway for the bed-and-breakfast. Rue's cottage was past the main house and garden. The sight of everyone gathered on the porch brought a smile to his lips. Seeing the two families laughing and sharing a moment was a foreshadow of his future.

"I think I'm going to head home," Jace said when Logan pulled behind his truck. "It's been over forty hours since I slept in my bed."

"I'm grabbing Mom and Dad and heading out myself."

The pair climbed out of the truck and made their way to the group. Jace noticed Claire flexing her hand as he came closer. It was time for her to rest. Rue, too, looked as if she was ready to call it a night.

After making plans for the next afternoon to hang pictures and shelves, everyone said their goodbyes. Jace helped Claire to his truck and buckled her in. With a final wave, they headed out.

"I'm taking a hot shower, then passing out," Claire announced.

"I said the same thing to Logan."

Claire reached for his hand and gave it a squeeze. "Thank you for everything. I love you."

"I love you too, but you don't need to thank me. Rue wanted to be with her family. I'm glad we could make that happen."

"She's your family too," Claire said around a yawn. "I miss Luna."

Jace chuckled. He missed his dogs too and thought hard about just crashing at Logan's, so he wouldn't have to take Oriole and Cammie home. He glanced over and saw the love of his life rested her head against the window. Her eyes closed.

She was right. Rue and Garrett were family. Now he just had to make it official.

Chapter Twenty-Six

Laughter and music filled the night air and spilled into Jace's home. Claire poured the virgin strawberry margarita evenly between four glasses and carefully placed them on a tray. It was the second batch she'd made that evening. If they kept at this pace, she'd have to replace all his mixer.

She gingerly lifted the tray. Her brief time as a server didn't help her at the moment and the tray wobbled. Carefully, she maneuvered her way to the sliding back door. Josie scurried from an oversized chair and opened it for her.

"Why didn't you just leave the door open?" Rue said from a lounger, a plate of wings and slaw balanced on her thighs.

Claire sat the tray on the outdoor coffee table before answering. "I don't want to explain to Jace why he has bugs. Of course, the laughter probably scared them away."

"I still can't believe he let you have girls' night here," Naomi commented from the end of the patio couch. "And he took the dogs."

"He promised if I helped talked the guys into chipping in for this projection setup, I could."

It's been two weeks since they helped Rue move to Oak Mountain. To say Claire was happy to have her aunt close would be an understatement. Rue chose that weekend to spend at Hawkins Ridge. She and Josie spent most of the day putting together flower planters for Rue's porch and lawn. It would be easier for her to tend instead of planting them in ground.

Jace's brothers surprised him with the projection set up when they returned from Virginia. They've watched several baseball games during that time, but last night, Jace surprised her with a classic Sherlock Holmes movie night. Basil Rathbone was born to play the role in Claire's humble opinion. It was a perfect evening to round out a busy week.

Spring births on the various farms kept Claire and Logan busy. Examining mothers and their young to make sure everyone was healthy had them working until dinnertime. Claire took her medication religiously. The last thing she wanted was to be a spasming mess and useless to Logan.

Jace completed the contract with Wes Chambers and the resort yesterday. Beginning next month, they would supply the goat cheese, kale, and beefsteak tomatoes for the resort. Everyone liked Claire's suggestion of handing samples of dog treats when guests with pets check-in. The resort would keep a small supply to purchase on hand. If the demand warranted, they would stock them in their gift shop, which agreed to offer the soaps.

Speaking of the treats, Claire planned to work with Rue the following day on a cat option. Noah and Josie volunteered their cats to be tasters. The owners of Naomi's patients also asked about something for their cats as well. With the dog treats selling like hot cakes, it made sense. She expected the sales report from the accountant later the following week, along with her first check of her percentage. With Jace helping Owen with his duties, it freed up Noah's father to oversee the production of the treats. Claire was thankful.

"Jace told me the candidate accepted the offer this morning," Claire said, taking a seat next to Naomi. "I know everyone's excited."

Josie rolled her eyes. "We should have had a manager three months ago. Either way, I'm glad we settled on the couple. They're moving into the house Naomi and Maeve used when they first stayed with us."

The house was a two-bedroom and next door to Claire. She trusted the Becketts made the right choice.

"Since Rue is going to help with light office work two days a week, it will free up Izzy to handle the rush of vaccinations," Naomi added. "I think this expansion is growing faster than the guys expected."

Claire nodded. "Jace was talking about that over dinner last night. He said they want to hire seven people before summer."

"That's not including a new vet." Josie stood and relit the citronella candle. "Thomas is going to stick his head in on poker night to talk to everyone. We're concerned the boys are going too far. This is a family business and everyone wants to keep it that way. The path they're taking it will be too much for them and their spouses to handle."

Claire didn't know why Josie made spouse plural, but she didn't correct her. Rue, who had been quiet for the exchange and not familiar with how the property ran, spoke up.

"What will they do when they get older? Except for Fiona and Naomi's little bean, there aren't any grandchildren to pass the reins too. Is Fiona interested in running everything?"

Naomi and Josie spoke at the same time. After chuckling about letting the other speak first, Naomi replied.

"Fiona wants to follow in her father's footsteps and become a vet. She has no interest in running the property. There will be a thirteen-year difference between her and the newborn. While she's taking over, we'll be sending this one to college, so she'll have to rely on her father and uncles until she can get help."

"Even if Jace and Claire have a baby next year, it would be too young to help." Josie winked at a choking Claire. Naomi patted her back while her loving aunt cackled like a loon.

Once she had her breathing under control, she addressed Jace's mother. "We haven't talked about children. We're not even engaged."

"Oh sweetie, you're cute," Josie quipped. "Engagement is only a matter of time. You both are in your thirties. You can't wait too long."

"It would be nice if your kid grew up with Garrett's little one," Rue chimed in. Claire glared at her aunt.

"Don't forget, these Beckett men are fast," Naomi spoke around a bite of chicken. "I walked down the aisle seven months after I told Logan off when I first met him. I became pregnant almost three months later."

"They get that from their father. Thomas asked me to marry him on our third date. Since he didn't have a ring, I said no. We conceived Logan on our wedding night." Josie blushed, causing the women to double over in laughter.

Claire wiped her eyes and took in the three women she loved and saw as family. Josie's statement about engagement stayed in the forefront of her mind. Did she know something? Could he be planning a proposal? Was she ready to say yes?

When Claire pictured her future, Jace starred as the lead. They ate dinner together every night and had keys to each other's homes. She considered Oriole and Cammie as hers, and he felt the same way about Luna. It would make sense marriage was the next step. Was she ready?

She and Andy were engaged a month before she ended it. She didn't have time, nor the budget, to plan a wedding then. Now she had a little tucked away. She could afford something small with a simple, everyday white dress. But she knew Jace. He would insist on paying for everything. Unlike Logan and Naomi, this was their first marriage. Were they expected to go big? The thought of hundreds of people watching her walk down the aisle made her break out in hives. She didn't think Jace would want something large, either. Would Rue and Josie kill them if they eloped?

Yes. Yes, they would.

Claire mentally shook her head. No sense stressing over something that hadn't happened. Jace was the love of her life. If he was ready to pop the question, she would say yes.

Josie took a sip of her drink, crossing her legs. She finished her point once everyone had regained their composure.

"Truthfully, that's part of why Thomas is talking to them. My brothers sold their stake in the business early on because they didn't want this way of life. Logan was blessed that Naomi wanted to be a part of what they want to do here. Same with Jace and Claire." Josie tilted her head towards Claire with a grin. "There's no guarantee Naomi's baby or any future children will want this. He wants to make sure they have a contingency plan in place. In twenty to thirty years, if the next generation wants to pursue something else, Hawkins Ridge will survive financially and go back to being a family home with a few animals."

"There's always the possibility Noah or Caden will marry someone with children. Maybe they'll want to keep following in their footsteps," Claire added.

"One could hope." Josie smiled and clapped her hands. "Enough serious talk. Let's see what's on. I want to see what the hype is about this projection thing."

Claire pressed the button to lower the one-hundred-twenty-inch screen. When she turned on the TV, the three women gasped. It was the same reaction Claire had when Jace showed her. She handed the remote to Josie so she could finish eating.

Talk of the future excited and worried Claire. When parents force their kids down the wrong road, it creates a big divide. Claire didn't want that for their child. She didn't think Jace would, either. It wasn't something to discuss now and until she became an official Beckett, it wasn't her place to speculate.

She just wanted to focus on building a life with Jace.

"Drop it, Shorty, this instant," Logan fussed at the dachshund. "You aren't supposed to eat onions."

Jace and his brothers doubled over when every dog in the house barked their support for the dachshund. Cammie leading the chorus.

"Y'all could help, you know," Logan growled, shoving a finger into the dog's muzzle to pry his mouth open.

"You got it under control," Noah said, trying to catch his breath.

"Are you sure he got a piece of onion ring?" Caden asked, looking at the floor for evidence. "Maybe it's a dust bunny."

"I saw it fall off the plate when I was bringing it to the table. I turned around to pick it up, and he was on it." Logan scooped his arm under the dog's undercarriage and lifted him. "I swear I will call your mother and make her pump your stomach."

"Call his mother?" Jace howled, holding his stomach. "I dare you to call Naomi and tell her Shorty won't spit out a small piece of food."

"He doesn't do this around her. No. He waits until I'm in charge and forgets who sneaks him pieces of bacon."

"What in the world is going on?" Thomas yelled from the open back door. The volume of the barking and guffaws drowned out his arrival. Shorty, seeing Thomas, let the piece of food roll out of his mouth. The soggy splat when it hit the hardwood floor only added to the insanity.

Logan placed Shorty on his paws. All twelve dogs scurried over to greet Jace's father; even Balty. The glare Logan shot them promised no extra treats. He used a paper towel to pick up the piece of food and tossed it in the garbage.

"Hey, Dad," Jace said. He squeezed in between the herd of dogs to pick up Cammie, who was in danger of accidentally being stepped on by the larger dogs.

"Boys." Thomas scratched behind every ear before joining them around the kitchen island. He took Cammie from Jace, gave her a kiss, and set her on the floor. "What was with the excitement?"

Everyone took turns telling him what led up the disagreement between Logan and Shorty. By the end, the patriarch of the family was shaking his head.

"That's probably the reason Logan specialized in farm animals at vet school. Household pets ignore him," Noah teased.

"Please tell me you weren't going to call your wife to handle the dog." The corners of Thomas' lips twitched. He took the beer from Jace's hand. "Get yourself another one."

Jace shook his head and headed to the fridge. Logan turned off the water after washing his hands. He yanked the towel from the handle on the oven.

"Shorty is not a normal dog." Logan looked at the dachshund, but a smile graced his lips. "If he acts up, I threaten to tell Naomi, and he stops. This time he was just showing off for everyone."

"And what a fine job he did," Caden quipped.

Jace took a pull from his fresh beer. He looked forward to spending time with his brothers. Though they saw each other during or after work, this was their time to reconnect. Business was always discussed the first thirty minutes, then no more for the rest of the night. They even set a timer.

Caden's medical discharge from the military started the first poker game. Jace and Noah drove home from college that weekend. They used a coffee can full of pennies for the ante. It wasn't about winning, but being there for his brother.

Since then, every month, like clockwork, they got together. The coffee can grew to a water jug. They returned their winnings to the jug at the end of the night. They added any spare or found pennies. When Jace turned sixty-five, since he was the youngest, they agreed to cash in the pennies and go on a fishing trip.

"So, what's up, Dad? Are you playing?" Logan asked before popping an onion ring into his mouth.

Thomas shrugged. "I'll play. I came here for a reason, though."

"We figured as much." Jace pushed the party sub towards his father. "Did we miss a birthday?"

"No, but I want to discuss your plan for Claire's later. Your mother, Owen, and I were talking."

The brothers groaned. Whenever the parents got to talking, it wasn't a good thing. For them to send Thomas to deliver the message, it usually wasn't good. The four men picked up their plates and ate. No one would interrupt Thomas once he started talking.

"We want to say we're proud of what you boys have done with the business. You're working towards your goals. The town is noticing and saying nothing but positive things." Thomas paused and slid a serving of the sub onto a plate. He took a bite and finished after swallowing.

"However, we're worried it's getting too large and eventually it will be too much for you four. Hawkins Ridge is a family business. Hiring someone from outside to manage the property was necessary. Vince and Maya will be valuable additions to how things will run. They had good ideas during the final interview."

Jace and his brothers nodded in agreement. Harold's son went to college with Vince and referred him. He and his wife managed a working ranch in Kentucky for the past fifteen years. Both were in their early forties and looking for a slower pace. Everyone looked forward to working with them.

"Our point is the next generation isn't ready to run this," Thomas continued. "Fiona already said she wants to be a vet and not be responsible for everything else. The way you four are going, you'll either have to give some control to someone, not family, or draw too much attention. People will try to make you fail. Neither are acceptable."

Jace understood where the parents were coming from. They talked about the same thing earlier, before the Shorty incident. It supported their concerns, knowing the folks noticed, too. Logan set his paper plate on the counter and spoke for them.

"We actually talked about that tonight. Now that we've added the resort, we're going to pause on new contracts for a while. Between the pregnancy, the new managers, the dog treats, building a foster home database and getting the therapy program off the ground, we don't want to over commit."

Jace cleared his throat, drawing their attention. "The contracts signed in the last six months are multi-year. The break will give the managers time to get a handle on things. I plan on doing more around here to help lighten the load, especially with the foster homes and treat production. I still need an assistant to help with administrative tasks."

"We also talked about employees living on the property," Caden piped up. "We want to limit the people living on the property. Except for the managers who have to live here. Employees who've lived here until now can stay. We need them for when emergencies happen overnight. Otherwise, keep the remaining houses for people we're hiring from outside the county. Give them eighteen months to find something in town. We'll help them, of course."

"We're expanding our family. Their safety is important." Noah shrugged. "Who knows? Maybe Caden or I will find our special person or even adopt."

Jace took a long pull of his beer. They all talked about adoption through the foster care system before Naomi and Claire came into their lives. They wanted to give kids in the system a chance at a future. Logan felt putting the pressure on Fiona alone would lead to her resenting Hawkins Ridge. Back then, none wanted marriage. Things had changed. Noah and Caden were open to the possibility of getting married again, but neither was actively looking.

Jace wanted a child with Claire, but he wanted to talk with her about adopting a few years down the road. His heart told him she would be on board.

"Speaking of expanding the family, that brings me to Claire's birthday." Thomas pointed his bottle towards Jace. "You still plan on proposing? You sure it won't embarrass her with all of us there?"

Jace considered the same thing when he decided. "I talked to Rue about that when we went ring shopping. She said Claire wouldn't mind because it will be a family dinner. If it was in the middle of a restaurant or out in public with strangers, she wouldn't like it."

"Good enough. Tell us what you want us to do when you figure it out." Thomas popped his last piece of sandwich in his mouth and stood. "Alright. Let's see if you boys learned how to play poker."

Just like that, any conversations about work or the future of Hawkins Ridge were over for the night. Logan passed out bully sticks to the dogs while the rest cleaned their mess. Everyone refreshed their drinks and moved the finger snacks to the dining room table. Thomas turned on a baseball game as background noise. They'd watched the Orioles win earlier that afternoon. Jace dished out pennies for his father before taking a seat.

Chatter started about trade options and batting order while cards were being dealt. Jace couldn't wait to share this moment with his child. First, he had to get Claire to say yes.

Epilogue

O*ne Month Later…*

Claire twisted her lips as she stared at her reflection in the mirror. How are you supposed to dress for a birthday dinner?

Rue told her when they went for manicures and pedicures, under no circumstance was she supposed to wear jeans. That's her go to outfit of choice. The knee-length, pink floral skirt accented her curves while camouflaging her tummy. She paired it with a white dressy tee and strappy sandals. She dried her hair so her natural waves cascaded past her shoulders. Claire used the hair comb Jace gave her to pull up a side.

She gave a final twirl as the hem of her skirt swished in the breeze. *You clean up nice,* she thought with a giggle. Pleased with everything, she switched to her pink frames and hurried out the door.

Maya Ruiz stood at the end of her walkway. A common lawn separated the two houses. The new managers moved in the day before. The Becketts were giving them the weekend to acclimate themselves to the town. Claire hadn't talked with them that much. She didn't want to be late to her own party since she saw Garrett's truck parked beside the main house. However, she didn't want to be rude.

Maya was a natural beauty. A mix of African American and Puerto Rican, she styled her long ebony hair into a low ponytail. A wide smile greeted Claire as she came closer.

"Hi, Claire. You look nice."

"Thank you. I prefer jeans to a skirt any day, but my aunt strongly suggested I dress up." Claire absently ran her hand down her skirt.

"I think I own two dresses and two skirts. We live in jeans."

"Then you'll fit in perfectly here. Is everything okay? Did you need something?"

Maya shook her head. "Waiting for Vince. We're going to check out the burger place in town. Josie invited us to dinner, but we didn't want to impose. Besides, we wanted to drive around and see if there are rentals."

Claire's brows furrowed. "Rentals? I thought you had to live on the property." The other woman laughed, shaking her head.

"No. My sister wants to leave Philadelphia. Long story, but she wants to give small town living a shot. She considered moving to Kentucky to be close to us, but we got this job." Maya shrugged. "Now she's considering here. Vince and I think it's what she needs."

"We can help you look for something. Josie is a fountain of information. I'll mention something this evening and see if we can at least get you names of places or people to contact."

"That would be wonderful. Thank you."

They turned their heads at the sound of the front door closing. Vince Ruiz would have many older women fighting for his attention if he wasn't married. Tall with salt and pepper hair and a large, muscular frame. He twirled his keys around his finger as he walked towards them.

"Evening, Claire. Happy birthday."

"Thank you. I think they are going overboard for my thirty-third birthday, but I can't argue with Josie."

Vince's deep laugh echoed in the air. "Everyone I've spoken to has said the same thing."

"Speaking of Josie, Claire is going to ask her about rentals for Sienna," Maya said. Claire nodded.

"She helped find a place for my aunt, who moved here almost two months ago. She'll know of places that won't have a 'For Rent' sign in front of them."

"That would be wonderful. Thank you. We better let you go."

Claire checked her watch. "I hope they aren't holding dinner for me. Have a wonderful night."

She hurried across the gravel road and jogged up the back stairs. Various conversations and laughter greeted her as she slipped through the door. No matter how stealthy she was, Luna knew her owner was in the building.

"I was going to call you," Jace said as he walked behind the dog. He dressed in a pair of black twill pants and a periwinkle blue button-down. His dark blond hair swept his shoulders in a messy, stylish way. "You look beautiful."

Claire's cheeks heated. She rolled on her tiptoes and pressed a kiss to his cheeks. "Sorry. I saw Vince and Maya on my way and chatted. Remind me to talk to Josie. They are looking for a place for her sister, who wants to leave Philadelphia."

"We'll get together with her tomorrow," Josie commented from her side. Claire hadn't seen the woman approach.

"Thank you. I hope you weren't holding dinner for me."

Jace linked his fingers with hers. "No. We're going to eat in fifteen minutes."

He guided her further into the open space. All her loved ones milled between the kitchen and living room. She immediately noticed Sara sitting at the dining room table, Garrett rubbing her shoulders. Her cousin-in-law rubbed her protruding stomach. With the due date in a week, Claire tried to get Sara to stay home. Naomi's tummy, though only five months along, surpassed Sara's. Logan announced two weeks ago they were expecting twins. They kept it a secret because Naomi's doctor said the heartbeat for baby two was weak and wanted to run tests. Turned out it was hiding. Once the babies repositioned themselves, number two's heartbeat was as strong as number one.

Claire handed out hugs to everyone, expressing her gratitude for their presence. She hated being the center of attention, even with family. But they went out of their way to plan something special for her. It was a first.

Growing up, Rue would bake a box cake and cook a special dinner of spaghetti for their birthdays. It may not mean a lot to kids today, but it meant a lot to Claire. Sharing this day with her aunt was the cherry on top.

Rue slipped a glass of iced tea in her hand and linked her arm with hers. Jace let out a sharp whistle, ceasing all conversation.

"Thank you all for being here for Claire's birthday. It means a lot, and we're able to share this with all of you." Jace turned to her and lowered himself to one knee. Her hand went to her mouth.

"Buttercup—"

"You aren't," Claire interrupted. The first tear rolled down her cheek.

"Let me finish before you cry." He took her hand and smiled. "Buttercup, fourteen months ago, you strolled onto the property and into my heart. I didn't know what I wanted in life. I thought living the life of a bachelor made me happy. You showed me I was wrong with a simple smile. Your love is something I didn't think I deserve. I still don't, but I am honored you have given me a chance to be the man you deserve. You've made me a better person."

"You've made our family better," Thomas piped in as he passed Cammie to her. Attached to her collar was a tiny burgundy pouch.

Jace deftly untied the package and passed the Pomeranian back to his father. He pulled out a square box and flipped the top open. Claire lost all control of her tears.

Nestled in a white gold setting was a single pink diamond. Jace removed the ring and slipped it onto her finger.

"I can't imagine my life without you. You're my best friend, my rock, and my heart. Claire Elizabeth Everson, will you marry me?"

Words clogged in her throat. She nodded and threw her arms around him. Cheers and applause, including barking, erupted from her family and friends. Jace kissed her passionately, and she didn't care that everyone was watching. Unfortunately, the kiss ended too soon as he rose to his feet, lifting her with him. Surrounded by everyone offering well wishes and admiring the ring, Rue was the last to congratulate her. Her aunt dabbed at her eyes with a tissue.

"I'm so happy for you. Your mother would be so proud of you."

Claire hugged her. "None of this would have happened without you. You gave me the strength to keep going."

"You had dreams. I just nudged you in the right direction."

"Thank you for telling me to take a chance with him months ago."

Rue ran her thumb across Claire's cheek. "You always wanted to. You just needed a reminder that no matter what, you're a survivor."

Jace took that moment to wrap his arm around her. Rue patted his cheek and went to set the pots for dinner. Claire looked at her perfect ring and rested her head on his chest.

"Thank you for a perfect proposal. I love you."

"I love you, too, and can't wait to build a future with you."

Neither could she.

The End

Afterword

Thank you for reading Claire's Forever Love. This is the second book of the Hawkins Ridge Animal Sanctuary series. Each brother will have their own chance at finding their forever love.

The Asher House, an organization based in Oregon, partially inspired the idea of the sanctuary. What Lee Asher and his staff are doing is amazing. If you have not seen their videos on YouTube or social media and you love animals, check them out.

I have a soft spot for all animals and I'm embarrassed by the rabbit hole I go down watching animal videos on Instagram. If you are interested in sharing your home with a furry friend, please visit your local shelter. So many dogs, cats and a variety of other friends are desperately looking for homes. If you don't have the space, consider volunteering your time. They are always looking for people to take the animals on walks or simply just sit with them. Too busy? Consider donating food, blankets or toys. Something to let the underpaid and overworked staff know they are not alone in their love of animals.

Yes, I did name Balty, Oriole and Cammie after my love of the Orioles. Thanks to the MLB ticket, I was able to see every Oriole game in the 2024 season here in Albuquerque. Keeping fingers crossed for the 2025 season.

Want to keep up with what's going on in the series and be the first to see cover reveals and sneak snippets? Sign up for my monthly newsletter. or follow me on Instagram at @rubyjameswrites.

Acknowledgements

There are so many I want to thank. First, my husband Paul. I wouldn't be able to follow my dream without your love and encouragement. I am thankful every day for agreeing to meet you for that glass of wine 2 decades ago. You are my second chance at love.

To Becky, thank you for letting me use Duke's name and your business idea of homemade dog treats. You have been a cheerleader since day one, and I am forever thankful for your friendship. I am still waiting to hit the lottery so we can buy the small island, set up our sanctuary and stop adulting.

My friend Dawn. There may be gaps in texts, but we always know who to reach out to when we need that encouraging voice. Thank you for your service to our country and your friendship.

To my mother. The woman who taught me how to be a strong black woman. She is the muse for several mothers, grandmothers and aunts in my stories. I wouldn't know how to love and be myself if it wasn't for her. I miss her every day.

To my father, thank you for letting me be me and encouraging me to follow my heart. I miss you.

My LERA (Land of Enchantment Romance Authors) group. Present and past members have been nothing but encouraging. All of this, every book, is because my group of fellow writers talked me off the ledge when I wanted to give up. You've all made me a better writer. Thank you.

Melody Jeffries, my cover artist and friend. Your smiling face will always pop into my mind whenever I hear the Friends theme song. Your artistic vision for my covers is appreciated. Continue to have faith.

My new editor, Ramona Mihidi. Thank you for improving my voice instead of changing it. I am thankful I found you when I was close to giving up on my writing dreams. I am looking forward to growing as a writer with our support.

To my ARC team. Thank you for being my first 'fans.' It means more than I could ever express.

Most importantly, thank you to <u>every</u> reader who has pur-chased or borrowed one of my books. I am thankful for helping me make my dream a reality,

Also by

Point Harbor Sweet Romance
From Illustrating To Love
Maybe More Than Friends
Ronan's Queen
Seasoned New Beginnings
Point Harbor Box Set
Hawkins Ridge Animal Rescue—Sweet and Clean Small-Town Romance
Sheltering Naomi
Claires' Forever Love
Rescuing Sienna's Heart (Noah and Sienna-Early Summer 2025)
Blair's Sanctuary (Caden and Blair-Fall 2025)

About the Author

Ruby James is the pseudonym of a middle-aged woman living in the Land of Enchantment (New Mexico). Having grown up in the Washington, DC, area, she made the move to Albuquerque in 2006 alongside her future husband. With a background in healthcare, a bohemian woman who adores classic rock, Marvel, bacon, and coffee. She and her husband share their home with the Queen of the Castle, a tuxedo cat named Random.